NO RHYME OR RIESLING

BLOOD, WINE, MAGIC: BOOK 4

JUSTIN GODEY

This is dedicated to friends forgotten and those that have drifted away.

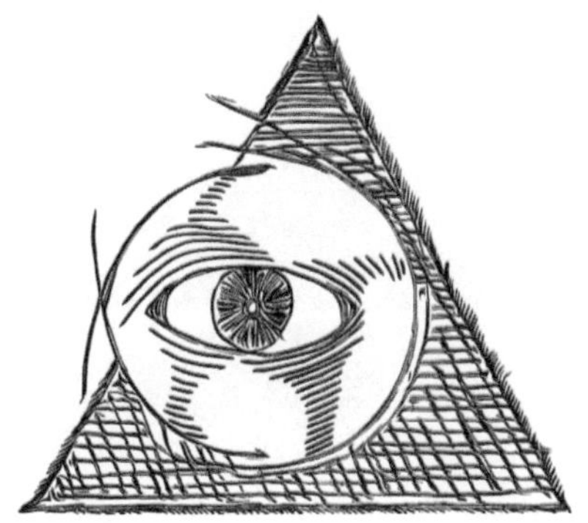

PROLOGUE

"Is it my story you want or Miles'?"

"Both."

"I can only tell you my story. Those are the rules. Sorry."

"Whose rules?"

"My rules."

"You sound just like him."

"*Or he sounds just like me.*"

"I think that is exactly what he would say."

"No, he'd say something like, 'Well, as ghosts don't exist, you must be a projection of my unconscious mind trying to express repressed blah, blah, psycho-barf.'"

"You're stalling. Please go ahead and tell me your story."

"Fine, let's begin my story at the end. I don't want to keep you in suspense, biting your nails, wondering how it ends. That's no way to enjoy a story, so it ends here: everybody dies. Everybody's story starts and ends the same. You are born, some stuff happens, and you die. The middle part? That's just filler. There is no happily ever after. Happily ever after just means nothing interesting happened, and

then they died. So that is my story. I was born. Some stuff happened. I died."

"That's a little reductive, isn't it?"

"Not what you were looking for? Fair enough. Here's an ending: I was startled awake by a horrible braying sound and a deep rumbling in my head. It was just my snoring—that is the sound that usually dragged me from slumber in those days. I was sitting in my recliner. It was a LaZBoy, but I didn't consider myself lazy. I never was. I was just old and tired—so tired.

The television was still playing reruns of an old sitcom I enjoyed in my youth. I'd tried watching modern programming, but it was so fast, violent, and confusing. The rote oldies were comforting, passing reminders of my youth.

I got up and made my way to the kitchen, which took me longer than I thought it should. My joints didn't work like they used to. I stopped and looked out the window. A young person was walking their dog past, and I watched and reminisced.

A car drove by. It was red and fast, and no one was inside it. Technology had shaped the world into a place I barely recognized anymore.

I continued to the kitchen and removed a prepared meal from my refrigerator. I took the meal to the microwave oven and began heating it. My refrigerator started to scream at me, an annoying bleating sound it made when the door had been left open too long. My kids got me that new refrigerator a year before. Or was it the year before that? I don't remember anymore. I remember thinking that I missed my old one. It didn't scream at me. I muttered dark curses at the complaining appliance. It didn't seem to care and continued its unrepentant squawking.

The microwave beeped, letting me know that my meal was done. I closed the refrigerator to stop it from screaming, but the microwave kept beeping. Everything made so much noise, but honestly, I miss it now.

I took the meal out and slowly carried it back to my recliner, where I sat and started to eat it. I took a few bites; they tasted like ash in my mouth. I used to love food and relish every bite. But at that point, I barely ate. Nothing tasted good; the texture was rough, and the chewing was painful and hard. I set the prepared plate aside; maybe I'd eat it later. Probably not.

I stared at the screen, letting it hypnotize me, but I didn't really process the material much.

I felt heavy and tired. I felt like I was being pressed into the chair by an enormous person sitting on my lap, compressing me, smothering me. It was suffocating. Life was suffocating.

"Today is the day," a character on the TV said. The laugh track roared behind them. I don't know why that was funny, but it did seem true. That was the day—my last one. I hadn't planned on it, but at that moment, I knew it was time.

I dug deep and pushed through the weight on my chest to stand. I hobbled my way to the phone, and I called my kids. Neither answered; they were probably at work. I left them both messages telling them that I loved them, that I was proud of them, and that I'd miss them. I felt like it should have been emotional, but it wasn't. It felt like talking about the weather.

I made my way back to my recliner and sat wondering if there was anyone else I needed to say goodbye to, but there wasn't. My friends and siblings were all gone. I didn't know anyone anymore. I considered calling Blaire, the lady who brought me meals three days a week and checked up on me, but I decided not to. She would have made a big deal out of the whole thing. She would have called an ambulance and there would have been a whole hubbub. Instead of dying peacefully there, by myself, I'd have spent my last hours in a hospital, plugged into a machine. There is no grace in that.

I felt dizzy and thought I might fall down; then I realized that I was already lying reclined in a chair and falling would be impossi-

ble. The weight on my chest was immense. I wanted to close my eyes. I was so tired.

But I still had a few things to do. I wrote a quick note apologizing to whoever found me. I told them they were worthy and that I was proud of them. I don't think people say that enough while they are alive. I had so much more to say, but I was so tired. 'I'll finish it later,' I told myself. I knew I wouldn't, and I'd have liked to, but right then, I needed to sleep.

I sat back, turned up the volume on the television, and closed my eyes for the last time."

"Hmm."

"Is that better? Is that the ending you were hoping for?"

"You're still stalling. Tell me the truth."

"Ah, well. It would have been a nice ending. You're right. That's not how my story ended, but it's the ending I deserved"

"What are you avoiding telling me?"

"What are you, my therapist? Dr. Ghostshrink PhD? I fell off a bridge. I was eleven years old. I had barely lived. There isn't much filler there to tell. In the end, there was no peace, only confusion and terror."

"Hmm. I see. So what's it like, death?"

"Being dead is boring."

"What's beyond?"

"If you want to know the secrets of the universe and what comes next, I am sorry that I can't tell you. I didn't get to go on. I was dragged back, kicking and screaming, to the border between hither and yon. Now I'm stuck here answering stupid questions. If you are looking to hear that you'll get your happily ever after, I'm sorry, but you just don't seem the type. If you want to know how to live a better life, the dead are probably not the right people to ask."

"So, what can you tell me about Miles..."

"Fuck off and go find someone else to seance."

CHAPTER 1

I BURST INTO MY APARTMENT.

"Miles!" Hank's familiar voice greets me. Hank is a mannequin, a detailed silicon and latex copy of me. He's more than a mannequin, though; he's a simulacrum—a magical effigy that I use to funnel dark magic into to protect myself. I don't think they usually talk, but Hank does. I waffle between believing that Hank is a demon, or something that I inadvertently trapped in the simulacrum, and believing he is a projection of my deteriorating faculties.

"Hold on, Hank, I have to look at something important."

"This is more important, Miles, trust me."

I pause. Hank rarely says something is important.

"Okay. What's up, Hank?"

"It's about Genevieve, Miles."

"What about Genevieve?"

"She called a guy!"

"What? That's not important, Hank! I don't care. We broke up, it's not my business. Are you spying on my ex?" I yell. Who does Hank think he is? Who do I think I am? After all, he is the voice of my own internal insecurity. Why am I raising my voice?

"No," Hank says, sitting quietly for a moment, finally breaking the silence. *"I hate this. You never listen to me! It's like you only hear what you want to hear!"*

"Well, it's like you only say what you want to say! That sounded a lot less stupid in my head!" I yell.

"*No, it sounded exactly that stupid,*" Hank says. He sounds like he is going to continue, but he doesn't.

I wait for a solid minute. Not a peep from Hank. I stare at the mannequin in the corner of my room. "Well?"

Silence. It's no wonder my neighbors won't make eye contact, let alone talk to me. I return to my desk and pull out the cards the mysterious Hierophant sent me. The Hierophant wasn't his real name, but an alias for the heist he hired me for. I don't know what his name was and I probably never will. These were sent before I realized he was an immortal abomination and destroyed him. I didn't get paid or get many answers, so hired is probably the wrong word. What I did get was a lot of headaches and a deck of handmade block-printed Tarot cards.

I lay them out before me on my desk. I don't keep my desk well organized to begin with, so they are laid on top of papers, pencils, and old toaster pastry wrappers. I count them again, fifty hand-made Tarot cards. It's not a full deck, and there are repeats. There are no instructions, but it seems obvious they are intended to be five sequenced, ten-card readings. This is a story or a message, but it is oblique and requires context and interpretation. I am also guessing at the order and alignment. The inverted cards might be upright and vice versa, but the specific reading is not the point here.

These aren't like any Tarot I've ever seen. The Major Arcana are quite different from the well-known Rider deck, though the Minor Arcana are basically rote.

I am only assuming these are from the Hierophant, because I cannot imagine who else would send me a deck of custom Tarot cards. However, this art looks different from the art of the deck that he used during our heist. I doubt it is the same artist. It was sent to me before we completed our caper at the home of Hollywood producer Jim Devora. It appears to lay out the events of that caper before they even occurred, seemingly prophetic. But as with most prognostication, more than a little stage magic is involved. The Hierophant intended to kill me, so he knew the only way I would get this message was if I somehow lived, which, in turn, would mean that The Hierophant had somehow died, which he had. Or maybe he was already dead. Or maybe he was never living to begin with. That will remain a mystery forever. What if I had died? It was certainly a possibility. The whole thing got pretty touch-and-go there at the end. Best not to dwell on what-ifs. I'm getting sidetracked.

I grew up around Tarot, but I am no expert. I don't read Tarot cards, or really buy into them as a fortune-telling mechanism. However, the Hierophant clearly wanted to say something to me with them, so I decide to do my best to interpret his tale. I pour through the cards.

The first four of the five sets refer to the days of our caper. I set them aside; the fifth set interests me the most. This, I believe, is a portend of the future still to come. The last question I had for the dragon Goldsmith was where I would find answers. Goldsmith said the answers were in the cards, and I know this is what he was referring to.

"Okay Ward, here we go."

The Six of Wands: success, public recognition. I have

received public recognition due to our caper, but not in the positive way I interpret from the upright card.

The Two of Cups, reversed: disharmony, break ups, distrust. Genevieve and I broke up. Did the Hierophant predict this? Or is it my apophenia filling in the blanks?

The Knight of Swords, reversed: a lack of focus, burnout. This is a pretty good description of my life right now.

The Tower: clearly depicted as the Donjon, an onyx replica of the Syzmek building that I have seen in my dreams—where Circe is inexplicably trapped and a place I haven't found my way back to. It's a thing only one friend and I know about. The Tower is struck by lightning and destroyed, causing disaster and upheaval. Two figures plummet from the tower. Their features are unidentifiable, but I have the sense that they are both intended to be me. The Syzmek building is probably my most public, and certainly most lucrative achievement. I designed an intricate magical protection system for the whole thing, a sixty-story building in downtown San Francisco, built to all the most modern specifications for Syzmek corporation. It has been hinted to me that Syzmek CEO Walt Carmichael, one of the world's richest and most powerful men, may too be a dragon.

Is Carmichael in cahoots with Goldsmith? Goldsmith is a weird old hermit who lives in a rundown house in the woods. So, that seems unlikely. They are more likely adversaries in a game where I am just a pawn or even less significant. I'm not completely sure what the significance of the Tower card resembling both the Donjon and the Syzmek building is, but I am certain there is some.

I shake these thoughts from my head and return my attention to the cards.

The Five of Swords: conflict and winning at all costs. This one is a bit of a mystery to me.

The King of Pentacles, reversed: financial ineptitude. Well, that tracks.

The Fool, reversed: recklessness and risk-taking. A man who looks suspiciously like me walks blindly across a narrow suspension bridge. Another figure, who also looks suspiciously like me, plummets off the side of the bridge, his compatriot blind to his fall. The bridge's ropes look frayed, and its planks look rotted. I recognize the bridge. I know where this place is, a place from my childhood. I glance over at Hank. There are no mysteries here.

The Six of Cups: revisiting the past, childhood memories. As I look at this card and back to The Fool, I can feel the hairs rising on the back of my neck.

The Three of Pentacles, reversed: I interpret to mean that I will be working alone, or unable to rely on others. I want to say this is how I do my best work. Lone wolf and all that, but that isn't true. Without the help of my friends and the kindness of strangers, I'd be long dead, or worse.

The Hanged Man, upright, a figure hangs, arms and legs bound, with a stick running between them so that he hangs like a pig about to be barbecued. The figure, of course, looks like me. He has a serene look on his face and even a hint of a smile. This is shocking, as another figure is impaling The Hanged Man with a spear. The blood drips down into a wine glass below.

A new perspective awaits. Revelation.

The cards are woodblock prints. A tremendous amount of time and effort must have gone into carving each one. I believe the cards were made specifically for me; making a single-use set of cards seems like a lot of effort for the result. Couldn't he have just written me a letter? Perhaps this is intended to be a message that only I could interpret, and I'm certain I have.

The Hierophant's message in these cards is that I need to

revisit my childhood. If I want the answers I seek, I have to dig up my past, or at least some of it.

This isn't new news. I've come to this conclusion before, but when I did, I was with Genevieve, and somehow, the idea of going with her was comforting. It might almost have been fun. I could walk her through my youth and have support. Have comfort. It could be the idea of bringing some of the aspects of home with me that made it more appealing. But the Hierophant's message implies I will be making this journey alone. The idea of going back alone makes me feel sad, sick, and, if I am honest with myself, scared.

There is a saying that you can't go home again. Meaning that once you've left the place where you grew up, it will never truly be home again. Was I ever at home in my childhood? Home is supposed to be a place where you feel safe, comfortable, and welcome. I don't know that I ever did. Or in looking back at my youth, it doesn't feel like it in hindsight, but there was a time when I felt at home. The expression that hindsight is twenty-twenty is a lie.

Do I want to trust a message from a mysterious magical being that I betrayed and destroyed? Goldsmith said that was where I'd find answers. But Goldsmith also said I had chosen my side, though I haven't chosen anything. I'm not even sure I know what sides he was talking about. Not exactly. Though I suspect now that he meant I was under Syzmek's thumb for bailing me out of the Devora debacle. Goldsmith has never lied to me, so far as I know, but do I want to trust a dragon that has turned its back on me?

My world feels like it is falling apart, and I don't know how to put it back together or move forward. As unpleasant as it might be, a trip down memory lane could be the way forward.

It would only be for a long weekend. You can endure anything ten seconds at a time. So, to get through three days, I'd only have to endure it twenty-five thousand nine hundred and twenty times, give or take.

I don't care what the cards said; misery loves company. I don't want to go alone, so I get my phone and call Jeff.

"Hey, Miles," Jeff answers after a couple of rings.

"Hey, Jeff, what are you doing this weekend?"

"Chase invited me to this disc golf tournament, camping trip thing he does every year."

"Since when do you play disc golf?"

"Since a couple of weekends ago. It's fun. Why'd you ask about this weekend?"

"I've decided to make a last-minute trip to where I grew up. I was hoping for some company."

"You aren't taking Genevieve?" He asks curiously.

"Oh," I say darkly and pause for a minute. "No, we broke up."

"You broke up? When did that happen?"

"Yesterday."

"Miles," Jeff says sympathetically, "I'm sorry, man, that sucks."

"Yeah, she was going to go with me, but now, obviously, she's not. And I guess I don't want to go it alone."

"I'm sorry, Miles. I'd go with you, but I can't do it this weekend. Could you go later?"

I think about that for a minute. There is no logical reason that it has to be this weekend. I could go anytime. However, I need resolution. I need something to change, and this is my next step.

"I appreciate that, Jeff. Thanks, but no, I need to go this weekend. It's something I have to do."

"Okay, well, if that changes, let me know. I am really sorry about this weekend, but you know..."

"No, I hear you. This is pretty last minute."

"Sorry," Jeff says softly.

"All right, well, I'll talk to you when I get back. I am going to make a couple more calls."

"Okay, good luck."

"Thanks, bye," I say and hang up. It's rather abrupt, and it feels rude, but I am also annoyed with Jeff. Intellectually, I know he has plans, but he's my best friend, and I expected him to drop everything and go with me on this trip. I feel betrayed that he's got plans with Chase already. Chase, the 'Snack-King' of Napa. Chase, who took my place at the poker table. Chase, who seems funnier and more successful than me. Chase, who has access to an endless supply of delicious treats. Chase, who, if he weren't so nice, I'd hate him. Damn, Chase even took that away from me.

I could call Alistair, but he's got a family and kids. I don't know that disappearing for a weekend is something he can manage. Besides, his husband, Jon, finally likes me a little bit. I'd hate to ruin that so quickly.

I could call Mike. He always says I need to call him about things other than weird stuff. But this is kind of weird stuff. It's not magic and mystery, but I didn't exactly have a quiet suburban childhood.

"Mike doesn't even like you," Hank's disembodied voice chimes in.

"It's a growing trend."

How many more friends do I have? I could call Emily. Would that be awkward? We almost dated, but we have become friends. It wouldn't be a romantic trip, and it wouldn't be weird. Would it?

"You'd make it weird."

"You mean that you'd make it weird."

"Well, it would be a group effort," Hank chuckles.

"But you will be here, not there. So it'll be fine. I am calling Emily."

"Harumph!"

I call, and Emily's phone rings and rings, and just when I am about ready to give up and disconnect, she answers the phone.

"Miles! How are you?" She says, her voice fraught with concern.

"You've talked to Genevieve," I say flatly.

"Yeah, she called me last night," her voice softens.

"It's fine. I am in the 'burying my feelings' portion of the breakup."

"Do you want to talk about it?"

"Nope, that's the point of burying my feelings."

"Oh, um, okay. So what's up?" She asks curtly. She clearly doesn't think much of my avoidance tactics.

"Well, I have to return to my childhood home, or I want to. No, I don't want to go back, but this is something I feel like I need to do, and Genevieve was, I think, going to go with me, but then, well, you know. I'm not excited to go alone, and I was looking for a friend to come with."

"Oh, when are you going?"

"I was planning to go this weekend."

"You mean, like, the day after tomorrow?" Emily asks.

"Yeah," I mutter, "I guess it's Wednesday, so yeah, I was going to head up tomorrow."

"Oh, Miles, I am sorry," Emily says, sounding sad, "I would like to say yes, but I have to fly back east for a SERGEI thing. I am out of town until next Wednesday."

"A SERGEI thing?"

"It's a board meeting, strategic planning, all that boring business stuff."

"Oh," I say flatly.

"I'm sorry, I could go next weekend."

"Thanks, but this is something I really feel like I have to do now."

"I'm sorry, Miles. It's so last minute. If you decide to go another time, I'd be happy to come along," she says. It's probably my mood, but I have difficulty believing she'd be happy to do it.

"It's okay," I say, "I'll figure something out."

"I'm sorry, Miles."

I hang up on her without another word.

"You're being kind of a whiny brat, you know that?"

"Go away," I say. "I guess the Hierophant's prophecy was right and I am going this one alone."

CHAPTER 2

"I've got two major problems ahead of me," I mutter to myself.

"Is your ability to count problems one of them?"

"Stay out of my inner monologue," I say petulantly to Hank.

"He said, out loud, to the voice in his head."

I turn my back on my simulacrum and start typing on my computer. The first of my two problems is that I know the name of the place I am looking for, but I have no idea where it is. I grew up in a place called Stanyon's Hollow. It isn't on any maps or in any tour guides. I know that to get to it, one drives to a little rural town called Covelo and then winds their way on an old dirt road into the mountains. Hidden somewhere in an undeveloped area the size of the state of Rhode Island is the hidden community of Stanyon's Hollow.

My father and I left Stanyon's Hollow when I was twelve or thirteen, and I have tried not to think of it since. When we lived there, it was a community of a dozen or so families that pooled resources to provide clean, fresh water, share food, and assist each other with labor, like home repairs and the like. It does not exist in any census data or have any legal status. The roads in and out were entirely maintained by the residents.

The second problem is that even if I can figure out how to find it, I have no idea how I'd get there or where I might stay.

"You can pitch a tent. Now that Genevieve's gone, it..." Hank begins, but I cut him off.

"No. You can be quiet now, Hank. Too soon."

"You have no sense of humor, you know that?"

Leave it to Hank to bring up my abrupt breakup with my girlfriend while I try to distract myself from it. I have terrible taste in imaginary friends. I grunt at him, then type "Stanyon's Hollow" into my web search.

"Well, I'll be," I mutter as I stare at the screen. The first link that comes up is to a listing on the AwayFromHome vacation rental site. "Cozy yurt in Stanyon's Hollow. Private off-the-grid getaway."

"I thought you said this was going to be challenging."

"I thought it would be. Listen to this: originally settled by Nathanial Stanyon and the Stanyon Logging Company in 1898, Stanyon's Hollow began as a small logging camp. It was abandoned in 1932 as a result of the national economic downturn of the Great Depression. It was rediscovered in 1968 by the Thule Collective, a group of like-minded, back-to-land-focused individuals. For over fifty years, Stanyon's Hollow has been a bastion for those looking to retreat from society and live a more simple and rustic life. Now you can get away from the thrum of city life in this rustic yurt, with a million-acre backyard called the Mendocino National Forest."

"Sounds like the setup for a Deliverance remake."

"I wonder if Burt Reynolds is available."

"He's like 80."

"How do you know so much about old movies? You're a mannequin."

"Well, you are never around, and there isn't much else to do."

I click the button to book the yurt, but an error comes up.

"Dammit," I grumble. I click it again, but I get the same error. I try reloading my browser and restarting my machine, but nothing works. Then, just as I am about to give up, I notice a 'Chat with the host' button on the screen. I click it.

"Hello," I type.

Three little circle bubbles float in the chat window for what seems like forever. Finally, text pops up in the chat-box.

Hello! I am Tiffany. How can I help you today?

Hi Tiffany, I am trying to book your Stanyon's Hollow yurt for this weekend, but it keeps throwing up an error.

Sorry about that. Since they did maintenance last week, the site has had many problems.

What should I do?

Send an email to Tiffany@awayfromhome.bs, and we will book it manually.

We exchanged a few emails. Then Tiffany called me, and it becomes clear that Tiffany is not a real person but an AI bot. I gave her my credit card information. Soon after I received the final confirmation email, a weird sensation of relief and trepidation wash over me simultaneously—intense ambivalence.

The confirmation email includes directions, something that seems otherwise unavailable, the combinations of three locked gates that must be passed through to get to Stanyon's Hollow, and detailed parking instructions. It is a mile hike from the parking lot up a dirt path to the Yurt.

The email has many other details; for example, Stanyon's Hollow has a co-op general store and 'other amenities' guests are welcome to use. Every Saturday night, there is a community potluck where every family brings a dish to share.

"It's weird that a back-to-land, off-the-grid collective has an AI managing bookings, right?"

"They probably just outsource it to a service."

"But still...their website has problems, but their AI is working fine?"

"The world is a weird place, Hank. I'm talking to a mannequin about going to a place a dead sorcerer told me to go through a deck of tarot cards. Glass houses."

Aside from the AwayFromHome listing, the only references to Stanyon's Hollow I could find are an article on the Thule Collective and a newspaper report about a marijuana plantation raid twenty years ago. I begin the article on the Thule Collective, but they were just a group of anti-establishment nuts in the sixties. It isn't very interesting, and I don't finish reading. Besides my memory and these three data points, Stanyon's Hollow doesn't seem to exist.

After I've perused all the rental details, I get up and pace my apartment.

This is happening.

When I mentally committed to this, some part of my brain thought I'd try to find the place, fail, and give up. In hindsight, I realize I was only pursuing this to tell myself I tried. But now it is suddenly real, and I am terrified. I don't want to go delving into my childhood, a period I've spent a lifetime trying to forget. I don't want to do this alone.

"You could ask Magdalena," Hank says, suggesting my neighbor, a time-bending eternally-teenage assassin.

"Yeah, I don't know if Magdalena is the person I want to share this experience with. Also, I don't think she's gotten back from France," I say, remembering that she was magically transported to Europe while escaping Jim Devora's vault.

I go next door and knock anyway, but there is no answer.

The rest of the evening is spent packing. Knowing there's a long hike up a trail to get to this yurt, I get everything I need into one backpack. Two pairs of pants, two shirts, an extra jacket, four pairs of socks and underwear, and some basic toiletries. I pick up my courier bag containing all my work tools. I heft it and consider bringing it, but it's a bit of extra weight, and I won't need it, so I hang it in my closet. Then, after sitting for a minute, I remember my trip to Portland, where I got tricked into helping get rid of an imp. I really could have used my work things and regretted not packing them then, so I grab the bag and put it with my backpack.

Once that is complete, I pace nervously, watch online trash, and overindulge in salty, crunchy snacks. It's about one in the morning when I finally fall asleep.

I find myself waking at about eight. After a quick shower, I sit down to a cup of stick-flavored tea. I recently quit coffee completely and reduced myself to a single cup of black tea every morning. The headaches, cold sweats, and rigors from withdrawal have passed, but I feel tired and dopey all the time. It's like there is a haze in my brain that won't lift. I know it would only take a single cup of coffee, or ten to twelve cups of tea, to fix that, and the temptation is immense. I think about how much coffee I drank leading up to the Devora job, and I can see it had become a problem. The tea makes my stomach feel slightly queasy, so I grab a toaster pastry on my way out the door.

"Wish me luck!"

"Take me with you!"

I imagine, for a moment, bending Hank into the passenger's seat and driving north with him. His joints are articulated, and it could be done. But I couldn't hike a mile and a half up a dirt trail dragging him, so he'd sit in the car. It would get me looks. It might get me pulled over, and many uncomfortable questions would be asked.

"Sorry buddy, you're staying here."

"Story of my life, just another piece of home decor," Hank says, doing his Eeyore impression again.

"I've never seen anything like you in a Martha Stewart magazine."

"You've never seen a Martha Stewart Magazine."

"Touché and ciao!" I say as I grab my bags and march out the door. Hank calls something after me, but I can't hear him over the pounding of blood in my head.

I toss my bags into the passenger seat of Magdalena's car because it has no back seat, and I haven't figured out how to pop the trunk yet. Magdalena said she was giving me the car because she owed me one, but it doesn't feel like my car. Petite, fast, and bright red, it looks like coke-dealer-Barbie's ride. This will always be Magdalena's car, even if she signed the title to me.

No sooner have I started the engine than my phone rings. It comes in over the hands-free unit in the car, which confuses me because I never set that up. The caller ID informs me that it is Russ.

"Hello," I say as I click the button on the steering wheel to pick up.

"Hey Miles, man, what's going on, dude?" Russ says.

"Not much. I'm just heading out of town for the weekend."

"Bummer, I wanted to hang out. The old lady is visiting the oldest in San Diego, and I'm super bored."

Do I want to invite Russ with me? Actually, I cannot think of anyone who would be less weirded out by Stanyon's Hollow than Russ. Why didn't I think of calling him?

"Well, I mean, do you want to come with me? I am going to

where I grew up for the weekend for an adventure of self-discovery. It's a long story. But I could use some company."

"Shit man, yeah. Get to see what gnarly corner of the earth forged Miles Ward? How could I say no to that?"

"Oh," I say, slightly surprised by his eagerness. "Okay, then. I was just heading out. Can I come by?"

"Yeah, I'll throw some things in a bag and see you soon!"

"Pack light. There's some wilderness hiking from the parking lot to the rustic yurt I rented."

"Sweet dude, say no more!"

"Well, all right then, I'll be over in a few," I say.

And with that, it looks like I have a traveling companion after all. Take that prophecy!

CHAPTER 3

"HOLA, DUDE!" Russ chimes as I park in his empty driveway. This is a new turn of events. Usually, I have to find street parking three blocks away.

He's got a rucksack on the ground next to him, with a sleeping bag bundled on top. He's wearing a flannel shirt and jeans with an orange stocking cap. The cap sticks up in a dome above his head, making him look like one of the ceramic gnomes peeping out at me from the overgrown jungle in front of his house.

"Hey, Russ," I say as I press a button to unlock the door for him.

"Nice car, man," he says with a whistle. He looks the car over thoughtfully.

"It's not mine. It's a loaner," I say, unsure if I am lying or not.

"Friends with your dealer, huh? Pop the trunk, dude."

Once more, I search the dashboard and find no indication of how to open the trunk.

"I'm not sure how."

"Here, lemme have a look," Russ coos.

I open the door and get out, and Russ climbs in and looks the console over.

"Wow, this is a lot of car. You sure you can handle it?" He says, leaning down low and putting his hand under the dash where I can't see it. Suddenly, with a soft whirr of a motor and the faint hiss of pneumatics, the trunk slowly rises like a campy B-grade vampire from a coffin.

"Wow, you got it," I say as I heft Russ' backpack. It is surprisingly heavy. It has several mesh pockets on the outside, and just glancing at some of the things in it makes me feel unprepared. Binoculars, a little folding shovel, and a canteen all catch my eye.

Russ gets out of the car, and we walk to the trunk together. I am about to heft Russ' pack into it when he puts a hand out.

"Hold on, dude," he says.

"What's up?" I ask.

"Does this trunk seem a little shallow to you? Look, there's a keyhole."

"It's probably just the spare."

"That would have to be a full-sized spare. There's no way this car carries one of those, and spare tires don't lock like that. That's a serious lock, not some flimsy little cabinet latch."

I look more closely at the trunk. I probably wouldn't have noticed it if he hadn't pointed it out, but the trunk is strangely shallow, and the lock looks far heartier and more industrial than you'd expect to secure a tire.

I take the key out of my pocket. Just looking at the car key, I know it won't fit. This was the only key I found in the car, hidden under the dash, where Magdalena indicated it would be in a voicemail.

I shrug at Russ.

"I don't know. Like I said, it's not my car," I say helplessly. And it's true: I don't know. But I have a guess.

"All right," Russ says, "I mean, it's not like it's a trunk full of guns, right?"

"Yeah, right?" I laugh nervously. It is probably a trunk full of guns, or worse.

Russ eyeballs me suspiciously.

"Whose car did you say this was?"

"Magdalena's."

He looks at me quizzically.

"My Hizarin neighbor," I say because I don't see any benefit in lying to Russ about this.

"So it *is* a trunk full of guns."

"That would be my guess."

"Cool," Russ hefts his backpack into the trunk. I can't tell if he's being sarcastic or not.

"I don't have the key, though."

"Cooler."

I get my bags from the passenger's seat and toss them into the trunk.

Soon, we are on the freeway.

"So, I don't mean to backseat drive or anything, amigo, but you are driving very fast."

"Yeah, sorry about that. This car seems hard to drive at anything but reckless speeds."

"I'm sure you know this, but you probably don't want to get pulled over with a trunk full of guns."

"We don't know it's full of guns. Knowing Magdalena, best case scenario, it is only guns."

"Uh, huh," Russ' voice is skeptically low.

I make a concerted effort to drive closer to the speed limit as we wind our way through Petaluma toward Highway 101.

"So," Russ interrupts the silence, "where are we going, man?"

"Right, we've got a lot to catch up on."

"Well, I mean, I know that you saved some sleazy movie guy's life. I don't live under a rock," Russ says.

"Yeah, that's not exactly what happened. I mean, I guess in a very indirect way it is."

"I figured there was more to the story. Give me the rundown, daddy-o."

Daddy-o?

"Okay. Let's see. My Hizarin neighbor, Magdalena, recruited me for this heist. We were supposed to raid Jim Devora's secret vault. It was run by this guy who only identified himself as The Hierophant. There was a whole Tarot motif."

"Cool."

"It was supposed to pay a lot of money, but it didn't. I'm more broke now than when I started."

"Eyes on the road, mind on the story, man," Russ says as I hit the rumble strip on the side of the road and swerve to correct.

"Right. Anyway, there was something off about the whole thing, but Magdalena wasn't going to back off, and I didn't want to leave her high and dry, so we got in there. The vault had these crazy wards on it. Well, it turns out The Hierophant was an undead sorcerer, or like a djinni, or something."

"Awesome."

I glance skeptically at Russ. Awesome isn't the response I would have to that.

"Then I realized that this guy wanted something out of the vault, and its whole function was to keep him out. I don't think he was going to let us live, let alone pay us. So I activated the wards on the vault, and he turned to dust. But then we were trapped in it. There were police, armed mercenaries, hell-hounds, and a militia. It was a hot mess."

"Well, that is bongos, but it doesn't tell me where we are going."

"I'm getting there. So then, the rest of the group escaped, but I passed out. I ended up in the hospital. There was this whole thing where this scumbag Hale is now my lawyer. My face was on the news. I had to leave town, so I went with my girlfriend, Genevieve, to Atlanta."

"Oh!" Russ exclaims suggestively, "That's why I haven't seen you around lately. Too busy getting busy."

"No!" I exclaim, then recant, "Well, yes, but that's not the point. In Atlanta, we broke up. I am still confused about how that happened. There was alcohol and a catfight in the middle of a mixer. I went for a walk and had a hotdog."

"Dude. You're rambling."

"Yeah, sorry. Since I quit drinking coffee, I've been feeling a little spacy and distracted. Staying on track is hard."

"You quit drinking coffee?" He exclaims, "You? Dude, that can't be good, man."

"Ugh," I groan. "Anyway, so then I came home. Oh, and right, did I mention that the Hierophant sent me a package before he died?"

"No, you neglected to include that important bit of information."

"Sorry."

"No problem, continue."

"I got this package before we went to Atlanta. It was from the Hierophant, or I am intuiting that it was from him. Anyway, it was a custom Tarot deck," I pause for a breath before continuing. "It was filled with images and stuff hinting at aspects of my life he couldn't have known. What I got from it was that I needed to go to where I grew up to get answers in my life."

"And you are trusting some maybe-undead-sorcerer-that-you-killed's last wishes? Does not sound like wisdom, dude."

"That's what I thought, but then a dragon said that the cards held the answers I seek."

Russ laughs uproariously for a full minute before he stops to gasp out, "A dragon? Seriously, dude?"

"You insert yourself into people's dreams and have helped me deal with vampire assassins and Greek monsters. Dragons are where you draw the line of credulity?"

"Fair, that's fair, mi amigo. Anyway, what answers do you seek, man?"

"I," I start to say. It is a good question, and the truth is I can't really answer it. "I don't know. You know how you know you have questions, but you aren't even sure what they are until you find the answers. Like, you walk into a bakery and see they have a single source Kenyan coffee that they are doing a special pour-over for, and this perfect cinnamon pecan roll, and you know you were looking for something but didn't know that was it until you saw it?"

"Sounds like a you thing, but yeah, man, I get it. You're having an existential crisis, and you need to figure out where you came from to figure out where you're going. We've all been there."

"Hmm, have we? Well, that is why I am heading now to Stanyon's Hollow, the remote shithole I grew up in."

"Awesome, this sounds like my kinda party!"

"Really?" I ask, dubiously.

"I mean, it might be the 'shrooms talking, but yeah," Russ laughs.

I roll my eyes. Great, I am taking a jaunt down memory lane with a tripping hippy.

"Shrooms, Russ?"

"Just a little."

"What?" I ask. "Are you micro-dosing?"

"No, I'm meso-dosing," he gives me a goofy grin and a thumbs up.

"Meso-dosing?"

"Meso is between micro and macro, dude."

"Oh," I say, bewildered. Either he hasn't taken much, or he's very used to functioning on psychedelics because I wouldn't have guessed. Probably both.

"Want some?" He asks, holding up a plastic zip-top baggie filled with what looks like dry brown sticks.

"No, and even if I did, Russ, I'm driving!"

"Doctors orders, dude!"

"You're not a doctor, Russ."

"The hell I'm not. PhD in organic chemistry from Clegmont University," he says matter-of-factly.

"Clegmont University?" I ask. I've never heard of it.

"Where'd you get your PhD from?" He says petulantly.

"I don't have a PhD."

"Uh-huh. QED, dude. Don't judge, man!"

I roll my eyes and fall silent. Russ doesn't say anything, and I turn the radio on. Music begins blaring at me. It's some kind of aggressive and vulgar rap music that I am not familiar with. It's a female artist, and she's very graphic in her descriptions of basically *all* aspects of her life. I stab at buttons until I get to something less distracting.

"Can we get a pit stop? I'm having a biological imperative," Russ chimes in a few minutes later.

"Sure, I should gas up before we leave the highway. There should be a gas station soon."

"Cool, cool," Russ declares, leaning back in his seat. He stares, glassy-eyed, at the horizon.

Magdalena's car is quiet. There is a constant thrum of tires on the asphalt and a whisper of air sliding over its streamlined roof, but that's it. It's somehow soothing, and I feel almost hypnotized by the broken yellow line on the highway. My mind wanders to the heist and how terribly it went wrong, that smug bastard Hale grinning at me on the corporate jet, and Walt Carmichael.

Is Carmichael the one pulling Hale's strings? Why did Genevieve break up with me? How many licks does it take to get to the center of a Tootsie Roll Pop? Was it always just a fling, and I didn't see it? Or did something change, and I didn't see it? Regardless, it's clear there was something I didn't see. Wait, does that mean Walt Carmichael is a dragon? Is Hank right? Is Genevieve already seeing someone else? Hale had much to say about the Blethspah Amah, the mysterious chosen one, who is secretly my friend Jeff. Why is "nonchalant" a word in English but "chalant" isn't? Can I believe anything Hale says? Does anyone actually like the taste and texture of Twizzlers?

"Gas station, dude," Russ says, breaking me out of my eternally derailing train of thought.

"Huh?" I say, confused at first.

"This exit is a gas station. I gotta pee."

"Oh, right!" I say, remembering that I promised Russ we'd stop. I swerve violently over the double white line onto the offramp. The little car clings to the road like a soup stain on my only tie.

The off-ramp takes us to a gritty-looking overpass. There are sheets of gravel bits on the shoulder where cars don't normally drive. They'd likely slide if someone drove over that, even at moderate speeds. The concrete edges are broken by patches of weeds cropping up between cracks. The whole area looks neglected and unmaintained.

We come to the gas station a quarter mile down the road. It's dingy-looking, and while it bears the sign of a bigger chain, it's a one-person operation. There are six pumps, but only two of them work. Pieces of lined, yellow, legal paper are taped to the others, with the words "Out of Ordr" written in black marker. If the E were missing from just one, it would seem like a mistake, but there isn't an E on any of the signs, making it seem intentional.

I find an operational pump, and while I start filling the car with premium fuel, Russ heads in to find the bathroom. I ponder the intentionally misspelled signs. Did the author think that was how you spelled order? Or did they think misspelling them on all the signs was funny? I am inclined toward the latter. A motion in the corner of my eye draws my attention. It's a bird-a big black one. A crow or a raven; I never learned to tell the difference. It flies away, leaving me looking blankly at the skyline. The mountains loom above us, each peak larger than a city's acreage. On each one, you could wander until you were lost, forgotten, and swallowed up by the trees. A hundred people could march up there at once and never see each other again. That's just one mountain, and there are dozens of them. There is so much space, but I find it much more comfortable to be surrounded by people; ignored but never forgotten.

"Miles, man," Russ says, his tone one of concern.

"Yeah?"

"You're zoning out. The pump has been done for like five minutes and you're just starin' off into space."

"I was just thinking about how much area is up in the mountains; how you could drift off like debris tumbling into space."

"Sure, man. I don't know. You don't seem like yourself."

"Yeah," I say, dragging my mind into the present. "It's been a rough week."

"I hear you. What's say we hit the road?"

"You're right. We have promises to keep, and miles to go, and all that," I say.

"Miles to go," he says smirking. It takes me a minute to realize that it's because it's my name. I smirk back, and we get into the car.

"So tell me about this place we are going to, dude. What's it like?"

"Stanyon's Hollow. I don't remember it well. My dad and I left when we were twelve or thirteen."

"We?" He asks.

"I mean, I was twelve or thirteen. The Hollow is the kind of place you get to by turning off the main road onto a side road, and off the side road onto a dirt road. Then, you go through a locked gate and turn left at the tree that looks like J. Edgar Hoover. Then, you turn right at the next fork and through another locked gate. Then, you turn right again at the big rock, but if you see a pond, it means you've gone too far. Then, you follow the road above a scree to a third locked gate. Then, you follow another road..."

Russ interrupts my rambling."Got it, dude. I did the trimmigrant thing back in my misbegotten youth. It's a place where people don't want to be found, I dig."

"Anyway, I remember there were a lot of woods, a gorge, and this wide-open parking space with a bunch of old cabins around it. Reading online, it was a logging camp originally. When I lived there, it was like a common area. From there, trails went up to different houses. There were some families, and we'd play with the kids. But a few houses belonged to people who, like you said, were there because they didn't want to be found. None of them wanted kids around and they'd shoot rock salt out of shotguns at us if they saw us."

"Shit."

"Yeah, they never actually aimed at us. Nobody ever got hit, but it scared the hell out of us. Anyway, that's about all I remember."

"You keep saying we, dude. You have a sibling?"

I stay silent for a long while, thinking. I hate talking about this, but it will come up sooner or later, so I should get it over with.

"Yeah, a brother. A twin brother."

"Dude, you have a brother! How come you never mentioned him before?" He says excitedly.

"He died. Up there," I say. I can feel tears beginning to well in my eyes. I fight them back with an angry groan.

"Oh, woah dude. Sorry. I wasn't trying to open up old wounds, man."

"No, it's fine. I'm pretty sure that's why I am coming up here," I mumble.

"Okay, right on. Well, you know, if you want to talk about it..." Russ leaves the invitation implied but unspoken.

"Thanks. Once we get there. Right now, I should really focus on driving."

"Probably should, yeah."

We settle into an uncomfortable silence as Magdalena's car eats up the road like fire spreading over a gasoline pool.

CHAPTER 4

On paper, State Highway 162 leads through Covelo to Willows, but in reality, it becomes a dirt trail through the hills after Covelo. Covelo could be any tiny town off any major throughway, lost and almost forgotten by the rest of the state. There isn't much left of it besides a few rows of buildings on a dusty street. The town has seen better days, though I couldn't tell you when.

We don't stop. Instead, we turn north at an intersection onto a little road into the hills. A few miles up the road, it turns from asphalt to gravel. I have to halt multiple times at forks and refer back to the directions I was given before moving on. Soon, the gravel road turns to raw, rutted dirt.

Magdalena's little car was built to fly on paved roads, but these dirt roads aren't the terrain it intended to cover. I must be careful to keep it from bottoming out on potholes or shaking itself apart on rutted, washboard sections of the road. Eventually, we come to the first gate. It’s a modern aluminum cattle gate, and it's more of a suggestion to stay out than an actual barrier. As the instructions said, it would be unlocked, so we only have to stop and open it.

The road then begins a steeper ascent into the mountains, winding its way back and forth up the face of one particularly rugged slope. The foliage is thick, but blackened stumps, intense copses of underbrush, and burn scars remind me of the wildfires that tore through here a few years back.

We come to the second gate. It's an old logging gate; a hearty thing made of six-inch diameter, hollow iron tubes. The open tube walls themselves are three-quarters of an inch thick. A bulldozer would need to take a few passes to get through this one. It has been painted and repainted dozens of times, and in each rusted chip, you can see the myriad layers of red, green, and yellow that it has been over the decades. This gate is locked, with the lock hidden inside of an iron enclosure too narrow to fit bolt cutters into. While this secures the lock from being easily cut off, it also makes entering the combination difficult. Russ and I have to take turns at squeezing our fingers in to put the numbers into the lock. Eventually, however, the gate opens with an ominous screeching groan.

At last, we come to the third and final gate. This one is new and was not here when I was a kid. I'd have remembered it. It's a wooden gate that looks more like a frontier palisade than anything. Upright wooden logs, cut to a uniform length of about ten feet high, make the surface of the gate. It is held shut with an imposing chain that appears to be made of hand-forged links, and an immense lock on it. A wooden arch above the gate bears a sign that reads, "Welcome to Stanyon's Hollow."

"Sending some mixed messages there," Russ says, pointing at the gate. He's right. The gate is anything but welcoming.

"There is some other script below that," I say, opening the car door.

Russ follows my lead, and we get out of the car and walk to the foreboding gate.

"Is that magic?" Russ points to the smaller script on the sign.

"No," I squint at the tiny symbols on the bottom of the sign, "It's Enochian."

"That's not magic?"

"No, it's just a made-up alphabet; the words are actually English. It's just a character substitution. More or less."

"What's it say?" Russ asks curiously.

"Hold on, it's been a long time since I've looked at Enochian," I say, trying to dig in my brain for that all-but-forgotten knowledge. "In my work, it's usually a sign that you are dealing with an amateur. Gamers and people who want something to look magical use it a lot."

"What's it say?"

"It says," I say, bumbling over the letters, "New...Um, Thole? No, New Thule."

"Thule?"

"Yeah. Way back, Stanyon's Hollow was the home to a group called the Thule Collective or something like that, back in the sixties. It must be referencing that," I say.

"Thule Collective, it sounds familiar. One of those sixties radical groups? Back to land? Down with the government, that sort of thing?" Russ asks.

"Yeah, something like that. I don't think they were ever very big. Didn't get in the news. No senators were kidnapped or celebrities murdered. I only know about them from the little history the AwayFromHome listing gave."

"Well, that's interesting."

"That is one way of putting it," I begin to unlock the gate.

"And why Enochian? I mean, who knows Enochian?" Russ gives me a bad case of the stinky side-eye.

"Just us weirdos," I say as the gate swings silently open. Its timbers are mounted on a heavy steel frame on the inside. A series of springs and pneumatics allow it to swing quietly and smoothly. It's much less rustic than its facade would lend one to believe.

I pull the car through and then close the gate. It's an easy prospect, and although the gate probably weighs a thousand pounds, it pulls closed with very little force, thanks to the mechanical aids it is built upon. Two square holes in the gate are big enough to pass one's hands through and lock it from the inside.

After we return to the car, we silently drive for a couple of minutes.

"So," Russ's voice sounds strained like he's slightly anxious. "How's the Dreamwalking going?"

"Nothing, still the same. Ever since Circe. Nothing."

"Why do you think that is?"

"Honestly? I think it's a mental block. All that scared me. It feels like going to the doctor. Part of me says I should, but another part keeps finding excuses not to."

"Why's that, dude?"

"Why?" I ask, incredulously, "Because it's scary, that's why. Whenever I Dreamwalk, something tries to trick or kill me, or who knows what. It's not fun or pleasant. I know it's your thing, but the Dreamtime seems to have it out for me."

Russ nods, "Yeah, I can see that. You got that energy, man."

"What does that mean?" I raise my voice in annoyance.

"It just means, dude, that you are you, and like, most of us walk across a bridge, and it's just a bridge, but you walk across it, and a troll jumps out, you know?"

I don't love the timbre of his metaphor. I grunt in response. We round a large bend, and the road dips down abruptly into a small valley filled with trees.

"This, I remember," I say as I glimpse the roofs of cabins through the trees, "This is Stanyon's Hollow."

The car descends a short, slightly muddy slope. Two large Douglas firs stand on either side of the road, like looming guardians. I remember the trees from my childhood. My father called them Romulus and Remus, though I could not say why. They were always the symbol that we were almost home. Romulus and Remus seemed larger back then, though empirically, they must have been smaller, and would have grown some over the decades.

We pass between the two large trees and into an evergreen hollow. A narrow dirt road opens up into a large clearing, where the road loops back in on itself in a circle. On the outside of the loop are several cabins. I vaguely remember them. One is the communal bathhouse, where there are showers and facilities to bathe, as most houses here have no real plumbing. Some are used to store tools and things used by people in the community to upkeep paths and common areas. There are about a dozen cabins in total. Simple, uniform structures, with a single door and two windows on the front. I estimate that each is fifteen by twenty feet in footprint. I am surprised by how well-repaired they all look. I vaguely recall some of them were abandoned and all but falling down when I was a child.

The biggest change and surprise to me is that in the middle of this loop, there is a large barn-like building. It looks very new and I am certain it wasn't here when I was a child. It's twenty-five feet in height, making it the biggest structure here. It is made from thick, hand-cut boards and has a number of high windows. On the front are two huge sliding barn doors and a sign that reads "Community Hall."

"This is cute," Russ says. I give a noncommittal grunt in response. Maybe it is an intrinsic dislike of change, but something about this new building doesn't sit well with me.

It is late in the afternoon, and the sun was already setting when we were on the road, but down in the recesses of this hollow, it is basically dark. I drive around the loop to where a large area has been cleared as a parking lot. A sign tacked to a tree says "Guest Parking" with a relatively level and clear space for a car. As the directions instruct, I park there.

We get out, and I stretch briefly. Russ follows suit, then stretches backward and lets out a grunting howl. I give him a quizzical look.

"Just expelling the negative chi man!" Russ gives me a goofy thumbs-up.

"Let's look around before we get our bags and hike up to the yurt. According to the instructions, it's quite a way."

Russ is walking toward the circle of buildings before I've finished my sentence.

"This is the bathhouse," I say as we walk by a cabin with a large water tank on the roof and a sign above it that reads "Bathhouse."

"I can see that, and that's the laundry and the community store." Russ points at each cabin in turn, "And that's the Bathhouse."

"We already covered that."

Russ holds his nose and waves a hand at me comically, "Yeah, man, but I felt like it was important for you to remember."

"Jerk," I say, laughing at his goofy antics.

"This place is seriously anachronistic."

"Reminds you of Woodstock, I bet."

"Dude, how old do you think I am? I was like five," Russ scolds.

We both laugh.

"There is a potluck community dinner in the hall tomorrow

night," I read from the instructions I received through Away-FromHome and point at the community hall.

"They have a community library," Russ indicates a building labeled 'Community Library'.

"This is much more sophisticated and communal than when I lived here."

Russ nods.

"Is anybody here?" Russ calls out in a moderately loud voice. We wait a moment, and there is no response.

"People are probably settling in for the night. Walking around here in the dark is dangerous. There are gorges, scree, and lots of places to fall. Also, rattlesnakes, mountain lions, and bears."

Russ walks over to the library and tries the door. It is unlocked, and he goes inside. I go into the community store. It is a small, single-room building with a table next to the door and a few rows of old, steel-cased shelves, like you might have found in a market forty years ago. They have many dings, scratches, and little patches of rust. On the shelves are stacks of canned and dry goods. There are also some baskets with fresh fruit and root vegetables. One basket has an assortment of things and a little sign that reads "For Guests." It has more text on it, but I cannot see it well in the dark.

I take my phone out to use it as a flashlight. I am not surprised to notice that there is no cellular service here. With the flashlight, I further examine the sign. It says this is a community effort to ensure everyone has supplies and that guests are encouraged to take something if needed and leave anything extra. One basket is complimentary. It has some apples, small red potatoes, and a turnip. None of them look commercially grown and I am guessing it is a surplus from people's gardens.

Russ is leaving the library just as I come out of the store.

"Anything interesting?" he asks.

"It's like a take-something-leave-something sort of community storage. There are a lot of nonperishables, canned goods, and dry goods."

"Cool," Russ says. "The library mostly includes dog-eared fiction, romance novels, sci-fi, and the like. There are some school books, too."

We wander around and peek into the windows of some of the other buildings that do not have signs. One is a daycare or a schoolhouse. There's a storage place that has many tools, including gas-powered chainsaws, blowers, and other devices I don't recognize. Nothing around here is locked.

"It is starting to get pretty dark, dude," Russ says. "We should probably make it to that yurt, man."

"Yeah," I say.

We make our way back to the car, and after only a little fumbling, I open the trunk. Russ takes a few things from his huge backpack and then hefts it onto his back. His silhouette in the darkness looks like a giant, bipedal turtle. He arranges one of the things he got from his backpack on his head and clicks it on. It is an electric headlamp. He also has a pair of collapsible aluminum hiking sticks.

I swing my much smaller backpack onto my back and my courier bag over my shoulder. I fumble around in my courier bag and produce a small penlight. I glance from my penlight to Russ' headlamp and back. He's really much more prepared than I am.

I lock the car, and with my penlight and printed instructions from AwayFromHome, I start leading us up the path. One hundred feet, one slightly twisted ankle, and one branch in the face later, I suggest that Russ should lead.

We trudge in silence up the winding path. At first, it makes its way over the loamy soil of the hollow between ancient fir trees. Soon, we exit the hollow and are briefly on the edge of a large meadow, but the path quickly departs. It leads up a switchback trail that ascends a steep slope dotted with scrub, rocks, and trees, like day-old stubble on the face of the earth. As we rise, the sky gets slightly brighter, and the gibbous moon casts a pallid light across the land.

To my surprise, Russ moves up the mountain's face like a goat. I expected that he would be the one to lag and fall behind, but I was wrong. This is clearly not his first time backpacking.

We are well up the slope, and the trees and scrub have given way when Russ stops at a large rock. He hefts his pack down and takes out a water bottle to take a sip. I huff up and stand next to him. I try to look impatient, but secretly, I am thankful for the break. I dig a warm can of coconut water out of my pack, pop it open, and take a large sip. The slightly sweet, slightly salty water tastes delicious running down my throat, and I realize this is the first liquid I've had since my mug of stick water this morning.

"Check it out," Russ says, pointing down to the valley below us.

I look at where he is pointing. I can see the large meadow that we skirted the edge of. It's a huge area shaped roughly like a teardrop but slightly curved. We must have passed through the narrow end, but there is a square structure in the large, bulbous end. I can't make it out in the gloom, but it is certainly man-made.

"What is that?" I ask.

Russ fishes the binoculars out of his pack and squints through them at the meadow.

"Solar panels, dude," Russ says with a whistle, "Like a lot of them. They got a solar farm up here."

"There was no electricity down at the community hall, though."

“Yeah, I dunno, it’s a little weird dude.”

"Yeah, weird," I say because I don't know what else to say.

"No doubt. Well, maybe we will run into one of the locals tomorrow, and we can ask them," Russ says. "Let's get moving. It will get really dark soon, and this slope doesn't look like it will get less treacherous."

He starts up the trail, and I stand looking at the moonlit meadow below. On the edge of the meadow, out of the corner of my eye, I see motion, an amorphous black shape flitting in my peripheral vision. Nothing is there when my eyes refocus on that side of the meadow. I'm certain there was something. It wasn't just a trick of the light. I stand silently, carefully scanning the entire meadow and its boundaries for further signs of movement.

"Something wrong, dude?"

"No," I say, "I just thought I saw something."

"Plenty to see, man. We should get moving while we still can."

"You're right," I say, turning away to follow Russ up the hill.

It's only a few hundred more feet of climbing by penlight until we come to a precipice. The mountain we are on is basically flat-topped, like a mesa, though I don't think it is naturally so. The top is covered with more trees. The trail leads us into a grove of oaks and manzanita and then forks. The instructions indicate that we should take the right fork, and so we do. Another dozen yards, we come to a large rock formation jutting up among a stand of live oak. The trail curves around the rock formation, and a large yurt is nestled among the rocks and trees.

The yurt is built on a raised wooden platform with storage

bins below it. A wooden staircase leads up to the front flap of the yurt. The yurt itself is plain and white. It has canvas walls and a roof stretched over its wooden frame. It is round with a high peaked center. It reminds me a bit of a circus tent. I can see that it has flaps on the roof, and the flaps are currently open. It will probably be chilly inside.

I lead Russ up the stairs and push the flap back to enter the yurt.

CHAPTER 5

The interior of the yurt is one large room. A large, four-post bed stands against the wall opposite the door. Worn and dented redwood boards have been bolted together to make a sturdy, utilitarian frame. It once was stained and sealed, but age has worn and chipped it away until a patina of small, high-gloss, curly-cues are all that remains.

A small, pot-bellied cast iron stove is mounted on a four-foot by four-foot aluminum sheet to prevent embers from catching the plank floor on fire. The stove's chimney pipe leads up to a vent hole in the yurt's roof. The space around the vent hole is secured with a silicon gasket to prevent the pipe from burning the canvas roof.

There is a large ice chest and a small sink. A jug of water stands next to the sink, capable of holding probably five gallons. The jug is clear and only half full. It has a spigot hanging out over the sink and a handwritten note that says "Potable." The sink has an obvious drain pipe running under the canvas wall. The gray water must drain down the side of the hill. I'm pretty sure that isn't up to the health code, but who will find it out here?

Next to one of the tan canvas walls, there is a small, round wooden table and a ladder-back wooden chair. A large, floral-patterned area rug covers much of the wooden plank floor. The space is spartan, and the decor is a little mismatched, but it is clean and dry. It will do for two nights.

"Sweet," says Russ as he drops his pack on the floor and begins poking around. In the back, behind the bed, he finds a nook created by a canvas wall.

"Check it out," Russ says as he enters the alcove. I follow him and peer inside.

It is little more than a three or four-foot wide, six-foot deep, canvas-walled closet. Seeing the closet from the entry flap in the dim light is almost impossible because the canvas wall blends in perfectly with the rest of the yurt. Inside is a folded-up cot with a thin mattress, a small bookshelf with an array of worn books, and three battery-operated LED lanterns.

I take the lanterns out and confirm that they are all working. They all have solar panels built into the surface and can be charged with a USB cable. Not that the latter does us much good up here.

As I begin placing lanterns around the room to light it up more, Russ calls, "Dibs!" and begins setting up the cot against one empty wall. I don't say anything, but I am secretly grateful that I don't have to share the big bed or argue over who gets what.

Once we've settled in, Russ begins to start a fire. I haven't done or thought about starting a fire in a wood-burning stove in decades. Russ, however, is a pro; he quickly makes a bed of newspaper from a stack in a small metal box beside the stove. He makes a circular tent of twigs around the paper and lights it. Once the kindling has caught, he carefully adds larger pieces of wood until the fire is blazing away.

"Dinner time," Russ says, as he opens his pack and takes out a small mess kit and a clear plastic bag filled with brown goop. He cuts the bag open, pours the goop into the mess kit, and sets it atop the stove. His goop looks disgusting, but it smells spicy and sweet as it warms up. It is a vegetable curry.

"You bring grub, dude? I got enough to share," Russ says politely.

"I'm good," I fish a silver packet of toaster pastries from my bag. I intend to toast them on the stovetop, but when I open the bag, they are all smashed and crumbled. So I wolf them down right out of the packet.

"Dude, you're having pop tarts for dinner? Have some curry with me!" He exclaims.

"Okay, thank you," I am grateful he is willing to share and glad he came along. Despite what I thought was a solid effort, I am unprepared for this trip.

I hunt around and find a box of plastic plates and cheap metal flatware under the sink. When Russ' curry is bubbling, he serves me a portion on the plate. I sit down and take a bite in silence.

I bite back a scream. The curry is spicy—so spicy I can see lights dancing before my eyes. I start sweating, but my skin feels cold. I glance at Russ, and he's eating it like oatmeal.

"Oh, yeah, dude, sorry I forgot to mention that I like a little spice in my curry. It's not too spicy for you, is it?"

"I. Think. I. See. God," I mewl miserably.

"Yeah, that's the spirit, dig in!" Russ shoves another heaping spoonful of the caustic curry into his mouth.

Somehow, I manage to choke down a few more bites before my stomach aches and my vision swims.

"What did you put in that? Ghost peppers?" I croak as I lay down on the bed and sweat.

"Ghost peppers are nothing. I used Moruga Scorpions, man; two million 'shoes, dude!"

"I don't know what any of that means. Thank you for sharing, but you need to know that your curry is nuclear waste," I inform him, holding my stomach. There is a gurgling sound deep in my bowels, and I feel an uncomfortable shifting, sliding sensation.

"You okay?" Russ' brow is furrowed with concern.

"No! Where is the bathroom?" I shriek, sounding more panicked than I intend, but exactly as panicked as I feel.

Russ quickly pulls the small folding shovel out of his pack and holds it out.

"I'd bet there is an outhouse, but if not, BIFFY!"

"I don't know what that means!" I say and dash out the door, ignoring his folding shovel.

Thankfully, I spot a small building a dozen yards behind the yurt. I dash there and make it in time. I am happy to discover this is not a hole in the ground with a seat over it, but a composting toilet in a small, insulated, and rather nice outhouse.

Twenty minutes later, I return, my entire digestive tract clear of toxic curry and anything else I've ever eaten.

"You good?" Russ is just finishing cleaning dishes in the little sink.

"All better now. Apparently, I ate a boot at some point, but it's cleared out now. You should put a warning label on that stuff."

"Sorry, man, I forget that not everybody likes the spice like I do."

"Uh, huh," I say skeptically. Some part of me can't help but wonder if Russ is pranking me or not.

"Wanna play some cards or something?" Russ asks, holding up a deck, "It's not like there's any TV or video games, or, I don't know, whatever it is you do with your free time."

"Sure."

So we sit cross-legged on the floor as Russ deals out cards.

"Rummy?" He asks.

"I guess, but you'll have to teach me as we go. Cards aren't really my thing."

After three humiliating defeats at a game I still don't understand, I've had my fill of Rummy.

"I think I am going to read for a bit," I say to Russ as I get up from the floor.

"Cool, dude, sounds like a plan," he shuffles the cards quickly and expertly. I'm always amazed at people who shuffle cards well. I feel proud if I don't end up flipping them all over the room.

I have a book in my backpack. I picked up a sci-fi novel at a bookstore in the Atlanta airport a few days ago. I selected it for the cover art, which features an action scene with a man, a feminine robot, and a large, furry creature that should probably be wearing a name tag that says "Not a Wookie. Promise." The cover looks action-packed. The actual story is closer to trashy romance. I've learned more about human-robot relations in the first three chapters than I ever desired. But, there are still some interesting bits, so I skip the parts that get graphic enough to make me uncomfortable.

As I lean back on the bed's headboard, Russ gets a book out of his bag. It's a beaten, well-worn book with a blue cloth cover and no cover art.

"What are you reading?" I ask out of curiosity.

"It's this sort of manifesto from the fifties: spirituality, 'expanding your mind' kinda shit. There's even some discussion of magic. It's kind of progressive, crypto-psychology stuff. The Collective Consciousness, it's called."

"Isn't the expression 'collective unconscious'?"

"Yeah, but he's sort of arguing that the distinction between the conscious and unconscious are semantic, so we are all one mind, one existence."

"Fascinating," I say, but it actually sounds both boring and bullshit at the same time.

"There's a lot in here about dreams that's fairly accurate," Russ concludes with a defensive tone. Maybe he heard the skepticism in my voice. "What you got there?"

"It's called Forward: Full Thrust. When I say it out loud, it is as trashy as it sounds, but somehow, when I bought it...I was expecting something else," my ears are burning.

"No judgment here, dude, whatever floats yer boat."

I turn silently to my book and continue reading the exploits of Captain Dick Canyon and his android first officer, S3XE, as they discover a planet whose entire male population was devastated by a viral outbreak five years prior. I need to be honest with myself, it isn't even close to trashy romance, it's straight-up space porn.

I get half a chapter in and feel uncomfortable reading it with someone else in the room. I put the book away and wish I had gone to Grape Reads to buy some of the Craven's Gate novels I had heard about. Trashy, fantasy psychodrama is more defensible than space porn.

I lay down and stare at the canvas ceiling for a bit.

"Hey dude," Russ interrupts my staring.

"Yeah?"

"Do you still have those pics of the Phantasmagoricon on your phone?"

"I do," I say, sitting up. "Why?"

"Well, this piece in this book sounds like a piece from the

Phantasmagoricon. You know the whole bit about the bubbles?"

"The bit about the bubbles? To be honest, I haven't read it. I keep trying, but it's so sprawling and incoherent."

"It is that man, it is that. Yeah, there is this whole bit about reality being bubbles, it's a little weird, but like, maybe, metaphorically speaking, you know, right on."

"And there's something similar in there?"

"Yeah, check this out," Russ stands up, one thumb holding the page open like he's reciting his favorite poem.

> Imagine a bubble.
>
> A perfect round bubble. Drifting on the wind.
>
> That bubble is an idea, a thought, a hope, a dream, a story. It exists alongside a myriad of other bubbles. This countless mass of bubbles are all contained inside another bubble.
>
> One of those bubbles is you.
>
> That bubble is surrounded by other similar bubbles. An infinite, endless cloud of other bubbles. All filled with hopes and dreams and stories.
>
> These bubbles all form, float, and pop inside yet another bubble that you call the universe. Which itself exists alongside other universe bubbles, inside other bubbles. Bubbles inside bubbles, inside of bubbles, until one of those is a bubble is an idea inside you. Or me, or him, or her, or we. Inside all of us.
>
> Infinite, recursive, and fractal.
>
> No bubble is forever.
>
> Bubbles pop. It's just a truth about bubbles.
>
> When they pop, what they were is absorbed into other bubbles. Our ideas go on to those we've impacted. Our stories

carry on in some form. Our bodies rot and are absorbed into the universe. Our energy disperses.

But just a little bit of the bubble passes beyond. It transcends the scope of the universe. But to do so, it must pass through.

Bubbles have barriers—flexible, dynamic, fluid barriers—but still barriers. We call those barriers different things. On people, we call them the 'Pneuma.' The barriers of the universe, we call the 'Chimeric Veil.'

When some of that energy passes beyond, it weakens the barrier. Even if that universe just suspects that a bubble will pop, it weakens the barrier to prepare for the passing.

When blood is shed, the universe expects death. It expects transcendence. Expecting transcendence, the veil weakens. A little soft spot forms. And in that moment, bubbles can be pulled from outside in. Or from the inside out. In the fractal, recursive ouroboros that is the universe, the distinction is semantic—drawing things from outside in or inside out.

That is what we call magic.

It isn't about if our bubble pops and we die. All bubbles pop.

It isn't about how, or when, or where we die.

It is about whether we are ready to accept it when that time comes. All the universe wants is for us to be at peace with our story when it ends.

That's why the willing sacrifice is so powerful. The universe respects when loss is accepted, even embraced as part of our story. The universe weakens its barriers when we are at peace with our story and ending. It wants those ideas to move on to another place.

And in that intersection of life and death, story and

ending, power can be obtained—power to manipulate the world around you or power to find peace within yourself.

"THAT'S A LOT OF BUBBLES."

"Yeah, no man, it's like that Phantasmagoricon. Can I look at the pages on your phone for a sec?"

"Sure," I say as I hop up and walk over to my phone tucked into my backpack. I take it out and look at the screen.

"Damn, the battery is at three percent. It must have run itself dead looking for a signal."

"And there's like, no electricity up here," Russ says, sounding disappointed.

"A lot of the houses will probably have generators, and you spotted that big solar array. The yurt doesn't have power, but we can find somewhere to charge it tomorrow.

I set my phone into low power mode. There is no sense in having the battery run down when there is absolutely no service here anyway.

I find the photos of the Phantasmagoricon on my phone and carry it over to Russ.

"I don't know how long the battery will last, but you can look till it dies."

"Thanks, dude, but I can wait till we get it charged. There's no rush."

I shrug and put my phone back in my bag. "Suit yourself."

I lay back on the bed and stare at the canvas ceiling again. It ripples slightly as the wind blows across it, making a light luffing sound, like a sail in the breeze. The stark white light of the electric lanterns casts faint shadows in the valleys of the canvas, that dance as they ripple. It is mildly hypnotizing.

"This William Baros guy was a nut," Russ says with a faint chuckle.

"Was?" I ask. The name William Baros sounds familiar, but I can't put my finger on it at the moment.

"Yeah. He died in the sixties. One of those Jim Jones situations, but with less press. He was sort of this philosopher type, and eventually, what he was saying got, you know, like a following. He set up a compound out in like, Montana or something, and started getting weird and messianic. Ended in mass suicide."

"His compound wasn't called New Thule, was it?" I say, half joking. The suspicious part of me focuses on the parallels.

"Nope. They were the Assemblage of Equilibrium and Aggregate Elevated Awareness, or AEAEA."

"That's a mouthful," I say.

"That is pretty much how this guy wrote. There are lots of big words, but used in a pretty confusing manner. That also reminds me of how the Phantasmagoricon is written. AEAEA had this whole thing about achieving peace by breaking down the barriers between the self and the collective consciousness and making all of humanity one giant, unified intelligence."

"Sounds like an excuse for a giant orgy. Not dissimilar to the plot of this book," I say, tapping my hand on my space-porn.

Russ lets out a snorting sort of laugh, "As a cult do, dude, as a cult do."

"It's early, but I think I am going to turn in," I say.

"You cool if I stay up and read a bit more?" Russ asks.

"Yeah, knock yourself out," I say as I get up and turn off all but one of the lanterns.

I change into pajamas and brush my teeth with the water from the jug, then climb into bed. I pull the blankets up to block the light from my eyes, and before I know it, the universe is fading into the blanketing fog of sleep.

CHAPTER 6

The wind is howling and whipping at my clothes and hair. My eyes are watering as my tears are blown away into the black night. My fingers ache, and my palms feel blistered from gripping tightly to the rough strands of rope in my hands. Before me, a row of crude planks leads out over a gorge, a veritable abyss in the stygian night. I rock violently back and forth in the gusts of wind. I am standing in the middle of a narrow suspension bridge, buffeted by a storm. I am paralyzed with terror. How did I get here?

On the far side of the bridge is a familiar figure. It looks like me, and dressed like me, but its skin is matte and rubbery.

"Come on!" Hank yells.

I try to move my hands forward and step, but my muscles are on strike. Terror is in the driver's seat.

"I can't!" I yell back.

"Of course you can, Miles. You just put one foot in front of the other!"

"No, I'll slip and fall!"

"You won't!" Hank yells. "And if you do, I'll catch you."

"You can't catch me, you're over there!"

"It's a dream, Miles. We can do anything we want. Come on."

"I can't!"

"You can; if you can't, I'll catch you."

"You can't catch me! You're dead!" I yell at him.

Despite the fact that he's ten yards away, it is dark, rain pelts my clothes, and wind tears at my face, I can see his face with perfect clarity. He looks sad, dejected, and defeated. The animated form that was Hank turns into a rubber mannequin, rigid and inflexible. The wind picks it up and hurls it into the night, plummeting it down into the darkness below.

"Hank!" I scream, "Hank, I'm sorry!"

The wind becomes a hurricane-force gale, bucking and shaking the flimsy bridge like a lost ship at sea. I slip and fall. My fingers catch one of the ropes that support the bridge. I am clinging with one hand, screaming. My fingers burn, and I can feel them slipping on the wet rope. I call for help, but the roaring wind tears my voice from my throat, and I can't even hear the words in my own head. I will fall, and this time, no one will save me. My fingers slip, and I am buffeted into the darkness.

I wake up screaming. I am sitting in the four-poster bed in my rented yurt. Russ is sitting up on his cot, staring at me in obvious alarm.

"Dude!" Russ says. "You cool?"

"Yeah, just a nightmare," I respond, my voice still slightly shaky. The memory of the dream is already fading. It feels more like a scene from a movie I watched years ago than a fantasy that passed through my brain.

"Was it?" A familiar voice says next to me.

I start and look over. Hank is sitting in bed next to me. He's dressed in identical pajamas. I glance back at Russ, but he doesn't seem to have any reaction to the animate mannequin in the bed next to me.

"Great, I'm still dreaming," I groan and flop back in bed.

"'Fraid not, dude," Russ says, climbing out of his cot. I am startled to discover that he sleeps unabashedly nude. I turn to face Hank while Russ pulls his clothes on.

"What are you doing here?" I whisper to Hank.

"Same thing I am always doing, protecting you."

"You mean hassling me and giving me a hard time?"

"Well, that too. A simulacrum's gotta have a hobby, right?"

"I'm still dreaming, aren't I?" I whisper to Hank, but Russ, who has gotten his clothes on, can apparently hear me.

"You might be in one of those somnambulatory states, where you are half awake and capable of motor function and speech, but still experiencing dream-like sensory input." Russ adds, "Sleepwalking."

"I feel pretty awake to be sleepwalking."

"You're not sleepwalking. You're not dreaming. I'm here like I always am. You just decided to respond to me for once."

"I respond to you all the time," I say, in a normal tone of voice.

"No, it's like you can't see or hear me unless we are near the effigy, but I'm always with you. How do you think you are protected from magic anywhere you go? You're connected to me. I'm connected to the effigy."

"Um, you okay, dude? You're talking to a pillow," Russ says, concern in his voice.

"I might be having a psychotic break, but yeah, I am fine," I nod. This doesn't seem to reduce Russ' concern.

"You aren't having violent thoughts, are you?" he asks with a touch of humor in his voice, but I can tell from his furrowed brow that it's to hide his alarm.

"So, I've mentioned that I have a simulacrum that protects me from magic; that I can channel magical energy into so that it doesn't affect me as much?"

"Yeah, you've mentioned it."

"Well, what I don't like to advertise is that it talks to me. I've always assumed that it was, like an imaginary friend, my own unconsciousness talking to me, or whatever."

"'Imaginary friend,' like I'm Puff the magic freakin' dragon or something. I'm insulted."

"It's not something I really talk about because it can be a little off-putting and make people question my mental well-being."

"I copy that dude."

"Well, normally, I only hear him when I am home, where I can see the simulacrum, the mannequin. But now, he's suddenly here. Normally, it's just his voice, but now I see him sitting in the bed beside me. He says it isn't a dream, and I am not losing my mind."

"Can't lose what you never had."

"And he's kind of a jerk," I roll my eyes.

"Okay, so you wake up screaming from a nightmare, and then this projection of your simulacrum shows up. That's got to mean something."

I turn to look at Hank, an eyebrow quirked in an unspoken question.

"Don't ask me. Like I said, I'm always here. You just don't seem to notice me most of the time. But since you are listening, there is something I have to tell you..."

"He says he doesn't know, that he's always with me, and I just don't usually notice him."

"Well, what did you dream about?"

"I dreamed I was on a suspension bridge in a storm, and Hank wanted to help me, but I wouldn't let him. Then we both fell into the gorge, and I woke up."

"Who's Hank?" Russ asks. I've never told Russ that I named the simulacrum.

"Um, Hank was my... is my simulacrum," I stammer

uncomfortably. It's the truth, but it's not the whole truth; it's probably not the relevant truth, either.

Russ raises an eyebrow. "I sense there's more to this story, dude. Do you want to talk about it?"

"No," I feel slightly nauseous.

"Suit yourself, man, but I can't help but wonder what you came all the way up here to deal with."

I look at Hank, his rubber face frowning in annoyance, and sigh. "Yeah, you are right. Remember that I said I had a brother? Well I named the simulacrum after him. Hank was my brother. He died when we were kids."

"I am sorry, man. Did it have anything to do with a bridge?"

I feel tears welling up in my eyes, and my vision narrows to a pinprick. My head swims.

"Yeah, he fell off a bridge. Or rather, I fell off a bridge, and he pulled me up, but lost his balance and slipped in the process."

"I am so sorry, Miles. That's like, awful."

"Yeah. The bridge is up here somewhere."

I glance at Hank, who has been very quiet this whole time. That is out of character; I usually can't get him to shut up. The imaginary mannequin shrugs at me. I jump off the bed and scurry over to my bag, where I fish out the set of cards that the Hierophant sent me.

"One sec," I say over my shoulder. Then, I rifle through the cards until I find the Fool card and throw it down on the foot of the bed. I notice with some alarm as I do that Hank has vanished. "And he's gone again."

Didn't Hank say he had something to tell me?

"This is one of the cards that you were talking about?" Russ asks.

I nod, "The Fool. That person walking off the edge of the

bridge is obviously me. The other person trying to help him, that's Hank, and that is the bridge in question."

"Spooky."

“Indeed.”

"So you want to find this bridge?" Russ asks.

"I mean, no, not really, but like you said, it's what I came here to figure out. So even though I don't want to, I will."

"Fair enough. Do you remember how to get there?"

"No, it was on the back trail that led to our house. We weren't supposed to go near it, let alone play on it. But, we were kids with little supervision and did a lot of stuff we were told not to."

"Well, it's over a gorge, right?"

"Yeah, it's pretty deep and very steep but not too wide. It didn't even seem that wide when I was a kid."

"Hmm," Russ says, going to his pack. He rummages around momentarily and comes out with a large, waterproof topo map and a handheld GPS. It's an older model with none of the fancy modern features, but it gets him our coordinates. I zone out, watching him, bleary-eyed and half-asleep.

"Fossil Creek? Line Gulch? Do any of these sound familiar?" Russ asks, listing the names of lines on his map.

I shake my head in a vague no.

"Simon's Folly? Bear Wallow?" He asks.

"Simon's Folly, that's it," I say, a memory shaking loose. "I remember my dad used to tell us a story about how the gorge got its name: a logger who went to relieve himself in the night didn't see the gorge in the dark and fell over. I am pretty sure my dad made it up. He added different details every time."

"That's just over the other side of the hill. I bet if we went left at the last fork, it'd take us there," Russ says after examining his map for a moment.

"Okay, well, maybe we go check it out after first light?"

"Sounds like a plan. That's a couple of hours away," Russ says. "You going to be able to get back to sleep?"

"No."

"Me neither. You want to play some more rummy?"

"No."

"Okay. I'm gonna read some more," Russ says, "that cool?"

"Yeah, that's fine. I need some time to think."

"Okay, think away, amigo, think away!"

I sit on the bed, eyes closed. I want to plan for the morning, but I keep replaying the last week in my head, second-guessing what I might have done differently to achieve a better outcome. It's a waste of time, and I'd much rather invest my mental energy in something more productive. Still, I just keep spiraling over the heist and what followed: the conference in Atlanta, breaking up with Genevieve, the plane ride home with Hale. The light is dim, and the gentle rustling of the wind on the canvas walls starts to slowly lull me into sleep. Just before I doze off completely, my eyes snap open to the sound of a voice.

"*Miles*!" I can barely hear the voice over the wind and the luffing of the canvas. "*Miles*! *Help*!"

I sit bolt upright and glance over at Russ sitting on his cot and reading quietly by lamplight.

"Did you hear that?" I ask.

"All I heard was you snoring, brother."

"Oh," I say and lay back down to rest.

CHAPTER 7

After a healthy breakfast of crumbled toaster pastries, and whatever weird blend of nuts, berries, and “medicinal” herbs Russ brought, we start the trail toward the suspension bridge. We leave most of our stuff in the cabin, so we are traveling much lighter than before. Russ brings his binoculars and a little hip pack that I assume has his daily ration of psychedelic mushrooms in it. I grab my courier bag and throw an extra can of coconut water into it.

The trail is little more than a meandering line cleared of star thistle and scrub. Manzanita and Scotch broom lean in heavily on the north side of our easterly path. The landscape is dotted with the occasional live oak and large, raw granite slabs that stick up from the earth like broken teeth. While the hollow down in the valley is lush and green, this part of the mountain is more desolate, yellow, brown, and gray.

We know we are getting close when a hand-painted wooden sign nailed to a tree reads, "Beware, dangerous bridge. Keep off!!!" We continue forward and encounter another similar sign, this one more dire: "Keep out. Danger! Fatal

Falling Hazard!" It is accompanied by a hand-painted picture of a stick figure plummeting to its death. Considering it is just a stick figure, the image is pretty graphic.

Despite the warnings, we press on and soon round a bend. There, we see the bridge and the chasm that it crosses.

The gorge is not wide, ranging from ten feet at its narrowest to twenty-five feet at its widest. I get within about twenty feet of the edge, and my legs will carry me no further. They root to the ground and will not budge, no matter how much I will them. If I am being honest, I don't will them much; my legs and I are in agreement on this topic. From my place, I can only see the wall of the gorge and not its depths. In my memory, the gorge is bottomless, but I know that cannot be true.

Russ does not share my fear and walks right up to the bridge. The bridge itself is a suspension bridge. Four thick, coated steel cables, two high and two low, run over the gorge. They pass through stout wooden posts and are anchored into the ground with huge iron spikes. Chicken wire has been run vertically between the cables as a makeshift barrier, and wooden planks fastened with heavy U-shaped bolts make the walking surface.

This is not the rope and plank bridge of my childhood. It has been rebuilt much more sturdily. Another addition that was not there in my memory is the wooden gates that have been erected on either side. They are made of rows of pine tree saplings screwed into a wooden frame and hung by metal hinges to the posts that anchor the bridge. A heavy chain and padlock seal the gate on this side. The other side is probably similarly secured, but I cannot see it. A hand-painted sign on the gate reads, "Danger: Keep Off."

Russ leans right over the edge. I feel nauseous just watching him.

"That must be over a hundred feet deep. Nothin' but rocks down there," he makes a long, appreciative whistle. He pauses to examine the bridge for a moment before returning to me.

"So," my voice quavers with fear, "we saw it."

"You okay? Was this too much?"

"Yeah, I am fine. I don't know what I came here for. There is nothing here but bad memories," I say. My chest feels like there is a weight on it. "Also, I am a little scared of heights."

"Understandable, dude. You want to head back?"

"Yeah, let's go down to the community area, get a shower, and eat something other than toaster pastries."

"Sure thing," Russ starts down the trail. He's about fifty feet down the trail when he turns around, "You okay?"

I'm still frozen in place. My mind is blank. Suddenly, Russ' hand is on my shoulder.

"Dude?"

The touch on my shoulder snaps me out of whatever daze I was in.

"Yeah," I turn around and start walking back toward the yurt.

We wind our way through the scrub and brush in silence, which is broken suddenly when Russ begins speaking.

"You know," Russ says thoughtfully. "If that bridge is so dangerous, why don't they tear it down?"

"I think my dad said it was a fire safety concern. Without it, there is only one way off the mountain for the houses on the other side of the gorge. The gorge wraps around the mountain to the north and east, and there are miles and miles of undeveloped wilderness."

"I guess that makes sense," Russ says, "But, I mean, look at the path; our footprints aren't the only ones here. This gets a fair amount of traffic for an emergency exit, right?"

I look down at the dirt where Russ is indicating. He's right.

On the dusty path, dozens of different shoe prints, mostly boots, have left impressions. I am a little frustrated with myself that I didn't notice that on my own. I'm usually pretty observant, but I've been so dopey lately.

"Yeah," I say, "You are right."

"If it's just an emergency exit for a couple of houses, why would so many people go up and back?"

"Good question," I mentally shrug.

We continue winding our way down the dusty little path. It descends out of the exposed, scrub-covered area and back into the green of the valley. We stop briefly at the yurt for bathing supplies before we descend the path to the hollow where we parked our car. The plan is to shower and see if we can bump into anyone.

I cannot shake the feeling we are being followed, though I am sure it's just nerves after visiting a place of such childhood trauma.

CHAPTER 8

At the bottom of the hill, the trail flattens out and turns a broad corner around a copse of trees. We can see the parking area as we come out of the bend. Magdalena's little car is still parked there, and its loud red paint and modern curved lines look out of place in the rustic setting. Next to the car there is an old, beat-up pickup truck that once was blue but now is a dull grayish color with patches of rust, like liver spots. There's also a slightly newer black sedan that wasn't here last night. It is coated with a patina of dust.

As we approach the bathhouse, we see three men at the community hall in the compound's center. They are doing some repairs on the building; it looks like they are replacing shingles in the siding. Two worn and dusty ATVs are parked nearby. Near the building with the sign that reads "Store," I see two mud-encrusted children playing in the dirt with yellow metal toy trucks. A flash of motion behind the store focuses my eye on two women hanging laundry on a line.

As we approach, one of the men notices us and points us out to his compatriots with a nudge of the elbow. One of the other men breaks away from them with a nod and begins walking toward us. The others continue squaring shingles on the side of the building.

The man approaching us is fairly tall, barrel-chested, and has the build of a man who is strong from doing manual labor but has never seen a gym in his life. His skin is tan and weathered. His hair is short, but shaggy, and black with streaks of gray. His eyes are a familiar, piercing blue. The red flannel shirt, faded blue jeans, and work boots make him look like a cartoon lumberjack.

"Hello!" He says jubilantly, "You must be the people renting the yurt!"

"Indeed we are," I say.

"Matt, Matt Milligan," Matt holds out a calloused hand. Suddenly, I know why his eyes look so familiar. Matt Milligan was my best friend as a kid—my only friend, really. He was the only other kid our age in Stanyon's Hollow. He looks old now, even older than me.

"Miles, Miles Ward," I say, shaking his hand. He has an exceedingly firm handshake, and the calluses on his hands are as thick as armor.

"Russ Russo," Russ introduces himself, offering a fist to bump instead of a handshake. Matt looks at him, confused.

"I don't like shaking hands, man," Russ says. "It's like a serious vector for communicable diseases."

Matt shrugs and fist-bumps him.

"Welcome to Stanyon's Hollow," Matt says, "Let me give you the tour."

"That's okay, man," Russ begins, "Miles..."

I realize he is about to say I grew up here, something I suddenly do not feel like sharing, so I cut him off.

"Russ and I poked around a little last night. We are heading to the bathhouse and the store there," I point, indicating the places of interest.

"All right then," Matt says. "Well, feel free to take or leave anything at the store. That's how we do it here. And tomorrow night, there will be a big community potluck in the common hall. Tyler, Robbie, and I are fixin' the place up for it."

He indicates the two men who are working on the building.

"Thanks, man," Russ says. I nod along in agreement.

"Well, I should get back to work. You boys should come to my place for lunch. We don't get many visitors, and my wife and I like to gab if we get a chance," Matt smiles broadly and welcomingly.

"Yeah, that would be great," I murmur.

"Cool, dude," Russ gives his goofy thumbs up.

"Come by around midday. We aren't real formal with time up here," Matt points behind the storage building. "There's a trail behind that building, with a bay on one side and a little pine on the other. You go up that, it goes straight to our house. It's the A-frame with the big awning; you can't miss it. Pam will be excited to talk to some city folk."

"Thanks," I say, "sounds great."

"Great, see you for lunch," Matt says with a little salute. "I should get back to work."

"We need to hit the showers anyway, man," Russ drawls.

Matt returns to his companions, and soon is hammering up shingles again. Russ and I make our way to the bathhouse.

The bathhouse is little more than a wooden shack. A dozen posts are planted in concrete, with boards between them to create walls. There are four stalls made up in this way, with curtains for doors. There is running water inside, and I am surprised and relieved to discover that both hot and cold varieties of water are offered; when I was a child, I had to get used to cold showers. PVC drains are set into the concrete pad to run the water away. There is no sewer up here. There are two plumbed toilets in stalls at the back of the bathhouse, so I am assuming they have a septic field nearby. These are all big steps up from the icy showers and outhouses of my youth.

After a brief but refreshing shower, I emerge. Matt and his companions have left, along with the ATV. I don't see the women hanging laundry anymore, either, but the kids are still there, encrusted in dirt and pretending to sword fight with sticks. The metal dump trucks now abandoned in the dust.

"What's next boss?" Russ says as he comes out of his shower, looking refreshed.

"I'm curious about those solar panels we saw down in the meadow."

"Yeah?" Russ says. There is almost an accusatory tone to his voice for some reason.

"There are no lights or electricity in these buildings."

Russ nods his agreement.

"But, that was a lot of solar. If it isn't powering all this? What's it powering? And they'd need a lot of battery power to store all that generation, otherwise, they'd only have power during the day," I scan the buildings and treeline for some signs of a power line, but find none.

"And that's curious, and so you want to go snooping around another person's property. Up here in the mountains," Russ drawls, "where we are probably the only two unarmed people for miles, and nobody would notice if we both just went missing."

"They have an AwayFromHome rental. They must expect us city slickers are going to wander off the path. It's just some solar panels."

"Okay, dude, I just wanted to make sure we were both looking at this the same way."

"Well, let's go drop our bath stuff off at the yurt, and we can figure it out as we go," I say.

"Sounds like a plan, man."

On our way back to the yurt, we stop at a little clearing overlooking the valley below. It has an open view of the meadow with the solar panels in it. It's daylight now and we can see it all unobstructed. Dots of yellow, orange, and purple flower buds make the field look like a huge abstract pointillist painting. However, the large solar array makes an ugly and angular gouge right in the middle of the painted meadow.

There are a lot of solar panels; from here, it looks like maybe thirty. I'm not an expert, but I know that is more than enough to power a house or two. It would take many backup batteries to store that much generation. There is no way anything up here is connected to a larger state or local power grid.

No other structures or man-made objects are visible from here. It's just a meadow filled with grass and wildflowers, three or four acres large and surrounded by a heavily wooded forest on three sides. The mountain face we are looking down from boxes the fourth side.

"I wonder what it's powering?" I say out loud.

"A huge indoor grow operation," Russ speculates, "is the best case. Worst case, a meth lab or something sketchier."

"Marijuana isn't illegal anymore. Why would they have a hidden grow operation up here?"

"You'd be surprised, dude. You would be surprised. Why do people still make moonshine? To avoid taxes and government oversight," Russ wags a finger at me.

"Huh," I scratch my chin. I guess I hadn't ever spent much time considering the economics of a marijuana plantation. "I don't know, that doesn't sound right. Does it?"

Russ shrugs, "I don't know. You could ask someone down

at the community center there, or you could ask that Matt guy at lunch. We are going to his place for lunch, right?"

"I think so," I nod.

"Oh yeah, man, did I misread, or did you not want to tell that guy you grew up here?"

"I got a little, I don't know, cold feet? Matt was my best, maybe only, friend growing up, and I don't know, it felt weird."

"Huh," Russ says with narrowed eyes. There is a tone of suspicion, and he's trying to make eye contact, but I avoid his gaze. "It's just, if he had been your best friend, I'd expect at least a glimmer of recognition at your name. But nada."

"It's been a long time," I say, still trying to avoid Russ' gaze.

"No, dude, you're being shifty. What's the dealie-o?"

I sigh a long, frustrated sigh.

"Okay, fine. Miles Ward isn't my birth name. I changed it when I turned eighteen and went out on my own."

Russ laughs, "Really, man? You always say that it's a coincidence that your name matches your job, but you changed it for branding?"

"No," I exclaim, "I wasn't doing the whole apotropaist thing when I changed my name. It was just a coincidence that it happened to match up later."

"Was it?" Russ asks skeptically.

"Yes, Miles, Was it?"

"Yes!" I exclaim, perhaps a little too enthusiastically.

"So, then, what is your real name?"

"Ugh. My real name is Miles Ward. It's on my license. It's on my social security card. My birth name was Mitchell Richardson," I say petulantly.

"Well, this day is getting more interesting by the minute!" Russ says.

"Do you want to go look at those solar panels with me or what?" I ask curtly.

CHAPTER 9

We trudge down the rocky trail in stone silence. As we round a hedge of Scotch broom, its noxious yellow flowers waggling in our faces and dusting our clothes with pollen, we see a figure plodding up the trail ahead of us. I stop dead still as I see a six-foot-tall penguin approaching us.

I blink my eyes hard and realize my mind is playing tricks on me. The person coming up the path is almost as odd a sight as a giant, flightless Antarctic bird would be. He's a tall, broad-bellied man, probably a little over six feet, but his height is difficult to judge because he wears a black stovepipe hat. His black jacket, slacks, white shirt, and light yellow cumberbund make him look much like a giant penguin. He has large, floppy, un-tied leather work boots on, making him shuffle side to side as he walks, like a waddling penguin. Anyone could have mistaken him for a giant bird in this light. That's what I keep telling myself, at least.

As he gets closer, I see that his hat is moth-eaten, his clothes are stained with food, dirt, and sweat, and he is not nearly as presentable as I first thought. His large, round, pocked face has a sour, eternally downturned mouth, and his eyes are downcast on his shoes so that he doesn't see us until he is almost upon us.

"Greetings, dude. I thought you were a penguin for a moment!" Russ exclaims as the man gets close. Russ nudges me with his elbow, "Hah, can you imagine? It must be the psilocybin."

"Yeah," I chuckle, "imagine that."

The man looks slowly up at us, as if we were the ones walking down the trail in penguin suits, his jaw slack. "Woah, hi."

"I'm Russ, this is Miles. How are you today, man?"

"We are renting the yurt," I add in helpfully.

"Oh, visitors," the man says. "Not supposed to talk to visitors."

"What's your name?" Russ asks.

"Gawain."

"Is that a first or last name?" Russ looks Gawain up and down carefully.

"It is just my name."

"Okay, great to meet you, Gawain; like I said, I'm Russ," Russ holds his fist out for a fist bump. Gawain either doesn't want to fist bump or doesn't register the motion as a greeting because he doesn't seem to notice Russ' hand.

"I'm Miles," I don't bother with a manual greeting.

"Hi, I'm Gawain. I'm not supposed to talk to visitors."

"Whatcha up to Gawain?" I ask.

"Preparing for the morning," he says flatly.

"Do you know anything about the solar panels in the meadow down there?" Russ points down the hill.

"Power for the morning. I am not supposed to talk to you."

I look the man over. His age is hard to surmise because his features are young, but the pockmarks and ruddy, sunburned face makes him look older. He could either be a prematurely aged twenty-five or a well-preserved forty-five. In any event, he's a grown man.

"Why aren't you supposed to talk to us?" Russ asks.

"Cause I say stupid stuff, and it scares the visitors."

"We aren't scared, Gawain."

"I'm glad," he says. "I have to go prepare for the morning."

"What does that mean?"

"I'm not supposed to talk to the visitors," Gawain says. "The doctor doesn't like it when I talk to strangers."

Gawain moves off the trail, stomping through some brambles to avoid us.

"I have a present for you," Gawain says suddenly, turning around. We turn to face him. He fishes in an inner pocket of his jacket and takes something out, holding it in a meaty hand. I reach forward, and he drops it into my hand. At first, I think it is a little wooden coin based on its size, shape, and texture.

"Thank you," I say, closing my hand around it.

"You are welcome. You should go before the morning," Gawain says and then trudges off.

"Gawain, wait, one more thing!" Russ calls after him, but Gawain continues trudging along in silence and vanishes past the brush up the trail.

"Am I tripping, or was that weird?" Russ asks.

"Pretty sure yes to both."

"Oh, yeah," Russ laughs.

I open my hand and look at Gawain's gift. It's a small, hand-carved wooden mask, about the right size for a fashion doll. I turn it over to see the front, and it is hideous. Gnarled protrusions jut out. Eyes, mouths, unidentifiable organs, and sphincters are carved all over it, seemingly randomly. The detail is fine, and the craftsmanship is surprisingly exquisite for such a hideous thing.

"That's freaky," Russ says.

"Yeah. Freaky is kind of my line of work, though," I put the small mask in my bag. If nothing else, it will make for a weird story later. "Should we follow him?"

"No, I think we let that guy go. I peg him as the victim of some trauma; he reminds me of some lobotomy patients I met back in the day."

"But, is it weird and suspicious that he's heading toward our yurt?"

"Yeah, but what's he gonna do, get in your clean clothes? No man, guy like that, you scare him he's unpredictable. Let's leave him alone, dude."

"Yeah, you're probably right."

As we start back down the trail, I try to shake the weirdness of our encounter with Gawain from my mind. It doesn't work.

CHAPTER 10

THE WILDFLOWERS in the meadow are deceptive. From the hillside, they were a beautiful array of colored dots. Once we are marching through them, I realize that half are thistles of one kind or another. The worst is the yellow star thistle, whose sharp thorns poke clear through my jeans, unabated by the fabric.

There is a narrow dirt path leading out to the solar panels. It's little more than a dusty rut between thistles, requiring we walk heel-to-toe through the field as if on a balance beam. If Russ is getting stabbed by the thistles, he doesn't give any indication—unlike me, who spends the whole march across the meadow cursing.

We approach the meadow's center, where the solar panels stand incongruously against the agrestal landscape. The structure is far bigger than I anticipated from a distance. It reminds me of the solar panel arrays they have above parking lots at the high school back in Napa. Eight large concrete pylons have been expertly set here, with big metal girders supporting a framework for the solar panels to sit in. Three large bundles of wire sink into the earth. It probably covers half an acre of land in total.

The weeds and thistles have grown over the place where the cables were buried, but looking at the angle they enter the ground, it is possible to estimate the direction of the cables. They appear to run to the far side of the meadow, away from the community of Stanyon's Hollow and into the forest beyond.

"You're right. They aren't powering the community center," Russ points at the angle at which the wires enter the ground.

"No, it looks like they run into the woods."

"I don't think we should try to follow them," Russ says, his voice touched with concern.

"Mmm," I grunt. I don't agree, so I'm intentionally vague.

"I feel like you should ask Matt about them. The only reason I can think to have this much generation out here is, well, some kinda drug operation, and it's gotta be big. Big operation means big money and big money means high risk. High risk means..." Russ drags a single finger across his throat and dramatically hangs his tongue out one side of his mouth.

"Yeah, I get it. You are probably right," I nod.

"Good. Anyway, it's almost lunchtime, dude!" Russ points at his watch.

"Already?" I ask.

"Yup, it's just after twelve!" he exclaims.

"How is it afternoon already? We haven't done anything."

"Yeah, we've been marching up and down that damn mountain all morning."

By the time we make it back across the field and to the community center, my socks have been mostly replaced by burrs, and my calves feel like they are on fire from thistle stings. We don't have time to hike all the way back to the yurt again to change, so I sit down on a log used as an implied barrier around the circular drive to assess the damage.

"I remember why I never came back," I mutter darkly, picking burrs out of my socks. There are more than I could possibly remove, but I hope I can at least get to a place where I don't feel like I am wearing sandpaper spats.

"Was it always like this?" Russ asks in a hushed and reflective voice.

"What do you mean? Covered in burrs and poison oak? Yeah."

"No. I don't know, there's something off, man. It's like, I don't know, the air pressure is too high or something," he pauses dramatically and cocks his head, "and you hear that?"

"What birds and crickets?”

"Exactly, like there's birds around, but there should be more. And there were crickets and shit last night, but no more than at my house, and I live in a city dude."

"Bullshit, there's plenty of wildlife; I saw a deer just this morning. Have you been watching horror movies?" I chide him.

"I don't know, man, this place is giving me the heebie-jeebies."

"Jinkies, Shaggy," I stand up. "I think you found a clue."

"Haha. If I'm Shaggy, that makes you Fred, dude."

"Shit. Let's forget the whole Scooby Doo angle," I start leading Russ up the path toward Matt's house.

"Or maybe Velma."

"Let's drop the Scooby Doo angle."

"Oh! I know why you want to drop it cause, no, you're the dog, man!"

I grunt and lead on in silence. At first, I am a little unsure of where to go, but once we turn the first corner, it all comes back to me like I never left this place.

The trail climbs to a bank above a small creek—nothing

but a trickle. The rocks on the side of the trail are covered with moss, and the trees around us keep the cool, damp creek air in. We don't overheat despite the constant walking. It's so cool that I suspect there is more water underground here than we can see. An occasional California Bay adds a sharp, herbaceous odor to the air, and it is a peaceful walk.

We are tipped off that we are approaching Matt's house when we see another toy dump truck loaded with plastic dinosaurs. It has been left in a small clearing on the side of the trail, looking like it is about to careen through a house made of bark and sticks.

Around the next corner, we come to a large clearing in the trees. A moderately sized, A-Frame house has a wooden shed leaning against one side. The A-Frame is dark stained wood, with huge sheets of metal roofing that come almost completely to the ground at a very steep angle. A single metal chimney rises from one side of the roof, a little tendril of smoke coming out.

There is a large, unsealed wooden deck in front of the house. The large awning Matt mentioned hangs over it, made of the same lumber and metal roofing as the house. Matt is standing on the deck in front of a charcoal grill. He's wearing a long, dirty apron with a slogan, but we are too far away to read it. Playing in the dirt in front of the deck is one of the children from earlier in front of the laundry.

We walk up to the house. It's in a small, man-made clearing. About fifty feet of heavy trees stand between it and a small cliff behind it, blocking the eastern skyline. It must not get light here until very late in the morning.

"Good to see you again," Matt motions with a pair of tongs at the child playing on the deck. "That's my daughter, Winnie."

Winnie ignores us. My vision swims and I grab the deck's

railing to catch myself before I fall from the sudden wave of vertigo that sweeps over me. Matt doesn't seem to notice.

“Pamela is inside, finishing up dinner. Oh, you brought wine. Pam is going to be happy to see that!” Matt exclaims.

I'm very confused because, while I am sure Russ has mushrooms, probably hashish, and who knows what else, we didn't bring any wine.

“It’s a cabernet; it’s pretty full-bodied and should hold up to that beef well,” Genevieve says from behind me.

Ice runs in my veins. I slowly turn to see Genevieve standing behind me in light tan hiking pants, a white tank top, and a blue windbreaker tied around her waist. She isn't wearing makeup, a look I am not used to seeing on her. Her hair is held back in a tight ponytail, and she smiles at Matt. My stomach lurches, and I feel a tightness in my chest.

What the hell is going on?

“Venison. And we aren’t particular about our booze here. As long as it isn’t Petersen’s elderberry wine, we’ll enjoy it,” Matt pauses and quirks an eyebrow at my expression.

I flap my jaw silently like, a stupified fish in a tank.

“Petersen’s?” Genevieve’s tone is jovial and relaxed.

“We don’t get a ton of provisions from town, so wine and the like is a rare treat. Ernie Petersen’s a fella here who makes his own berry wine. It’ll get you drunk, but that’s all I can say for it,” he explains.

“Sounds lovely,” Genevieve says flatly.

“Do you want to take that on inside to Pam?” Matt says. “You ladies can get acquainted.”

Genevieve quirks an eyebrow and hands me the bottle of wine. I think she's offended by the traditional gender roles Matt is suggesting. I stand there staring at her blankly. I don't know what to say.

"Are you okay?" She asks softly.

"I um, uh. Where's Russ?" I whisper back.

"Who is Russ?" Her face contorts with concern.

I look around; there is no sign of Russ. Genevieve is standing exactly where I last saw him.

"What is going on?" I ask.

"You don't look great. You should go sit down," Genevieve says with extreme concern.

“No, I'm fine. I’ll bring the wine in,” I hold the bottle up. "I can get some water inside."

Genevieve crosses her arms over her chest, "You sure you are okay?"

"Yeah, I'm fine. It's just been, you know, a lot," I turn and walk inside with the wine.

The front entrance is a large sliding glass door covered in plastic decals of famous stained-glass windows. I couldn’t tell you where they are from specifically; ecclesiastical construction isn't exactly my area of expertise, but they all look familiar. I slide the door open and walk into the entryway.

Over my shoulder, I can hear Genevieve begin interrogating Matt.

“So, Matt, what brought you to live here in Stanyon's Hollow?”

“Well, I was born and raised here. My grandfather was one of the founders of our community,” Matt begins, but I don't hear what else he has to say, as I close the large sliding glass door behind me.

"I'm losing my mind. What just happened?" I murmur to myself.

"You aren't going crazy. There is something weird going on here," Hank's voice says from beside me. I startle and glance around, but the space is empty. I have an odd sensation that Hank is right beside me.

"Yeah," I mutter, "I'm not sure the disembodied voice in my head is going to assure me of my sanity."

"Sure, I hear you. But seriously, something isn't right. Be careful."

I sigh and look around, trying to get my bearings to reassure myself that I am firmly rooted in reality.

"It's a dream. I am dreaming," I say, more loudly now.

"It isn't, and you aren't."

I will myself to wake within the dream like I did when I was learning to Dreamwalk with Russ. I concentrate with all my might on waking.

"You look constipated."

"Damn," I mutter. I slap myself hard in the face; my cheek burns with the sting, and the side of my eye socket feels hot. "This doesn't feel like a dream."

"I told you it's not a dream. I don't know what is going on, but Russ was here; now he isn't. Genevieve wasn't here, and now she is. And she seems to like you again. Like I said, something very wrong is happening."

I glance over my shoulder out the large glass door. Genevieve is watching me, her brow furrowed in concern. I grimace a broad, fake smile and raise the wine bottle in salute. She gives me a forced half-smile for my effort. I should get this wine to Pamela and try to figure out what's happening.

The entire front half of the A-frame is one large space. It has a high, vaulted ceiling with three unusual wooden mobiles hanging down from the roof. The mobiles are built around three chandeliers with old incandescent bulbs. They depict scenes, but I can't see the details in the dim light. Two kerosene lanterns currently light the room, and a pile of coals crackle in a large cast iron stove off to the side.

Two doors, one open, are to the right and left of the stove. The opposite side of this large room has a stairwell leading up.

Several old, worn sofas surround this large front room, with end tables piled with books. The books are mostly dog-eared paperbacks, and a quick glance reveals them to be mostly 90s sci-fi and romance novels.

The room smells amazing, with spicy vegetables and sweet corn. I can hear the clanking and clattering of dishes from the open door to the right of the hearth.

"Hello! Pamela? I'm Miles," I say loudly as I walk toward the door.

"Come on back!" I hear a husky female voice.

I follow the voice through the door and into a small kitchen. There is a large sink, a stove, and a refrigerator that is clearly older than I am. I wonder briefly how they have a stove and refrigerator in a house that does not always have electricity.

"Hi!" I say as I come in.

Pamela is a broad-shouldered woman in worn jeans and a ruggedly constructed blouse. She has the build of a shot-putter. She's got a beige-colored canvas apron on, and her hair is held back with a bandana. She eyes me as I come in, and I can't help but get the sense that she is not impressed until I hold up the bottle of wine.

Pam smiles broadly and motions toward a large wooden chopping block in the middle of the kitchen. Beneath it hang an array of cast iron pots and pans.

"You can put that there," Pam says, waving her knife at a cabinet door to her right. "There are glasses in there and an opener in the drawer below."

I put the wine down on the block as indicated. Behind Pam, there is a window, and beyond the window, I see a small, open-sided wooden structure. Inside of it are a number of large metal canisters, maybe four feet tall. A pipe runs from one of the canisters into a conduit in the structure's concrete foundation. I squint, and I can see a "flammable" sticker on the sides of the tanks: propane. That's how they power their stove and refrigerator.

"Well, make yourself useful! I'm not much of a conversationalist until I've had a glass or two!" Pam says with a smiling and humorous demeanor.

"Right," I begin, digging out glasses and an opener.

I fumble with the foil on the bottle of wine and glance at the label. Genevieve bought this bottle from Holzhom Winery when we visited Jeff the last time she was in Napa. I manage to get the cork out without breaking it, a true personal achievement. I carefully decant the wine the way I always see Mike doing it so I can try to look professional. I pour slowly and carefully so as not to over-aerate it.

I bring a glass to Pamela and carry one for myself.

"To those who have left us and those who have joined us!" Pamela says, as some sort of toast. She holds her glass up. I tap my glass to hers.

"Cheers," I say, and I take a sip.

Pam chugs her wine down quickly and hands the glass back to me. I carry it back over to the chopping block and set it down. With a towel to protect her hands, Pam abruptly opens the oven and pulls out a large pan of cornbread. The cornbread smells sweet and delicious, but there is a hint of kerosene in the room, making everything less palatable.

I pour Pam another glass of wine and bring it to her.

"Matt tells me you are the yuppies staying up at the yurt."

Does anyone use the phrase yuppies anymore?

"That's right. I guess. I don't think of myself as a 'yuppie' per se, but I suppose everything is relative."

"Well, I tell you, you'll not find a quieter place to lay your head."

“Yes, it seems very peaceful. Are you from Stanyon's Hollow?” I ask.

“What? No, Matt and I met at college and got married after. We used to visit his folks; it’s just so peaceful and quiet. When it came time to have little Winnie out there, we decided that it’d be best to come here, away from all the hustle and bustle and crime.”

“That makes sense,” I say, but it’s a lie. Having grown up here, raising a child here wouldn't be my choice. However, it’s not my place to judge, so I smile and nod.

“Why don’t you take those glasses on out, then come back and help me with this food? Soup’s on!”

As I walk over to the cabinet, I have an instantaneous bout of vertigo and have to grab the counter to steady myself. Pamela doesn't seem to notice. I take a few deep breaths and then retrieve two more glasses from the cabinet.

"You might want to bring a couple of extras in case anyone else mysteriously shows up," Hank whispers to me.

"Knock it off!" I hiss.

"Hmm?" Pamela replies.

“I was just saying I think you knocked it out of the park with that corn...bread...thing that you... um made. Okay?” I stammer uncomfortably.

I carefully balance three wine glasses and the bottle between my outstretched fingers, and bustle past Pamela on my way outside before I say something else to look like a lunatic. The bottle feels weird in my hand. It isn't the Cab that I just poured. I examine it: It isn't a wine bottle at all; it's just water.

Matt is leaning on the railing of his deck, and Russ is in a chair nearby. I look around. Genevieve is nowhere to be seen.

“It was a lot the first couple of years. Being nineteen and sitting down at a computer for the first time, with everybody else thinking I'm nuts. But I got through it," Matt says as I hand him a wine glass full of water. "Thanks, Miles."

I give Russ a glass and place the bottle on the deck's railing. Russ looks at the wine glass filled with water and back at me, his face scrunched with confusion. I shrug at him.

"You're welcome," I say. "I am going to help Pam bring dinner out."

"Perfect timing, the meat's almost done!" Matt waves toward the house with a large two-pronged fork. "Oh, and she likes Pamela. She tolerates me callin' her Pam, but she prefers Pamela."

"I am going to go help Pamela bring dinner out."

I speed walk back into the kitchen, my mind racing. What the hell is going on? First, Russ is here, then Genevieve is here with wine; then Russ is back, and there is no wine. One of my most deep-rooted fears is discovering that I am schizophrenic. I've secretly always suspected it since Hank started talking to me. I've always wondered what it would take to make me break. Apparently, returning to this place was it.

I come back into the kitchen almost at a sprint.

"Let me see if we have a palatable vintage in the cellar for our guests," Pamela says in a feigned British accent.

"Perhaps some elderberry wine?" I ask in a similarly bad accent, I can hear my voice cracking. Pamela doesn't seem to notice.

She laughs a shallow, forced laugh, "Matt told you about that stuff, did he? It'll warm a winter night if you don't go blind."

"He mentioned."

"We do appreciate the touch of class when it's available," she smiles as she opens a bottle of wine from the cupboard. "Now, would you be a dear and carry the salad and the quiche?"

She motions to a counter space where there is a large egg pie and an immense bowl of wet-looking vegetables. I pick the bowl of veggies up and it smells like vinegar.

"We pickle a lot. That's what we call salad half the time up here."

The smell of acetic acid has new connotations for me, and I instinctively glance around for magic sigils, but I don't see any in the kitchen here.

"It looks great," I say. That's not a lie. Everything looks delicious, and the smell would be equally great if not for the pervasive undercurrent of kerosene and the permeating fear that I am losing my grip on reality.

I take the two dishes and cradle my water-filled wine glass in the crook of my arm.

When I get outside, Matt motions to a corner of the deck that wraps around the south side of the house.

"We usually sit at the outside table with guests."

I walk around the corner of the house. The deck extends on this side to the back of the house. There is an immense wooden table here, cut from a single slab of some large tree. Based on size alone, I am guessing redwood. But it has been weathered and stained so many times over that it is hard to identify the wood.

I set the two dishes down, extract my glass from my elbow and set it down as well. Pamela is close behind me with the cornbread and a stack of plates and utensils. She balances it all effortlessly and somehow manages to have a free thumb and forefinger to pinch the stem of her wine glass. I see that she has filled it with a yellowish-green white wine. She takes a sip without dropping any forks, which I find impressive. My expression must communicate my admiration for her technique.

"I worked as a waitress for a lot of years," she says by way of explanation.

She sets her burden down and finishes off her second glass of wine—or is it her first? I'm confused now. Russ comes up with the bottle; it looks like a Sauvignon Blanc. Pamela takes the bottle from Russ' hand and refills her glass, pausing to fill Russ' as well.

"Thank you," Russ says.

"Welcome. I'm Pamela; you must be Russ. Is that right?"

"That's right, Pammy, good to meetcha," Russ says.

I can see Pamela stiffen when Russ says "Pammy." This is clearly some kind of trigger, and Pamela's posture and demeanor become far less amicable than they were.

"And it's Russ, not Russel or Rusty or something? Cause I'm a Pamela, not a Pam or a Pammy."

"That's right, dude, sorry."

"Anybody that's too lazy to say your name is too lazy to respect you," Pamela puts on an overly folksy accent and smiles too broadly. I don't think she cares for Russ.

"Sure thing!" Russ says, seemingly oblivious.

"Isn't that right, Matt?" Pamela says as Matt comes around the corner with a large platter of meat and his daughter Winnie in tow.

"Yes," Matt says uncomfortably. He must have been just within earshot for the exchange.

"Winnie, be a dear and show our guests where they can wash their hands," Pamela says, "and make sure you wash your hands too."

Winnie gets up and starts shuffling into the house silently. Russ and I follow. The child shows us to a bathroom and does a lackluster job of washing her hands. I feel like maybe I should say something, but as a childless man, I have no idea what etiquette around instructing other people's children is. It's certainly not the first time Winnie did a poor job washing her hands, and it probably won't be the last, so I let it slide.

I wait for Winnie to depart, and then I frantically interrupt our handwashing.

"Russ, what the actual hell is going on?" I am trying not to scream.

"Dude, chillax, what are you talking about?"

"I... Goddammit, I don't know, Russ, but it's weird. One minute you are here, then Genevieve is here, and you are gone, and then you are back, and she's gone. I think I am losing my freaking mind."

"You didn't steal one of those cookies from my bag, did you dude?" Russ raises a skeptical eyebrow.

"What?" I ask, trying not to scream. "No, I didn't eat your stupid cookies. This isn't drugs. I don't know what it is."

"Okay, dude, settle down," Russ says calmly. "I know a bad trip when I see one."

I close my eyes and take a few deep breaths.

"Okay," I am trying to maintain my calm, "could I be dreaming?"

"Well, man, I mean, I'm not dreaming. I know that. So we aren't like, in the Dreamtime."

"Okay, but what if you aren't real?"

"Pretty sure I'm real."

"I'm pretty sure that's what a hallucination would say, too."

Russ thinks for a long minute. "Listen, dude, if I'm not real, then there is nothing I can say that can convince you I am or am not, you know? You either have to accept that you're in reality and figure it out, or accept that you aren't and just go with the flow. That's life, man. I mean, are we the dreamers, or are we the dreamed? You know?"

"Okay, for some reason, that convinced me that you are

really you," I say earnestly. Honestly, it was probably the most Russ response he could have said. Unexpected, incoherent, but still somehow predictable. Either wise or the stupidest thing I have ever heard. I'm not sure which one.

"Okay, so what do you need from me, man? You need Niacin? I got some. You need Narcan? I got some of that, too."

"Why the hell do you have Narcan?"

"You never know, man, you never know," Russ shakes his head sagely.

"No, I don't need either of those. I'm going to just keep going and hope it was a one-time thing."

"All right, dude, let me know if you need something."

"I will do that. In the meantime, let's try to be normal. What do you think of Matt and Pam?"

“They seem nice enough,” Russ shrugs.

“Yeah, I guess.”

“Somethin' feeling off there?”

“I don’t know, it’s a little weird. I mean, I grew up with the guy, and it took me a minute to really recognize him. We've aged, but he doesn't seem to recognize me at all.”

“You changed your name, dude; I am guessing you've changed a lot?”

“I don't know. It's all just... weird."

“Maybe in the bathroom, during lunch, isn't the place for this conversation; maybe we should talk about this later,” he looks pointedly at the lack of space between us.

“Agreed.”

We dry our hands on a small hand towel and return to the dining table.

Matt seems to be waiting for our return because he excuses himself to wash his hands upon our arrival.

The two have drained the entire bottle of wine while we were washing up.

"I guess we are going to have to break into the elderberry wine after all," Pamela says sadly as Matt returns from the bathroom.

"Do we?" Matt says, sounding resigned and trepidatious. The vibe has changed wildly since Russ called her Pammy.

I quickly retrieve the bottle of Goldschlager that I have stowed in my bag, and place it on the table.

"Are distilled spirits acceptable?"

"Better than a stick in the eye, I always say!" Pamela declares.

"We should start with grace," Matt says, giving Pamela a brief but disapproving glance.

Matt and Pamela each take one of Winnie's hands. Matt reaches out for my hand, and Pamela, after a moment's hesitation, for Russ'. Russ and I exchange glances. Russ shrugs, and we all join hands in a circle. Matt, Pamela, and Winnie all close their eyes. I glance over at Russ who has his eyes half-lidded and looking down. I feel awkward and uncomfortable, and with eyes averted, I keep watching the group in my peripheral vision.

"Thank you, oh lord in morning, for these strangers who have come to break bread with us. Thank you, oh lord in light, for the bounty of the earth we eat. Thank you, oh lord in evening, for the flesh upon which we feast. Thank you, oh lord, in night, for seeing us through to the next dawn," Matt says.

I glance over at Russ, who is looking at me, a single eyebrow quirked. He's as confused and slightly alarmed as I am. That was a very strange prayer, in my inexpert opinion.

"Amen!" Matt, Winnie, and Pamela all say in unison.

"Amen..." Russ and I both murmur in response.

We begin to eat.

"We met a guy this morning–Gawain, I think," I offer as a way of small talk.

Matt looks pensive, "Gawain? I don't think I know a Gawain."

Pamela shakes her head, "Gawain, nope, doesn't ring a bell, and I'd remember that. Might be one of the Roscums."

"They aren't really part of the Hollow. They got a place over the mountain—big family. Yeah, probably a Roscum," Matt confirms.

Pamela seems eager to drink the Goldschlager as fast as she can. I get the sense that she is uncomfortable with Russ and me being here. She becomes more boisterous and bawdy with each drink. Matt gives her disapproving looks and occasionally reminds her that their child is at the table. Soon, it feels like this late lunch is stretching into an early dinner as the natural light dims on the horizon. It is getting dark, probably an hour or more early, due to our location nestled in a canyon.

Pamela tells many loud and dramatic, but ultimately pointless stories about her youth and college years. The louder and more boisterous Pamela gets, the quieter and broodier Matt seems to get. There is a point where the whole affair is quite awkward as it becomes clear that Pamela is not happy living in Stanyon's Hollow and would like to move back to Portland or Seattle. She feels trapped here.

Once the meal has concluded, Matt offers to put Winnie to bed. He doesn't wait for a response from anyone before he whisks the little girl off to sleep. It seems late, and I am wondering where the afternoon went. Russ and I sit and continue to listen to Pamela's sprawling drunken tales. With the little girl gone, they get wilder and more bawdy.

"This one time, my sorority sisters and I...well, we'd had a few drinks, and heard that one of the frats, Gamma-Beta-something, or was it Sigma? I don't know. This frat was having a party, so we decided to crash it. But then Leslie; she was kind of the crazy one in the house, I mentioned it was a sorority, right? Anyway, Leslie was still mad at one of the frat guys who had dumped her and wanted to play a prank. I think his name was Bodie, Brodie... something like that. We all thought it would be funny because we were drunk. We were so lit. So, Leslie, right, her first plan is she's going to pull the fire alarm, and we are going to turn on the sprinklers when everyone runs out. But does Leslie pull the alarm? No! She sets a fire in the bathroom! That was so Leslie! Well, it turns out that it's not a party, it's like an orgie or something," Pamela snorts and howls with laughter.

Russ and I exchange a somber glance. She catches her breath and continues. "Next thing we know, there's a bunch of drunk, naked people running out of the house. They are all covered in oil, and we set off the sprinklers, so people are slip-sliding on the grass and falling down. There's smoke pouring out of the windows; police and fire trucks showed up. Luckily, Leslie's dad was a major donor to the school, the library had their family name on it, and we didn't get in trouble."

Pamela's stories get bigger and less believable as late afternoon becomes night. For every insane story Pamela tells, Russ has a story he wants to share, but each time he tries, she speaks louder and more insistently, drowning him out. I've never seen Russ get annoyed, but his irritation soon becomes apparent. I am getting very uncomfortable with the whole scene.

My eyes wander over the house and woods. It's all familiar like somewhere I've seen in a dream. I have memories here, but every time I start to latch onto one, it flits away like dandelion fluff in the wind.

I'm broken out of my reverie by Matt tapping me on the shoulder. "Hey, Miles, mind helping me clean the dishes?" he says quietly so as not to interrupt Pamela's tale. I nod and pick up some plates from the table.

As I follow Matt into the house, I glance over my shoulder at Russ, sitting with his arms crossed and his face crosser, glowering petulantly at me. At the same time, Pamela brutally assaults him with a story about getting pulled over outside of Needles.

Inside the house, Matt carefully scrapes the plates and dishes into a large bucket in the kitchen.

“We have a gray-water system; the less solids in it, the better,” he explains. "Tomorrow, I’ll take this all down to the community compost pile. It’s a hike because we don’t want it near the houses.”

I nod as he hands me a plate. I start scrubbing it clean in the sink.

“Bears,” he explains as if to answer a question I never asked.

“Makes sense,” I say, though I am not sure it does. I’m feeling very awkward about this whole dinner. I feel like I should have something to say. So much seems familiar, and yet I have no clear memories to draw upon.

“Miles,” Matt says, his tone changing to something that sounds concerned.

“Lots of people come to Stanyon's Hollow. They all have their reasons. Some people leave, like I did. Some come back again, also like I did. For some, this is a place to rejuvenate and heal; for some, it is a place to escape. For some, it’s home. We don’t ask people why they come or go. That’s their business.”

“It sounds very...” I pause, thinking of the right word to finish that sentence, “philosophical.” That’s the best I can come up with, but it sounds lame and dodgy in my ears.

“I guess...” he casts his eyes down at the plate he is scraping, furrowing his brow. "I guess what I am trying to say is, I don’t know why you came back. And I don’t know why you changed your name. And I don’t know why you act like you don't remember me, but it's okay. Whatever you came here for, it's okay. And if I can help you find it, I will."

I feel suddenly rigid and tense. I feel like an imposter who's just been discovered.

"Thanks," I say.

We sit for a solid minute in silence. He scrapes plates and hands them to me. I scrub and stack them.

"I'm not pretending," I rub my hands together nervously. "I don't remember much. It's more like remembering stories my dad told me."

He nods. "I guess with everything that happened, I can see why you might repress a lot of that."

I feel queasy. I have a sudden wave of vertigo, and I have to hold onto the counter. There is a tightness in my chest, and my heart feels like it's racing in my rib cage, pounding against the sides like an inmate fighting to escape. Again, he doesn't seem to notice.

"With everything that happened," I whisper.

"With your brother and your mom."

I duck my head and scrub the dishes like they have wronged me. We finish cleaning in silence.

"You wanted to charge your phones. I'll start the generator," Matt says quietly, to change the topic.

He leaves as I finish the last couple of dishes and put them in a white, rubber-coated wire rack to dry. I lean against the counter and take a few deep breaths. I feel a dizzying wave of vertigo and sickness wash over me. That conversation made me feel ambushed. So much for my attempt to go unnoticed here.

I return to the table outside, where Russ and Pamela are sitting. When I return, Pamela boisterously and drunkenly finishes up a story, and Genevieve laughs uproariously. Once more, Russ is nowhere to be seen. Pamela and Genevieve seem to be as thick as thieves, and her dislike for Russ does not carry over to Genevieve.

“Pamela was just telling me a very in-depth tale about a tree that fell in a storm last year.”

“Oh, that must have been terrifying. Was it near the house?”

“Yeah, it fell right there,” Pamela indicates a large cleared patch fifty feet to one side of the house. I can see large logs still remain.

"You have to hear this, Miles," Genevieve laughs. "See, when it fell, it broke off, so it looked like a pen..."

Fortunately for my tender ears, a generator kicks on somewhere far on the other side of the house, drowning out the rest of the tale. A moment later, Matt comes around the corner of the house.

“You know what, Pam? I think you need some water and a lie-down,” he says with some concern.

“I’m just fine,” Pamela slurs slightly. She stands up and lurches forward. Matt catches her. “Okay, maybe a little nappy-poo won’t hurt."

“I’ll be back in a bit; you can plug your phones in there,” he indicates an electrical socket on the side of the house.

We nod and wait as he helps Pam up from the table.

“I’m sorry,” Pam tells us. “I’m sorry.”

“We don’t get visitors much,” Matt says by way of apology.

“And the wine was good. I mean, so good. I mean so good that it was good,” Pam rambles as she and Matt vanish around the corner into the house. We watch electric lights, now powered by the generator, turn on through the windows as they make their way through the house.

“I don’t think she’s happy here,” Genevieve says.

“Mmm,” I murmur in agreement, but Genevieve seems to take it as doubt.

“Yeah, her best stories are about the city. All the ones here are about trees that look like genitalia. I think she feels trapped here.”

“I understand that feeling,” I say pensively.

"Something else," Genevieve says darkly. "She's not as drunk as she seems, it's an act. While you two were inside, she said if she seemed drunk enough, Matt wouldn't break out the elderberry wine."

"Is it that bad?"

"I don't think that's it. She also said you and I should get out of here now that we should run. Miles, something weird is going on here."

"You don't know the half of it," I mutter. "We aren't going to run though, are we?"

Genevieve shakes her head no. "Not a chance."

We sit in silence for a minute.

"Genevieve, listen," I begin, "there is something I have to tell you, and I know how insane it will sound, but hear me out."

"More insane than all that?" She asks, with a concerned crease in her brow.

That familiar wave of vertigo passes through me. I can't tell up from down or left from right. I lay my head down briefly on the table to stabilize before it passes. When I sit back up to look at Genevieve, it's Russ again.

"What is happening?" I groan. "I can't do this, Russ. This will drive me crazy if I am not already there!"

"Dude, what's up?" Russ says.

"It happened again, the thing where suddenly you aren't here, and Genevieve is, but then, like mid-sentence, you switched back."

Russ nods sagely. "Okay, well, is there some kind of trigger?"

"We were talking about how Pamela told Genevieve not to drink the elderberry wine and how we should get out of here. I was about to tell her about this switching, and you. Then I felt dizzy like I was going to fall over, and then things changed. It's not just people, though; it's the wine."

"Huh?"

"I mean, like, Genevieve brought a bottle of wine, but you didn't, so we drank different wine. And Pamela gets along with Genevieve but not with you. I don't know. Maybe the change has to do with when I remember stuff or have connections with my time here?"

"Okay, dude, talk me through that."

“Well, like, Matt remembers me. He started talking to me about that, and I felt uncomfortable, and then, things changed,” I say.

“Oh?”

“Yeah, while we were washing dishes," I trail off as I see the dirty dishes still sitting on the table. Didn't we take those in when Russ was here? That doesn't make sense. Nothing makes sense.

"You were washing dishes," he nods in acknowledgment that the dishes have not been washed. "And..."

"And..he said he knew who I was and that he didn't care why I was lying. But now, it’s like a dream I had or a movie I saw when I was young. I don’t know.”

"You aren't making much sense," Russ puts a hand on my shoulder.

"Yeah, I know."

The last of the vestiges of sunlight have long vanished behind the mountains above us, and the wind is picking up a bit. Russ and I sit in contemplative silence. I listen to the muffled hum of the generator and the wind rustle through the trees.

Matt returns quietly.

“Sorry about that,” he says.

“No need to apologize. Being around new people can be challenging,” I try to sound empathetic despite being so tense that my nerves could be used for bow strings.

“Matt, dude,” Russ says, “why’d you lie about the bridge? I walked up there this morning, and it’s not some rusted-out, broken-down old ruin. It’s pretty well maintained.”

I stare wide-eyed at Russ and mouth, "What the hell?" at him at an angle I don't think Matt can see.

Matt looks taken aback. His eyes wander around, looking at the house, a tree, the sunset, anywhere but at Russ.

“It’s just... I recognized Mitch...I mean Miles, and...well, with what happened at that bridge, I just thought it might be a hard place to go.”

He doesn’t make eye contact with either of us. I don’t think Matt recognized me when we first talked to him. I think he wasn’t sure that I used to live here until during dinner, which means he's lying.

“I appreciate that,” I say to try to smooth things over. I don’t want to telegraph my suspicions, but he’s lying about this, and I want to know why.

“What do you mean ‘what happened at that bridge’?” Russ asks.

“It’s okay,” I say, trying to stop him from asking. My voice cracks a little, and either I am not heard or I am ignored.

“You know, his brother falling off it and everything. After that day, it took me years to walk by that place.”

My head feels like it’s swimming, and I look at him. I can imagine his face as a boy, a look of wide-eyed terror as he runs away screaming. I’m lying on swaying wooden planks; tears blur my vision and stain my face. I look down over the edge of the bridge...

“I’d like to go to bed now,” I say. “I’m tired.”

I stand up abruptly and grab my phone. It had only a few minutes to charge, and I’m sure that didn’t help much, but I have to get out of there.

“Um,” Russ says, jumping to my side. “Yeah, thank you for lunch, dinner, drunch, or whatever, Matt. I will walk him back to the yurt, dude; it’ll be too dark soon.”

Matt nods blankly. He still seems taken aback by Russ' bluntness. “Right.”

“'Night,” Russ says.

“Good night,” Matt says.

I say good night, but I’m pretty sure it just comes out as a mumbled mess.

I practically sprint back down the path from Matt’s house, with Russ plugging along somewhere behind me.

When we return to our yurt, we zip the door shut and tie it off. I go to my bag and pull out an old shoebox I threw in there before I left Napa: my prototype Ward-in-a-Box. It’s inspired by the little contract I had with my favorite bakery/coffee shop, Soothsayers. This box has everything I need to quickly and temporarily ward a building.

The open floor plan and lack of clutter in the yurt make it ideal for such an effort. I use double-sided tape to place little paper plaques at cardinal and intercardinal points around the yurt. On the inside of each plaque, facing into the room is the same picture of a sandy beach; the outside, taped to the wall of the yurt, is a sigil.

The sameness of the sandy beach creates the implied circle, and the rune on the outside designates function, creating an inclusive boundary. If I were to use the actual walls of the yurt to represent the circle, I would have to put the runes on the outside of the building, which would be too easy to take down. A drop of blood for each sigil, a quick examination through a gazing crystal, and voila, we are magically protected for the night.

The activity keeps my mind off the day's events, but the minute I sit down, it all comes rushing back to me. I sigh and fall back on the bed.

"Are you okay?" Russ asks.

"Yeah, just a lot of shit has been coming up for me today."

"Yeah, I picked up on that dude."

"It's okay. I need to do this, I think. I need to get through this stuff. I've been avoiding some things for too long."

"Well, if you want to talk about it, I'm here," Russ says, standing awkwardly in the middle of the yurt, hands in pockets.

"My brother and I used to play on that bridge," I explain in a low voice. "We weren't supposed to, but we'd get on either side and jump up and down, and it would be kind of like a trampoline. Matt was our friend and playmate. He'd come out and bounce the bridge, too. We'd take turns, two of us bouncing, and the third one would judge who bounced the highest. Henry and I were bouncing, and Matt was judging from the bank."

I pause to take a deep breath.

"Anyway, I got bounced and thrown off the bridge. I was like, hanging on, barely. I was so scared. I honestly don't even really remember being off the bridge anymore. I think I remember it more because my father didn't let me forget it for the rest of his life. He reminded me of it at every opportunity. Anyway, Henry pulled me up. I got back up on the boards and looked around, and he was gone. Matt ran off screaming for his dad. It took me a bit to realize that Henry had somehow fallen off the bridge while pulling me up. He saved me and fell off doing it. I could see him there at the bottom, on the rocks..."

Russ doesn't say anything. He stands there quietly.

"I think I just want to get to sleep. I know it's early, but I'm exhausted."

"Sure, dude, sure. I'll sit over here and read my book if that's cool."

"Yeah, that's fine," I murmur. After a moment, I add, "Thanks for listening, Russ."

"No problem, amigo. I'm always happy to lend an ear," he sits down against the wall and takes out the book he's been working through.

I lay down and pretend to sleep, but really, I am trying hard not to think about Stanyon's Hollow, my family, my childhood, or anything else. I'm not remotely successful.

CHAPTER 11

"MILES! MILES!" A voice hisses, barely whispering next to me. My eyes flutter open. I must have fallen half asleep when I wasn't paying attention. It is pitch black.

"What?" I whisper groggily. I don't recognize the voice, but I am immediately alarmed.

"There is something outside."

I sit slowly up. I can't see anything. My brain is straining to take things in. I do recognize the voice. It isn't Russ, and there is no reason that voice should be here.

"Mike?"

"Who else would it be? There is something outside. Come on, man, wake the fuck up."

My friend, Mike. Well, is he a friend or an acquaintance? We play poker together. It used to be weekly, but it's been more sporadic lately. Hank thinks Mike hates me. I don't think that's true, because Mike has helped me out of a pinch or two when he didn't have to. There is some version of reality where he comes into the mountains on a weekend trip to my childhood home, so he can't hate me that much.

"Turn on a light," I whisper back.

"I tried. The lantern isn't working; the battery is dead."

I know I put a lantern on the floor next to the bed; I lean over and pick it up. I flip the switch on. Nothing. It is still pitch black.

"This one, too."

I hear someone clamoring around in the darkness. I hold my hand in front of my face and see nothing. There is no light. The only time I've ever been in this much darkness was in a culvert a hundred yards under a freeway.

"My flashlight is dead, too."

"It is too dark," I reply.

"I know."

"I mean, it shouldn't be this dark inside a yurt on the side of a hill. There is something else going on."

"I know!" Mike breaks out of his whisper into a panicked, almost-yell.

The distinct sound of a long zipper slowly opening cuts through the silence.

"The door!" I gasp.

"Shit, shit, shit, I knew we shouldn't have come out here. How'd I let you talk me into this?" Mike is so quiet I can barely hear him.

I reach out into the dark where I think Mike is, based on his voice, and grab his shoulder. He lets out a little squeak of surprise. I pull him close and whisper very quietly, "Hide under the bed."

He slowly slides out of my grasp and onto the floor. I roll to the opposite side of the bed and reach down to where I remember leaving my courier bag on the floor. I have to grope around for a long second, straining my ears to hear something coming in through the door flap. The only sound I can hear is my raspy breath and the pounding of my heart.

I pull my courier bag up and quickly root around until I find my lighter. It's an old-fashioned one with a flint and liquid fuel inside. Something could be interfering with the electric lanterns, but that won't stop fire.

I flip it open and flick it a few times but see no spark or flame. That is very weird. I am about to flip the top closed in the dark, but I feel warmth. I back my hand away before I burn it. The lighter is lit; there is just no light.

I close the lighter, careful not to shove my hand in the flame, and then stop to think. I put the lighter away and search around in my bag again. In the dark, I find nothing that will be of immediate use.

I slip onto the floor and think about what might be useful. I strain my ears in the darkness. I have only been awake for minutes, but it seems like hours. My breathing is starting to calm, and I can hear things over my heartbeat now. I can hear Mike's panicked breathing from beneath the bed. Then, there is a rumbling sound from the front door, like the growl of an angry cat—if the cat were the size of a horse.

I urge myself to hear something, anything in the blackness, but I hear nothing more. After a moment, a dim light begins to emit from the darkness. At first, it seems like my imagination, but then it gets brighter and brighter, until I can see light emanating from the two lanterns and the flashlight lying on the floor. Soon, the yurt is bathed in the light of the electric lanterns.

"I think it's okay to come out now," I say, looking at the unzipped door and the ward symbols around the building. "I think the wards I put up kept...whatever that was, out."

"For the first time, I am not convinced that your whole 'magic' thing is bullshit, Miles," Mike mutters.

"Well, thanks?" I say, not sure if I should be offended or complimented.

"What the fuck just happened, Miles? What was that?"

"I have no clue."

Mike seems freaked out enough; it doesn't seem like the right time to tell him that I am jumping timelines, dimensions, or whatever kind of freaky Twilight Zone nonsense is going on, so I keep my mouth shut about it. We both sit on the bed. After a bit, I tell him we should take shifts, that he should try to get some sleep while I watch, and then I can wake him up in an hour, and he can watch. We can do this until daylight when we can determine what's next.

Mike agrees, but I am not sure he gets any real sleep. He does his best to lay there with his eyes closed, though. Two hours later, I rouse him and try to get some sleep. The adrenaline rush of the disturbance has passed, and I fall asleep more quickly than I expected.

CHAPTER 12

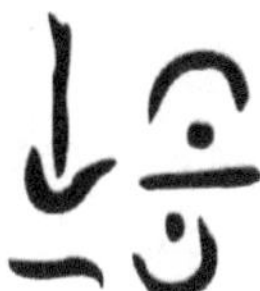

When I wake up, Russ has boiled water and is steeping a pot of tea. He holds out a cup for me as I climb out of bed. I realize that, somehow, I am already getting used to this companion-of-the-moment thing. I hope this does not become the 'new normal.'

"Thanks," I mutter. "Did anything weird happen last night?"

"Well, I mean, yeah, everything over at Matt's was kind of weird."

After what happened with Mike last night, I'd all but forgotten about yesterday.

"No, I mean here, in the yurt. Did something try to come in and get stopped by the wards?"

Russ looks at me for a moment. His face has a long, flat expression, one I associate with his thinking.

"No, nothing, dude," he says finally. "Why? What's up?"

"Just another timeline jump or whatever; I wonder what is going on there?"

Russ shrugs.

I sip the tea. It tastes like boiled sticks. I stretch and yawn. The yurt is much warmer than I expected a canvas building to be.

"You are right, though; Matt's was weird. Sorry about freaking out."

"Don't apologize, you had some shit come up. That'd suck for anyone."

I nod and drink more tea. I hate it, but I need the caffeine.

"Matt lied when he said the reason he told us to avoid the bridge was because he remembered me. I don't think he had figured out who I was at that time."

Russ nods thoughtfully and sips his steaming mug of tea, "Why, though?"

"A decade ago, I'd have guessed it was because they had a grow operation up there. I guess they might still have an illegal one, but these days, it's just not as big a deal. I think he'd just say it; it's not like we come off as cops."

Russ nods, "Something else, maybe? Cooking meth? There's money up here, man; a solar array like that doesn't get bought with bad elderberry wine."

"Maybe. That still doesn't quite add up, though."

"We should check it out. You think you're up for crossing that bridge?" Russ says.

"I want to find out what that solar array is powering. We should go see if we can figure out where the lines run."

Russ takes a sip of his tea and nods. He goes to the bag of food I left sitting on the counter and rummages around.

"Cold toaster tart, dude?" He asks.

"Breakfast of champions," I reply, nodding.

He tosses me a little silver packet, which I open. He grabs a packet for himself. I open mine up and dip the first one into my tea. Russ follows suit.

After a nutritious breakfast of processed pastries, we get

dressed and take an early morning stroll down the side of the hill to the community circle. A couple of men are back to working on the community hall already, but they seem to ignore us. Matt is not among them. Russ and I continue hiking past the parking area and back onto the trail leading down the hill.

Soon we are crossing the field once more, thistles and burrs jabbing at my legs. Once more, I feel annoyed that Russ doesn't seem as bothered by this as I am.

We arrive at the large array of panels standing alone in the middle of the briar-filled meadow. The solar panels feed into one large conduit that goes under the ground. We stand assessing them for a moment.

“If this conduit goes in a straight line, and it would be weird if it did anything else, then it leads toward that grove over there,” Russ says, indicating a large stand of trees at the far side of the field.

"Let's go," I say.

Russ groans in protest, then reluctantly waves his arms for me to lead on.

I nod, and we start silently walking in a line toward the stand of trees. Once we begin, it’s obvious we are following an area that was dug up some time ago. The grasses have grown back over it, but a slight mound is still running in a straight line across the field, making it easy to follow the conduit.

We come to the large stand of fir trees. They are old and tall and cast a huge shadow over us. Hidden in the treeline, I see another trail to this place that winds its way around the periphery of the meadow. One path leads toward the community center, and another branches off into the trees to the south. From the edge of the grove, it is easy to see that there is a structure within. I lead the way into the grove, motioning for Russ to be quiet as we go.

Inside the clearing is a fairly large structure– too big to be called a cabin, too flat and rustic to be called a house. 'Barn' might be the word I'd use to describe it. The electrical conduit surfaces again next to the barn and feeds into rows and rows of what must be batteries under a small lean-to against the exterior wall. We stop at the edge of the clearing and listen.

After a moment of silence, with no indication that anyone is around, I skulk toward the back of the barn, Russ close behind me. There are dusty glass panes in the wall, just above my eyeline. I stand on tippy toes and peek inside. Russ can't quite clear the window to see in.

I am perplexed by what I see in the dark. The interior has been painted white. It has white tiled floors and rows and rows of benches decorated with high-tech lab equipment. It reminds me of all Jeff's gear in his backyard shed, but bigger and more. Huge arrays of lights hang on chains from the ceiling. It has to be incredibly bright inside this place when it's turned on.

"There are gurneys and beds in the corner," Russ whispers beside me. He has pulled himself up with his arms, and his feet are dangling above the ground below him.

I hadn't seen them before, but I look at the corner farthest away from me and see what he's talking about. Four light blue curtains hang from the ceiling, creating a small, separate area. One curtain is drawn back, showing a bed and two gurneys. It's hard to see in the dim light, but once he pointed it out, it's obvious.

"Some kind of medical facility? A lab? Both?" I whisper.

Russ lowers himself back down and then shrugs.

"This is very weird, dude. We should go," he says.

I feel sick to my stomach and dizzy, like I am about to faint. I fall back onto my heels, put my hands on my knees, and lower my head between them.

"Are you okay?" Genevieve asks me from where Russ was standing.

I jump back with a start. Not this again. What the hell is going on?

"Yeah," I say, stepping back from her warily. "Just, um, catching my breath."

"I want to look around," she says, brow slightly furrowed with concern.

“I don’t think that’s a good idea,” I whisper back. I can hear my voice quaver, not from fear of being caught, but from the near panic, this weirdness is inducing in me.

“I’m going to risk it,” she says.

“What should I do?”

“Make sure no one is coming. Whistle if you see something.”

“I don’t like this,” I whisper back.

She turns and makes her way around the building. This thing with Russ and Genevieve swapping is confusing and concerning, but I have a couple of theories on what might be happening. Occam's Razor would suggest that I am probably suffering from some psychosis. I don't feel like I am psychotic, but I don't know if that is something someone is aware of when it is happening. This could be some dream state I am in, though again, it doesn't feel that way to me. I could be under the effect of a spell, something trying to change or subvert my mind.

I scratch my forearms and activate the warding sigils tattooed on my arms. I can feel them come alive, but there is no pressure or sense of force. Something strange is going on, but my best bet is to continue observing and trying to figure it out.

I crouch in the shadows and look back across the field toward the solar panels and the community beyond. After scanning the hillside, I make out the white tip of the yurt we are staying in, far up the hill. From the yurt, I follow the trail down the hill and find the location where we first spotted the solar panels. My heart jumps into my throat when I see a figure standing on the trail, looking down into the field before me.

I stay crouched, watching the figure. For a while, I'm not sure if it is a person, a shadow, or a tree, but then they move a little, and I can clearly make out arms and legs. I am certain there is no way they can make me out in the treeline, even if they have binoculars, but if they've been there long enough, they might have seen us cross the field.

I look behind me in an attempt to see what Genevieve is up to. There is no sign of anyone. I turn back to spy the figure on the trail, but the figure is gone. I carefully and systematically scan the hills, field, and treeline to see if I can find the figure again, but I don't.

Just when the stress of trying to find the figure is about to drive me insane, I hear Genevieve coming up behind me. I turn to confirm it is her and not someone else creeping up.

"Hey," I whisper when I see her face.

"Hey," she whispers back.

"Any luck?" I whisper.

"No, it's locked up tight as a drum. Why are we whispering?"

"I saw someone up on the hill. I think they were watching us."

"Oh, where?"

I point to the trail on the hill, briefly and quietly explaining what I saw.

"That is a long way away," she says in a conversational tone. "There's no way they can hear us from up there. Besides, if they were watching us and know we are here, playing dumb is probably a better bet than being all secretive.

"Fair," I say, trying to speak aloud but still whispering. I have a thought.

"Genevieve, what did we do last night?"

"You were stressed out after Matt's and went to bed early. I stayed up reading. Why do you ask?"

"I'm just curious," I nod. That is basically the same narrative as I have, but I was with Russ. "And do you remember why we came down here?"

She looks at me, brow furrowed in concern, "Because I wanted to go to the bridge, and you wanted to come to see if this was a meth lab."

I have other questions to ask, but I seem to be freaking her out. I decide to go forward as if everything I said to Russ, I have also said to her. If she gets confused by anything, that will be telling, I think.

"Why would these people build a secret laboratory, build a huge solar array, and then lie about it?" Genevieve breaks the silence.

"The meth theory is holding more water."

"Yeah, but you don't need an operation like that for meth; people cook that stuff in the bathtub of a camper trailer."

"But drugs seem most likely."

"It's a good theory, but I don't know. Let's not jump to any conclusions," Genevieve purses her lips. "Do you think this has anything to do with why Matt lied about the bridge?"

"My gut says yes, but like you said, let's not jump to any conclusions."

"We should head back," Genevieve grimaces.

"Okay."

"There is a trail that skirts the meadow; it's less exposed but probably twice as long," I point to the other trail I noticed.

"Let's just hurry across the meadow," Genevieve says. "If

we were going to be spotted, we'd already have been. Let's move quickly."

So we take off across the meadow, trying to hurry while looking casual. I'm less satisfied with our efforts than I want to be, and by the time we get back onto the trail to the yurt, I feel like I'm basically running.

When we pass through the community area, Matt is back with his companions, working on the community hall. We skirt on by so as not to engage. I feel like they are all watching us as we walk by, and none of them waves, not even Matt.

As we hike back up the trail to the yurt, I can't shake the feeling that I am being watched. I look over my shoulder and scan the treeline all around me, but I don't see anything unusual. I'm probably just feeling paranoid after seeing the person standing up on this trail.

When we get to the open bit of trail where I estimate the figure had been, I stop.

"Wait up," I interrupt.

Genevieve stops and turns around to face me.

"This is where I saw the person watching us."

She nods, and we look around.

"There are some bootprints right here," she crouches down near a flat spot just off the path. "Fresh."

I walk over and look. They are large boots, bigger than my shoe size—probably a man's boot.

"That's way too big to be Matt's," I say.

She nods, "I was thinking the same."

"What do you think we've gotten ourselves into?" I ask.

Genevieve smiles, "I think there is something secret and sketchy going on. But finding secret and sketchy things and getting to the bottom of them is kind of my thing."

"I guess. It's been like a week since we broke into the secret vault of a Hollywood director at the bequest of an undead sorcerer. Today, we are uncovering a secret mountaintop laboratory."

"And before that, you were battling a fire demon; before that, we got attacked by flying monkeys; and in the meantime, you burned down a bar. I'd call that a good run! What's your point?" She says with a mirthful laugh.

"That was my point. Things keep getting weirder," I sigh.

"That's literally the thesis point of the book I was pitching when we met. We are seeing the last hurrah of the unknown as magic and technology merge. All this stuff will normalize into something new. As with every change through human history, people can adapt or move aside for those who can."

"Was this really what you expected the future to look like?"

"No, not really," she concedes. "This is weirder and way more interesting."

I look down at the field below, specifically at the stand of trees that I now know houses a secret laboratory. From here, I can't even tell it's there.

"Too bad I don't have binoculars," I say, staring into the field. We are in the open and exposed here. My vision swims slightly in the sun.

I can hear Genevieve rummaging around in her bag. A pair of fancy new binoculars are shoved into my hand.

"Were you a Girl Scout?" I say, holding my head as the now familiar wave of vertigo washes over me.

"No, dude, Boy Scouts. Troop number eleven eighty-nine. Or was that the last four digits of my phone number growing up? Shit, I don't remember; that was a long time ago."

"Shit!" I jump and almost drop the binoculars, realizing I am standing on the slope with Russ again. I glance at the binoculars in my hand. These are older and more worn than the ones Genevieve handed me, but still binoculars. That's weird.

"Dude! You okay?"

"This has got to stop," I grab my chest with my left hand. "Yeah, I'm fine, Russ."

I hang the binoculars around my neck, "Can I ask some weird questions?"

"Go for it."

"What has happened over the last, say, half hour?"

"We went down to some creepy, hospitally-lab thing, and you saw some dude watching us from up here. We came up here, and you wanted some binoculars. What's going on, dude?"

"Do you remember how I said yesterday at Matt's it was like you got replaced with Genevieve?"

"Yeah, dude, I recall."

"It happened again, only for longer this time."

"Huh," he says pensively.

"Has anything like that been happening to you?"

"Well, that raven over there," Russ says, pointing to a blackbird in the tree that is watching us silently, "keeps telling me he has a secret to tell me. But it's not quite the same."

"What?"

"Yeah, I mean, it's weird and, frankly, pretty annoying. He says it's a trade, and I have to give him a secret of greater or equal value. But, like, how do you put a value on a secret?" Russ says, shaking his head, then he turns to yell at the raven, "How do you put value on a secret, dude?"

"Are we going crazy up here?"

"I don't know about you, man, but I might have overdone the juice this morning if you know what I mean."

"Okay, then, am I having a psychotic break?"

"In my experience, people either know they are losing it, or they don't know that they are losing it, but if you are asking, you're probably not there yet."

"I'm not sure that is comforting."

Russ shrugs.

I take up the binoculars and try to get a view of the laboratory. It takes me a minute of gazing around, moving, and gazing around until I get an angle with a good view of the stand of trees. I can make out some straight lines through the grove that must be parts of the barn. I can see the tree I was crouched behind, watching the figure up here. I was wrong. If the person had binoculars, they could have easily seen me.

I glance down at the ground. I'm only about eighteen inches away from the boot prints we found. I step over to them and look back at my hiding spot.

"If the person here had binoculars, they could have seen me down there," I lament.

"Did they?"

I shrug and return the binoculars to Russ, "I don't know. I could barely make out a person at this distance, let alone see if they were holding anything."

"Let's assume they did."

"Why would we assume that?"

"Well, if they didn't, then it doesn't matter. However, if they did, then they know we were down there, and like, maybe they like it, and maybe they don't, but we should keep our eyes open anyway."

I nod, "That makes sense."

Russ starts toward the yurt once more. I fall in step behind him.

"So," I say, "what's next?"

"Well, if you're up for it, we could see what is over that bridge."

I make a big audible sigh to demonstrate how little I like this plan.

“Okay,” I say, “I’ll give it a try. It’s just, well, this is hard for me.”

“Understood, amigo,” he says.

“But I agree, we need to figure this thing out or just get the hell out of here. Or rather, figure this thing out and *then* get the hell out of here, or just get the hell out of here now.”

“Curiosity killed the cat, cat. But ignorance killed the man, man.”

I quirk an eyebrow at him, "I've never heard it that way before."

"Just made it up."

We huff along the trail to the yurt in silence. Once we slip inside, I stop to check the wards I put up yesterday. They all seem to be intact. I dig a couple of Jeff's magic-sensing glow sticks from my backpack and put them into my bag. Russ tosses me an extra flashlight. I have one in my bag, but it can’t hurt to have extras.

“Are you ready, dude?” Russ asks me.

I grab a couple more foil packs of toaster pastries and put them in my bag.

“As ready as I'll ever be!”

CHAPTER 13

I FOLLOW Russ as he backtracks down the trail a hundred yards and then turns onto the trail to the footbridge. The bridge is still there, gated and locked.

While the ravine is not wide, it is deep. Two granite walls stand against each other in an eternal face-off, a giant split in the earth. A hundred or so feet down, a little trickle of a creek winds its way through the gouge in the stone, rocks jutting up like teeth from the ravine's floor. I'm feeling less paralyzed with fear today than yesterday, but still terrified.

I grip one of the bridge's support cables and lean forward to look down. A sudden wave of vertigo causes me to lurch back. I work to push down the image in my mind's eye of a body crumpled on the rocks below. I glance over at Russ, expecting to see someone else in his stead, but apparently, this was normal, run-of-the-mill vertigo, not the sensation that portends a change in my reality.

"Are you okay?" Russ asks.

"Yeah, just give me a minute," I say, my voice wavering in my head.

"Yeah, no problem."

I look at the bridge itself. It is far sturdier looking than I remember it from my youth but not sturdy enough for me to want to climb out onto it.

Russ hops up and begins to swing himself over the gate.

"What are you doing?" I ask in horror.

"Gonna give it a little test; ain't no thing, my man." He lowers himself over the other side while I have a panic attack. He steps out onto the bridge and hops around. "It's pretty solid, man."

The bridge bobs and swings slightly under his weight. My breath is fast and shallow. I try to calm down and take slower breaths. It's hard. The ogre of anxiety is trying to squeeze the air from my chest.

Slowly, carefully, I push myself toward the bridge.

"Did I mention I'm also kind of scared of heights?" I mutter pitifully.

"You had mentioned that. If we go quickly, this should be relatively painless."

"Quickly," I spit the word out like vulgar profanity.

Russ starts to speed walk across the bridge. It bounces and sways as he does. In forty seconds, he is across, and he beckons for me to follow.

"Come on."

I slowly lift myself to the top of the gate and lower myself over the other side. Normally, I could do this without thinking, but it seems to take forever. I'm gasping and sweating when I get over the gate. I turn and grab onto the support cables.

I look at my hands. My knuckles have turned white because I have a death grip on the cables. With an immense force of will, I open my right hand and move it forward. I put my first foot out onto the bridge. The planks give slightly as the cables stretch to support my weight.

I slide my second foot forward and am completely out over the precipice. A hundred feet below me, rocks jut up and wait to crush my bones and tear my flesh. I take another step, then another. The closer to the center I get, the more the bridge bounces and sways. My stomach starts to toss and turn, and vertigo sweeps over me like an ocean wave. My vision swims and narrows, and my knees get weak and buckle.

Fuck. I'm about to pass out on a suspension bridge over a chasm.

"Goddamit, I hate this," a male voice behind me says. I turn and look. A man is standing there. He's a little taller than me. He has dark hair, eyes, and a large scar extending from the bottom of his left eye to his chin. He's wearing a T-shirt that looks intentionally tight to show off his muscular figure and a large backpack. He's gripping the cables hard. He looks very familiar, but I've never seen him before.

I turn to look for Russ, but he's not there. Not again.

"Um, hey," I say to this new stranger.

"Jesus!" He yells and starts. "Goddamit, Miles, you scared me!"

That's weird. I am standing like five feet in front of him.

"Are you blind?" I ask him. He doesn't seem blind, but it's the most likely explanation.

"Asshole. What are you trying to do, get me killed? Is this some revenge thing?" He asks with gritted teeth.

"No. Sorry. I just... I am standing five feet in front of you. I'm wondering how you can't see me," I say earnestly.

"Because you are a ghost, or you know. Whatever you are. Aren't you supposed to be hovering around a mannequin back home?"

"Huh?"

I stare into his eyes and know why he looks familiar; he's got my eyes.

"Hank?" I say.

"You know I hate being called that. It's Henry."

I have a sudden, horrifying thought. I look down at my body, but it isn't there. I'm completely transparent.

"Well, this is a fucked up dream."

"What are you carrying on about Miles?"

"I've had some weird dreams, but this is a new one, is all I am saying."

He laughs, "That's rich. Can you tell me if the gate on the other side is locked?"

What the hell? I slowly turn and reach out to grab the cables, but I don't have hands. I don't have anything, not even a body. However, the intention to move seems to be all I need, and I drift slowly toward the other side, like a camera on a track.

I pass through the gate and turn to look at it. There is no chain or lock on this side.

"Nope," I yell back, *"no lock!"*

"Thanks," Hank yells back.

"And am I a ghost?" I ask as I float my way back to him.

"Hell if I know. A ghost, a projection of my unconsciousness, a demon? Don't you know?" Hank replies.

"Why am I here?"

Hank has made his way across the bridge, and I float in front of him as we talk. He sighs heavily.

"I assume," he says as he pushes the gate open, "because this is where you died."

"I died?"

"You fell off this bridge. I tried to pull you up, but you slipped," he says sadly as he hops to the ground by the bridge's support cables.

"What?" I say. *"I didn't fall. You fell. You're the ghost..."*

Hank furrows his brow and makes a concerned face. He's

looking near me, but not at me, as I hover by the now-open gate.

"Are you okay, Miles? This doesn't sound like you."

How suddenly am I the ghost–and Hank, alive? And how come living Hank is better looking than me? And more ripped than me? We are twins!

"*What the hell is going on?*" I yell.

"Jesus! You scared me, Miles!" Russ exclaims.

I blink. I'm standing in the same spot next to the gate on the far side of the bridge. Sitting before me is not Hank but Russ. How did I get here? Did I float over the bridge? There was no rush of vertigo when it changed this time. Without inner ears, maybe ghosts can't feel vertigo.

"What the...this is too much," I say, holding my head and falling to my knees.

"Yeah, dude, no shit. I thought you were going to pass out on the bridge. When you said you were scared of heights, I didn't think you meant, like, *scared of heights*."

I sit with my back to one of the support posts for the bridge.

"Me either. It scared me to death, apparently," I mutter pitifully.

"Well shit, how are we going to get back across there?"

"There's another path," I murmur. I am starting to remember now, "Or there used to be. It went to Matt's house but at a point down the hill past the gorge. I remember I used to take it as a kid."

"Well, let's do that on the way back then; we don't need anyone passing out on that thing."

"Do you believe in ghosts?" I ask.

"There is space for everything in the universe, man. I mean, even scientifically, our nervous system is made of energy firing in neurons and flying down the super-highway of our mind.

Where does that energy go when we die? All this," he motions at the world around us. "It can't mean nothing, right?"

"I've investigated a dozen or more ghost sightings. I've never found evidence of one. But now, I'm not so sure. Some things can continue living when their bodies have stopped working, right? The Hierophant, for example. So, who's to say there isn't some energy that could continue even after the body has decayed? What does that mean? I don't know. There must be something to it."

He nods, "Yeah, man, but maybe we don't have an existential crisis while swinging a hundred feet over these rocks, dude."

"It happened again."

"The whole time shift, dream, whatever thing?"

"Yeah, only this time I was with my brother, who, you know, died on that bridge. Only he was alive, and I was the dead one."

He nods and puts a finger pensively to his lower lip.

"Pretty heavy, dude. What do you make of it?"

"I don't know. What do you make of it?"

"It doesn't matter what I make of it. I think this is a thing you gotta handle for yourself, you know?"

"Way to pass the buck. Whatever," I grumble. "Let's go, I'll handle it later."

"Sure thing, dude."

I get up. I'm still a little shaky but mobile.

"You're right," I lead us down the trail into a thicket beyond the gorge, "it's just, I don't know. I've been thinking about Hank a lot lately. For a long time, I thought it was, you know, just me talking to the voices in my head, like an imaginary friend or something. But now I wonder..."

"Yeah, dude, I wonder too."

The trail is overgrown with brush. It is passable but

requires some ducking and weaving. The occasional broken branch and dusty footprint on the ground indicate that, while it's overgrown, it isn't unused.

Our path descends a small gully and winds between a half-dozen huge moss-covered rocks. One particularly large rock juts up like the fin of an enormous petrified shark. The rock wall is almost flat, about forty feet high, and runs probably eighty feet long. The path splits here, with the right fork winding behind the rock and the left fork continuing through the trees.

"To the right is where I used to live," I say. My memories are returning to me, and I remember this place, "The left path is the one that makes its way back to Matt's house."

I note that the right path has completely grown over, shrouded in a bed of loam and fallen leaves. The left path is littered with sticks and leaves but shows more signs of maintenance and recent passage.

"Well, let's see your childhood home," Russ says.

I start down the path to the right, crashing and stomping through the brush.

The overgrown path leads us around the lee of the shark-fin-shaped rock. There, moldering beneath the trees, are the ruins of a small cabin. The roof has caved in, the walls have rotted and buckled, and there is little left but a pile of collapsing timbers. I walk up to the front step, a low wooden platform that juts out before the rubble. I put one foot on the rotted step, but it falls through the instant I put any weight on it. Millipedes scatter beneath my feet, and I step back.

"This is where I grew up."

"Cozy."

"It's smaller than I remember. And not just because it's collapsed into a flattened heap. This can't have been more than three rooms."

Russ nods.

"The outhouse used to be over there," I say, pointing into the woods. From here, I can see no traces of the small wooden shed.

We stand in silence for a moment.

"Take all the time you need, dude," Russ sits down with his back to a tree.

"Thanks."

We sit quietly for a minute more. I'm waiting for some important memory to come flooding back to me, for some epiphany to strike.

It doesn't come.

Finally, after some unknown amount of time, I say, "I think I'm good here."

"Okay," Russ gets up from his resting place.

We start back up the overgrown trail. When we reach the fork again, we turn and take the other path toward Matt's house.

"Hey, buddy," Hank says. I start and see him standing next to me, just off the trail. He's straddling a small clump of ferns.

"What the hell!" I exclaim.

"Miles, are you okay?" Russ asks.

"No, I don't think so."

"You're fine. I just came to..."

"What's up?" Russ asks warily.

"Just, Hank's here. But you can't see him, can you?" I point at Hank.

"No, I can't. But when you say Hank, do you mean your brother or the dummy?"

It is an interesting question. I turn to stare intently at Hank.

"No, dude, that's not the relevant bit. I gotta warn you, keep

your head about you on this path. There's stuff you don't want to bumble into."

"Thanks for the warning. Can I ask you something?"

"Hit me with your best one."

"A little while ago, I had this... episode. Were you around for that?"

"You mean when you almost took a header off that bridge?"

"Yeah."

"Miles?"

"Yeah?"

"Miles, I talked you across that bridge; we had a whole conversation. I had to coax you step by step. Do you remember that?"

"No. You weren't there. I was the ghost, and you were the living one, and it was me talking you across the bridge. We didn't have the same experience that time."

"Maybe not. Are you okay?"

"I don't know, but the fact that my imaginary friend is concerned about my mental health can't be good."

I turn and look at Russ. I expect to see him staring at me with concern, but he's ten yards away, examining tree bark.

"It's the mannequin Hank, and he says there's something dangerous ahead and that I should keep my head about me."

"Cool, dude."

"It is a little weird. I can actually see him here, like an apparition. It's a first."

"Second."

"Second time; I saw him yesterday, too. But I thought it was just a hallucination or something. Now I'm not sure."

"Think that's related to the whole, you know, reality swap?" Russ asks. How is he less freaked out about this than me?

"'Cause you are losing what he already lost."

"Really?"

"Probably," Hank shrugs. *"I'm not a psychiatrist. Psychologist. Therapist. Whatever, I can't diagnose people."*

I sigh and trudge along. Whenever I turn my head to the right, Hank is walking next to me. I see a small flower wave back and forth as he brushes against it. I notice he steps over logs and moves around trees, but he is completely silent as he does so. I stop and step off the trail.

"What's up?" Russ asks.

"Yeah, what are you doing? You shouldn't stray from the path."

"I'm looking for footprints."

"Okay," Russ says and starts peering off that side of the trail.

I examine where I saw Hank step, looking for evidence of his passing. There are no footprints, broken sticks, or indications that someone walked alongside this path.

"I don't see anything," Russ says. "What's that mean?"

"I don't know. I see Hank walking beside me, and he moves around trees and logs, so I thought I'd see if there was any evidence of something physical passing through there."

"Oh, yeah, no. Sorry, I'm in your head."

"Clever, dude."

"No, apparently not really."

I turn to Hank, "Why? Why are you here now? Why do I see you?"

"You'll see."

"That's not helpful," I scold Hank as I walk again. Russ and Hank both fall in step.

"What's not helpful?" Russ asks.

"He says I'll see."

"Bogus, Hank. That implies you know but won't tell us, dude!" Russ calls into the woods. I appreciate Russ' seemingly unconditional support.

Hank shrugs, *"It seems like I can't tell you."*

“Can’t or won’t?”

Hank shrugs helplessly and makes a zipper motion over his mouth.

“Talking to the voices in my head isn’t helping.”

“Maybe it's ‘cause you should be listening,” Russ chimes in.

"Wise man."

“I know how this looks,” I say. “I can see the expression on your face.”

“You are having a moment of self-discovery, dude; I'm just along for the ride. Any expression you see is just the mirror for your soul, man, mirror for your soul.”

“I appreciate that. I was worried I was hallucinating, but I don't think that’s it. I think it is something else.”

"Well, I am definitely hallucinating," Russ says with a goofy grin.

I can't believe what a friend Russ is. He's come out to this remote shitberg with me, almost no questions asked, and is putting up with me freaking out in the woods, doing...whatever I am doing here, and without a lick of judgment. And he signed up for all this before the secret labs and mysterious bridges.

“But do you trust him?” Hank whispers in my ear.

It's a weird question, and now Hank is more into question than Russ.

“Why are you whispering?” I ask loudly. “He can’t hear you. Yes, Hank, of course, I trust Russ.”

Russ turns and gives me the double thumbs up, "I trust you too, dude!"

We come to another fork in the trail. I vaguely recall that the left path continues toward Matt’s house. The path to the right isn’t familiar at all, though.

“The right path looks more recently traversed,” Russ says.

“The right path?” I turn to ask Hank, but he’s vanished.

"What's he say?"

"He's gone," I shrug. "I don't remember the right path, so let's try that."

The right-hand path winds its way around some rocks and then does a handful of switchbacks down the side of a hill. Soon, we are in a wide, almost bowl-shaped depression roughly fifty yards across. I can see all the way across because the trees here are short, thin, and stunted.

At first, I wonder if this is all very new growth from logging. Then, I get to the trail at the bottom, where the loam and detritus from the trees sit on top of a silty layer of sand.

"It's sandy. I think the trees are all stunted because of the sandy soil," I stop and look around.

"This was probably the bed of a prehistoric lake," Russ speculates as he crouches down and picks up some sand. "It's coarse granite. Same as the rocks. Probably from back when glaciers ground their way across this part of the world," he adds.

"I didn't know you were a geologist."

"I did a lot of science stuff before I settled on chemistry, dude."

We continue down the path that seems to be leading to the center of the depression.

When we get to the middle of the bowl, we stop and look around. The wood looks positively primeval here. The air is silent and still.

"No birds," Russ says.

"Or crickets or...anything."

"That's very eerie."

CHAPTER 14

"WAIT, DID YOU HEAR THAT?" Russ asks.

I strain my ears; all I can hear is the faint sound of my heart pumping blood through my veins.

"No. And don't say 'exactly,' because we just covered that."

"No, no, man, that laughing. That creepy, children-laughing sound."

Now, it is my turn to be concerned for Russ. I turn and look at him.

"Meso dosing my ass," I start to say, but I am cut off.

"*Down the hollow...*" a faint, high voice echoes in the air, "*there's a path.*"

"That, do you hear that, man?" Russ demands, his voice sounding frantic.

"*Where children run and play and laugh,*" another voice joins the sing-songy chant.

"Yeah, now I hear it."

"*Through the wood and through the glen...*" Third and fourth voices join. High and lilting. Children's voices.

"Oh, thank god," Russ sighs. "I thought I was in real trouble."

"Yeah, I don't think that means we aren't in trouble," I look Russ in the eye. "I know this rhyme."

"*To Avalon and back again*!" The chorus of voices, juvenile and ethereal, fades into the breeze.

"From the trail, don't you stray," I recite. "In darkest night or lightest day. Where the path does not roam is the hungry Wugwum's home. See it when it wants to be seen: an evil eye and a tangled skein. It offers cakes and candy floss to lure you off into the lost..."

Russ is staring at me, his eyes wide in alarm, "What is going on?"

"It's a rhyme we used to chant as kids. It's like a Stanyon's Hollow version of Bloody Mary or, I don't know, the Headless Horseman. The Wugwum was like a spider creature that we said lived in the woods and ate kids."

"I have so many questions, but at the top of the list is probably this: why are there ghostly children's voices chanting it at us now?"

"I don't know, but I think I wet my pants a little," My tone is humorous like I'm just trying to lighten the mood, but there's definitely a hint of truth in it.

"Roger that," Russ says. "So what do we do?"

"Well, I see three options: we can continue on the path, go back, or go off the path to investigate."

"The creepy little children in the trees said don't go off the path, man!" Russ waves his hands emphatically.

"No, I recited that part of the rhyme; they just got to the 'Avalon and back again' bit."

"What the hell is Avalon?" Russ asks.

"In Arthurian legend, it's the island where Excalibur was forged. As kids, there was this place in the forest we'd always go, and we called it Avalon. The trek was long, and we came up with the rhyme to scare each other; it kept us on the trail so we didn't get in trouble."

"Is there more to the rhyme?" Russ asks.

"Yeah, but it gets pretty gruesome."

"Well," Russ says, drawing his last consonant out while he thinks, "let's hear the rest so we know what we are dealing with."

"Okay, you asked for it," I say. "Let's see."

For a moment, I subvocalized the first part of the rhyme again to jog my memory.

"...lures you off into the lost. It wraps you in its hungry...web. It eats your eyes and eats your... rhymes with web? Um, not a real rhyme...head. Eats your head. Eats your arms, fingers, and nails until all that's left is the tales of children who strayed from the path to run and jump and play and laugh. Through the woods and through the glen, to Avalon and back again."

"Well," Russ shivers, "that didn't make it better."

We stand stock still on the path, listening to the silence. Finally, after a moment, I interrupt.

"Let's just move on and hope that was..." I consider my words. "Well, I have no idea what I hope that was, but let's get away from it."

"Right," Russ says.

We proceed forward, but after about ten steps, I hear a faint susurrus in the wind.

"*Down the hollow, there's a path...*" a voice as faint as a zephyr whispers. Soon, another voice joins in, faint, quiet, and slightly off-key and out of time with the first. With each step, another voice joins, continuing the rhyme, also off-tune and out of time. The susurrus becomes a cacophony.

"If we go any farther, my head will explode!" Russ howls,

holding his ears as the horrible screeching rhyme gets worse with each step. "Let's go back!"

"No," I shout. "I don't know what is happening, but let's find out."

"Is that a good idea?"

"I am pretty sure we left good ideas behind with the bridge."

Russ nods, "Yeah, dude. That's fair."

I turn and rush off the path toward the source of the first lilting voice in the trees. Russ reluctantly follows behind me. I charge up the rim of the bowl-shaped area and through a stand of trees at the top, where we first heard the voices. As I break past the line of trees, the cacophony of voices silences like a box being closed and latched. Quiet returns to the forest so suddenly that it is jarring.

A brief wave of dizziness passes over me, and I stumble to a halt. I look around and find myself in Avalon.

The flat clearing between a dozen large fir trees is circled by a ring of giant carved logs. As I see them, I remember them from my childhood. There used to be five of them, with one fallen and decomposing. Now, only two remain standing. When last I was here, their paint was chipped and peeling; it is now all gone, and only weather-bleached wood can be seen.

The two standing logs have been carved into a bear and a rabbit. Two of the fallen ones can still be identified as a boar and a horse. The fifth, already decaying in my childhood, is now little more than a dirt pile, but it was once a mountain lion.

I hadn't read A.A. Milne back then, but it now occurs to me that they were intended to be hundred-acre woods characters. A bear, a rabbit, a pig, a donkey (not a horse), and a tiger; the bear looks very much like the protagonist in Milne's original work, not the Disney character. Somehow, this revelation takes some of the childhood wonder out of Avalon and replaces it with a level of surreality and more questions.

These characters are carved from redwood logs, but there are no redwoods for miles. And why would someone haul redwood logs somewhere so remote and carve them into Hundred Acre Woods characters? And why didn't my parents read Winnie The Pooh to me as a child?

My reverie is broken as someone comes crashing and huffing up the path behind me. I turn and am strangely not surprised to see my friend Alistair sweating behind me.

"What's the rush?" He asks.

I look him up and down. He's wearing a full, high-tech outdoor ensemble, which he probably bought at some boutique outdoor store. His pants are made of a specialty fabric with sections of meshing in key areas to let it breathe and one of those ridiculous-looking hats with the broad train to keep the sun off his ears and neck. He's carrying a backpack with a water sack built in and a tube that clips up on his shoulder. He has a broad white swath of zinc across his nose and an expensive and brand-new-looking pair of hiking boots.

"So, this is Avalon," he says between breaths.

"This is Avalon," I confirm and look around at the decaying old carvings, each larger than two men.

"Why'd you call it Avalon? A big fan of Arthurian Legend as a child?"

"No, I recall there was this old guy who would come around and tell tales by the fire. He said a lot of things. Said these woods were magic and that Avalon was out here. I think he used to say there was a witch's cottage in these woods, too, that she would bait children in and eat them," I explain.

"Isn't Avalon where Excalibur was forged? I took some classes on medieval literature when I was an undergrad."

"Yeah," I confirm, "that's the standard one. We'd always

come up here and forge magic weapons to fight the monsters in the forest. It was fun."

Alistair laughs good-naturedly, "How would you forge a magic weapon?"

"Oh, sure," I say, looking around for a large and sturdy-looking stick. I pick it up and walk over to him. "Kneel, Sir Alistair."

Smiling, he kneels down in his fancy ripstop khaki pants. I tap him once on each shoulder with the stick.

"I dub thee Sir Alistair the Kind. Go forth and use this stave to heal the sick and defend the helpless. May you never know wounds in this service!"

He stands up, and I place the stick in his hand.

"I accept the honor happily, King Miles!" He exclaims.

"Oh, don't call me King. Henry was always King. I was usually his court magician," I ponder this a little. I wonder what the Hierophant really knew and what was just him archetyping.

"Okay, good Miles the Magnificent!" Alistair hefts the stick a few times and leans on it. "This isn't a half-bad hiking stick."

"Do you do a lot of camping and hiking then?" I raise an eyebrow. Alistair has never seemed like the outdoorsy type to me.

"I love it, but no," he huffs. "Jon is a city guy."

"Yeah, I can see that."

"He's like, 'If you and your white friends want to go sleep in the dirt and get bit by mosquitoes, you go, but if you bring any ticks back in my house, uh-uh, we are gonna have words,'" Alistair says doing a surprisingly good imitation of his husband.

I chuckle.

"And if your boy Miles gets you in any trouble, you tell him I know where he lives, and I know where all the most painful parts of the body are," he continues. This part of his imitation may be too real. Jon is a nurse, and I am sure he has a good idea of how to put an aggressive patient down if he has to.

"Yeah, I am sorry," I say. I know my...eccentricity is a point of contention between Alistair and Jon.

"Sorry for what?" Alistair asks, looking confused.

"All the trouble and weirdness?"

"What are you talking about?"

"The lab...The Wugwum?" I say, confused. I motion in a circle around us, "Avalon?"

"I don't know what all you're talking about, but we hiked up here to see this childhood memory, Avalon, and it's kind of cool."

"Children singing in the forest?"

"Are you okay?" Alistair says, his brow creasing with concern.

"There's been nothing weird on this whole trip?" I ask, incredulous.

"Well, there is now," he states flatly, eyebrows raised at me.

"Okay, so I know how this sounds, but let me explain," I begin. Then I explain everything because, at this point, why not? In a few minutes, everything is going to change, and I'll be back with Russ, and this will have never happened. Or it will happen to someone else. Or it won't change, and I have had a psychotic break, and at least Alistair is a psychologist and the best person I know to deal with that. So I tell him about all the weirdness of the past two days: the time shifting, the weird sightings, the lab, the voices, the talking mannequin, everything. Finally, I conclude, "So, I am sorry to dump my psychotic break in your lap, but there it is."

"Miles, can I check a few things?" He asks.

"Um, sure?"

He holds my eyes open and looks at my pupils. He takes my pulse and inspects my head.

"I'm fine, what's up?" I ask.

"I'm just worried that you're having heatstroke, or an aneurysm, or a parasite or something. We should get you out of here and to a hospital to get checked out," he's, fretting like a mother hen.

"I'm coming to grips with it. This is getting normal. I'll get a wave of vertigo any minute now, then you'll be gone, and I'll be back in Weirdsville."

"Yeah, Miles, that's more concerning. Come on," he says, taking me by the wrist and pulling me back toward the trail.

"That's really not necessary," but I follow along anyway. We start to descend the embankment, and I stumble. Midstep, I feel that now familiar vertigo wash over me, and I collapse on top of Alistair. We roll down the hill in a tumble of legs and arms. When we get to the ground at the bottom of the hillock, I lay there, waves of nausea and dizziness sweeping over me. It was so much worse this time.

"Dude," Russ says flatly from below me. "Your elbow is in my junk, man."

"Oh," I roll off of him. "Sorry about that."

"You all done taking a leak or whatever you were doing up there? We should get back on the trail."

I continue lying on the ground, staring up at the tree branches. I got so distracted by Alistair I forgot for a second that I went up there looking for the voices.

"What about the Wugwum?"

"What's the Wugwum?" Russ asks. Oh, great. I've been assuming all this time that when I meet back up with Russ, it's the same Russ. But now, I am not so sure.

"The nursery rhyme? The voices in the forest?"

"Did you eat any cookies from my backpack, man?"
Oh boy.

CHAPTER 15

WE GO BACK into the sandy bowl and continue on the path as it cuts across the depression. We get to the far side and begin climbing our way up the trail. We escape the area that may have once been a prehistoric lake. There is a small sandy rise, and at the top is a somehow familiar-looking building. Worn wooden boards camouflage it from a distance, but as we close in, its outline becomes clear.

It's a small cabin, maybe fifteen feet on a side. It is made of planks roughly hewn from medium-sized trees that I'm guessing were cut from the surrounding forest. The building looks worn but maintained. It has wooden shutters hanging over the windows and a large piece of plywood hanging on rusted hinges for a door.

The cabin is not the most worrying thing, though. The air feels heavy as if gravity were pulling us toward the building. A feeling of primal wrongness, of some instinct screaming at me to run, pervades my senses.

"Do you feel that?" I ask.

"Yeah," Russ says. "No es bueno."

"I've seen this cabin before."

"Yeah?"

"Maybe, but no, more like in a dream. It's so familiar."

It takes an effort of will to overcome the horror that pervades my body, but I start to approach the cabin. Then I stop. To my right is what I first thought to be a tree stump, but upon closer examination, it is a post planted in the ground. "Hold on."

I scan the area and see a dozen or so such posts buried in the ground circling the cabin. Between the posts runs a single, contiguous piece of wire. I think this is to define the circle's perimeter, but just in case, I cautiously avoid it. I walk over to one post and take a closer look. It has a little wooden shingle hanging on it, and on the shingle is carved a sigil that I recognize: the King's Crown.

I continue to circle the cabin, looking at each post in turn. Russ follows me closely. Each post has another shingle on it, each with a sigil. After inspecting the first four, I already know what I'm looking at.

"This is a big inclusive circle. This is a warding barrier to keep something inside."

"But whoever built it put the sigils on planks so they could remove them," Russ observes.

"It's a cage–one intended to be opened."

We walk around the rest of the perimeter and examine the sigils on the shingles. Once we are done, I am confident about my assessment.

"I think this is intended to keep something magical in. Whatever is in that cabin could be dangerous."

I pick open one of the many scabs I always seem to have these days and dab a little blood on my finger. I trace over the warding tattoos on my arms. I can feel a little surge through my limbs like cold electricity.

I nod to Russ, and we step over the wire in front of the cabin.

"If we have to run, make sure not to trip on the wires," I point to the wire running between posts.

"No problemo, dude."

We creep up the front step to the cabin. It has only one door, the plywood plank. The stairs creak ominously as we walk up. The sound seems deafening as it breaks the silence. I am struck again that the normal chorus of birds and insects cannot be heard here.

The plywood door screams on its hinges as I pull it open. There is a weird reverberating sound as I open it, which I realize is a spring on the door that will pull it shut when released.

The cabin is one single room. It is dark and empty inside.

While holding the door with my left hand, I switch on the flashlight and scan the room with my right. It is not quite empty. There is a large circle of stones on the floor. Inside the circle is only blackness. At first, I think this is because the floor there has been painted black, but shining the flashlight on it reveals this untrue. It’s a pool of black shadows. The kind of shadow that swallows light and reflects nothing. It is unnatural, and looking directly at it makes me lightheaded and dizzy. I recognize this; it is a tear in reality, a vortex, a gate into the Dreamtime. It's just like the one in Portia's basement, except that it is huge by comparison—probably ten feet across.

Next to the circle and the immense pool of nothingness is a little wooden box on the floor. It, too, has runes carved into it. The box is coated with an ominous, rusty-black crust, staining the wood. I’ve seen this sort of thing enough times to know, without examination, that this is dried blood.

“Dude!” Russ says. "It's a permanent tear in the Chimeric Veil, like from the Phantasmagoricon!"

“Yeah, I've seen one like this before. Only it was much smaller."

We move over and crouch next to the circle.

“Don’t touch it,” I caution.

“Hadn’t crossed my mind, dude. Check this out; it's self-sustaining. Man, this is super dangerous,” Russ chuckles. "Anything goes into this, and something else comes out."

I look over the circle of stones on the floor. They are flat, roughly square slabs of granite. They look like they were cut from local stone. Each has a sigil carved into it, holes drilled into the corners, and they have been bolted to the floor.

"What do you mean?" I ask.

"Oh, well, like for something to come, like physically out of the Dreamtime through a gate like this, like for real, something of equal *Pezo* has to go in."

"*Pezo* means weight, like spiritual weight?"

"Yeah, that's right, a spirit in, a spirit out sorta thing."

"Lovely," I grimace.

“I know what that box is,” Russ stabs a finger at the blood-crusted object. “I’ve seen something like that before. It’s a summoning altar.”

I look it over and nod in agreement. I don’t recognize all the sigils, but it looks like a summoning ritual.

“It summons something big, but I don’t know what language that name is in.”

"It's meant to sort of, like, name or bait what they want to come out when they put something in. Without that, you get, like, whatever decides it wants to come out," Russ clarifies.

“So, someone opened a tear into the Dreamtime, created an altar to summon things through it, and sealed it in a cage,” I make a broad sweeping circle with my arm, indicating the ward around the building.

“I don't think they opened this. These rocks look old; this

tear is huge. I think this has been here a long time. I think they added the altar and the cage, man."

"Why do you think that?" I ask.

“I read about this in the Phantasmagoricon. This thing is, like, self-sustaining. It stays open by consuming, um, by, like, burning up reality itself. Like, I don't know, like fire burning its way through reality. It was probably tiny when it started and needed blood to keep it open, you know, for a while. But then it gets to a certain size, and it doesn't need it anymore, it just sort of starts sucking reality into it. Like a fission reaction that starts a fusion reaction."

"So why do you think it's been here a long time?"

"Cause it's fuckin' huge!" Russ says loudly.

I nod. We sit silently for a moment, staring into the unsettling, terrifying abyss before us.

“Do you think this is related to that laboratory?” Russ asks.

“It’s pretty far away. I would think if they were related, you’d put them closer together.”

“I think we should get outta here,” Russ stands up and backs away from the vortex.

"We should try to close it."

"Too risky. I'm not sure something with this much, you know, um, velocity can be closed. We'd risk getting sucked in. Then who knows what comes out."

"I am going to take some pictures of it," I take my phone out of my pocket. "Shit, my battery is dead; I didn't get to charge it yesterday. We could charge it at Matt's."

"What if he's involved in this?" Russ motions at the gate.

“Hmm. We could charge it off the car battery."

"That's a smart call, dude. Let's try that."

We leave the creepy little cabin on the hill. I close the door carefully so the spring doesn’t slam it shut. We skulk across the sandy dirt until we are outside the inclusive circle, and finally, we both take deep breaths of relief. The farther away from the cabin we get, the more the sense of wrongness and unease fades. Within ten minutes, the whole thing feels like a dream, gradually fading from my mind.

We walk back down the trail and through the little valley. When we come to the fork, we head down the path to Matt's house, following the trail as it winds its way around trees and large rocks. We reach a section where a series of switchbacks leads us down to the bottom of the gorge. The gorge has widened and lowered here, making the transition down one side and back up the other relatively easy. Soon, we find ourselves skirting a trail around Matt's house. We can see the house, but only at a distance, the trees heavily obscuring our view and, reciprocally, any view people there would have of us.

We finally make it to the community circle. It seems abandoned for the late afternoon, which I find odd. Since the community meal is tonight, I would expect someone to be there preparing.

We sit down in Magdalena's car. I plug my phone in and turn the car on. Russ pulls a book out of his pack and begins reading. Leaning back, I close my eyes. I doze off, and I don't know how much later it is when I am awakened.

Tap. Tap. Tap. We both start as someone knocks on the passenger's side window. It's Matt.

Russ rolls his window down.

"What are you two up to?" Matt asks amiably.

"Just charging my phone."

"I figured. Sorry, last night didn't work out. I saw you sitting here, and I thought I ought to come let you know we are having our community meal in another half-hour or so."

I glance in the rearview mirror. Around the community center, several people are bustling about. Russ must have gotten very sucked into reading to miss that.

"Thank you," I give Matt a thumbs up. "I think we'll probably just call it an early night. We've been hiking all day."

Matt looks toward the community center. He smacks his lips and then leans in a little closer, his brow furrowed with concern.

"You should be there," he whispers. "You're safer with everyone there than you are alone."

The hackles on my neck rise.

"Was that a threat, dude?" Russ whispers back.

Matt looks back at the community center. I follow his gaze and see an old man standing by the center, watching us. He's a big guy, probably in his early sixties. He's wearing overalls, a flannel shirt, and big boots. I can't shake the feeling that this is the guy who was watching us at the laboratory earlier.

"Not everyone here has taken to you as kindly as I have," he whispers cryptically. He pushes off the car and starts back toward the large building.

"Hey, Art!" I can hear him greeting the old guy in the overalls. I can't hear any more of his exchange, though.

"How's your battery?" Russ asks.

"About eighty percent. What now?"

"Well, the smart move would be to just get out of here," Russ glowers.

"The safe move would be to just get out of here, but that portal–we need to figure out what came through it if it's still here, and, if so, how to put it back before we close it."

"Sounds like you want to go to dinner."

"I guess so."

I turn off the car, and we make our way back up to the yurt to prepare for a Stanyon's Hollow community dinner.

CHAPTER 16

"DUDE, AM I RIPE!" Russ laughs as he pulls on a new shirt.

"Yeah, but with the baths right there next to the community hall, I don't know. It feels weird."

Russ shrugs in agreement.

"I think all the weird stuff going on with me is because of that thing in the cabin," I have been thinking about this since we left the inclusive circle.

"The whole suddenly-I'm-Genevieve thing?" Russ asks.

"And other people..."

"And the ghost of your dead brother."

"The kid voices in the forest," I add. Russ quirks an eyebrow.

"Know what's funny? You always say there is no such thing as ghosts," Russ laughs. "I told you there were more things in the world than Miles Ward knows."

"Yeah, or something like that. I never heard Hank until I made the simulacrum. Then I only heard him while near it until I rebuilt it, and then it started following me around Napa. But it's gotten so weird here."

“Yeah, I have been thinking about that, dude. So check this out,” Russ gets up, walks over to his pack, and pulls out the book he has been reading. He sits on the foot of the bed, and I sit down next to him as he begins thumbing through pages.

I look over his shoulder, it is the piece about the bubbles he read to me before.

“That’s the confusing, philosophical mumbo-jumbo you were reading last night,” I say.

“Yeah, William Baros,” Russ stabs a finger at the page in front of him.

“William Baros?” I repeat. “Why does that name sound familiar?”

"’Cause I mentioned him last night."

"No, I mean, it sounds really familiar, but I can't put my finger on it."

“I don't know, man, but I think he's the dude that wrote yer Phantasmagoricon. I also think maybe what we are seeing is these 'bubbles' he's talking about, kinda crisscrossing, bleeding over, you know?”

"Okay, so what happened to this William Baros guy?”

“He traveled around and did all this early self-help stuff. He grew a following, which evolved into one of those Branch Davidian style cult-of-personalities. The big rural compound in the woods, people leaving their lives to join, the whole nine yards. Had a similar ending, too: a mass suicide pact. But it didn’t get as much press as Jonestown or Heaven’s Gate, or the more well-known suicide cults," he explains.

"You alluded to that," I have an alarming thought, “Where was this compound?”

“I can see where you are going with that, man. Relax, dude; I already told you it was in Montana. Well, that was the one that they, you know, ended it on. They had a couple other compounds, but they got chased away. It started in like, Oregon or somewhere up north. Not here."

I sigh and nod, "Good. That would be too freaky."

"Where'd you get the Phantasmagoricon again, man?"

"From Circe," I say.

"Right, seven-foot-tall Hizarin chick."

"Something like that. We could try to ask her."

"But you trapped her in the Donjon, dude."

"I didn't trap her there!"

Circe, the very beautiful, very dangerous assassin. I once thought she was a vampire. Then I thought she was some dream projection. I have no idea what she is, but I know she is trapped in a giant black tower in the Dreamtime. A tower that seems linked to me, though I don't know how.

"Whatever, dude. My point is she's trapped in the Dreamtime, and I can't seem to Dreamwalk here. Heck, I don't even have dreams here, man. It's unsettling," Russ nervously flips pages in the book.

"That's weird, I have, I think. Or maybe that's all been more of this weird stuff."

We look at each other for a moment.

"I guess, thinking about it, that kinda makes sense," Russ says.

"Does it?"

"Yeah, man, there's like an actual tear in the Chimeric Veil, dude; we both saw it in that cabin. That's the problem."

"I don't understand."

"Think of it, like, um, like if you had a piece of plastic, stretched taught. Normally, like if you press on it from one side, it sort of makes a depression on the other side, right? You could, like, see through. But if you press right near a hole in the plastic, it just slides through. Normal dreaming is like looking at what presses itself up against the plastic and leaves a shape.

But here, it doesn't just leave a shape, it slides through and comes here. That's why you keep seeing weird stuff; shit is sliding through," Russ concludes.

"Okay, I think I understand that, but why isn't it happening to you?"

"Yeah, I've got a theory on that too."

"Okay," I say expectantly.

"So, you have this link to this ghost, or whatever, this thing on the other side of the Chimeric Veil, right? Hank. Well, that link is like a little thread–actually, let's call it a rubber band–it's stretchy, right? Let's say that reality is like water, right? If you have a band going through a hole and water pouring across it, it will drip down the band, right? It's going to pool around where the band ends. That linkage you have makes you like a focus for all the shit that flows through and starts weighing you down."

"But what about the whole *pezo* thing? Doesn't there need to be an exchange of spiritual weight?"

"No, no, man. Well yes, but sort of. Like, okay, do you know String Theory?"

"I mean, the pop science version, maybe," I say.

"Okay, this is like some heavy shit, okay, but there is this magic version of it. Every tiny choice or variation spawns off an infinite set of universes. But more than that, every thought, fantasy, and dream, they all spawn off versions of reality. But like, here, there is a hole in reality, right? And you've got this rubber band connecting you, through that hole in the space between realities, so every time something leaks in, the weight, it pulls you down, stretches the band. See?"

"No."

"So this theory says that we live in a kind of narrow web of quantum possibilities; that we actually flow and shift between different possible realities normally; it's just we only shift to the ones that are so close, at a quantum level, we don't notice. Like, you ever had that thing where you swear you put your keys in your pocket, but then you find them on the table and think you just made a mistake?"

"Sure, happens to everybody, right?"

"Yeah, exactly. Well, this theory says that you *did* put the keys in your pocket, but that ebb and flow in the universe just kinda nudged you over to a parallel one, where your keys were on the table, and that's like the only difference, and another version of you suddenly found their keys in their pocket, when they could swear they left em on the table, you dig?"

"Okay, sure."

"Well, you, my friend, seem to be jumping over pretty big bands of quantum divergence, huge gaps of probability. The theory states if you go far enough out on this infinite stream, there is a universe where anything and everything happens; there is one where you are a talking tube of toothpaste, somewhere."

"There is one where I am a ghost, and Hank is alive," I add, reflecting on my experience.

"That's right, man, but it's more like, well, like this book says, like clusters of little bubbles, right? Each cluster is defined by a set of circumstances, so the farther from your cluster, the more energy it takes to slingshot you. So, without truly cosmic energy levels, you can only jump between bubbles in your immediate cluster, ones that are quantumly similar. That is bubbles where you are basically the same you, in basically the same place, at basically the same time.

"Then why do other people change? You and Genevieve aren't 'basically the same' person."

"We are all sliding back and forth between our own quantum bubble sets, man. We exist in N dimensions, dude. Just the rest of us aren't jumping so far."

"I am not certain I understand any of that, but okay. So why me again?"

"Because every time energy comes in from outside, every time something comes through that portal, it comes running down that band. It's like a weight, pulling it down, making it taut, and then, Bam! Like you are a paperclip wrapped around the end, you go flinging into another bubble. But, like you said, *pezo* for *pezo,* so the other you goes flinging into your bubble," Russ concludes.

"Wait, so I am not in my original reality? Am I in some parallel reality? How do I get back?" I ask, a growing sense of dread building in me.

"If you believe the theory, and that's a big if, 'cause it's just a theory, then you don't get back. According to this theory, we shift between realities all the time. If that's true, then you'll keep slingshotting until that hole gets closed, the rubber band is broken, or we get far enough away from it. Or eventually, that hole will get big enough, and then it won't matter anyway cause the universe you are in collapses."

"Wow. Um. That is a lot to take in."

"Just a theory, dude."

My head hurts thinking about it. "Okay, I need to think about that. In the meantime, we should probably get down to that dinner."

"Yer sure you want to do this, dude?"

"No, but it seems like a good place to get some information."

We both finish getting dressed in pensive silence. We each slap on some deodorant.

"Let me ask you something," I say as we are heading out of the yurt.

"Shoot, dude," Russ says.

"How much blood would it take to open a portal like that?"

"To open it? Something like that would take the sacrifice of a willing life, man."

"That's what I was thinking, but to maintain it would require pretty regular blood sacrifices."

"Up and to a point, but there is a point where it doesn't need blood anymore, the flow of energy back and forth becomes so constant that it can't ever close or heal."

"Still, it means there is a better-than-average chance that there will be at least one necromancer at dinner with us tonight," I grit my teeth.

"And," Russ says, "what are the chances that they did all that without anyone else in the community noticing or at least being suspicious?"

"Hmm. There is no way all that goes on and nobody notices. There is no way that lab got built, and nobody noticed. It's really obvious the solar was built to power it, and Matt lied about that. I see your point; the whole community either knows and is silent or knows and is actively complicit."

"So, why are we going? We should go to our car and get out of here to report it, dude." Russ gives me a grim look.

"Report that they have a secret laboratory and a tear in the fabric of reality? I want to have more information, or we'd sound nuts."

"Dude, this isn't the first cult I've encountered in my day."

"We don't know it's a cult."

"Okay, if you say so. Looks like shit, smells like shit, I'm not gonna taste it to find out, man," Russ scrunches his face up in a disgusted look and sticks his tongue out.

I roll my eyes. "In my experience, nobody ever wants to believe this stuff is going on. It's so much easier to look away, especially if people feel like nobody is getting hurt. We need to find the victims. We need to find evidence."

We leave the yurt and zip the door shut. We are halfway down the stairs when I have a thought.

“Hold on,” I say.

I find a single leaf on the ground and return to the yurt's door. I thread the leaf's stem into the zipper tab, lay it at a very specific angle, and take out my phone to snap a picture of the zipper.

“I’ve got a photo. All this cult talk is making me paranoid, and I want to make sure nobody is coming in the tent when we aren’t here.”

"You do you, dude."

We turn and march down the trail to the community hall.

CHAPTER 17

When we approach, Matt is pacing nervously in front of the community hall. He is dressed in a nicely ironed flannel shirt and clean, hole-free jeans.

"Oh, hey! You made it!" Matt says when he sees us. There is something in his tone that bothers me.

"Yo, dude," Russ flicks his hand in the half-hearted illusion of a wave.

"What's up, Matt?" I ask.

Matt speaks in a low voice, looking around to ensure there is no one nearby.

"I'm worried, Miles. There's things going on. Art says he saw you down in the grove across Holton's field."

"You mean that crazy laboratory?" Russ stares blankly up into the trees. I can't tell if it's an act and he is intentionally being obtuse or if he's really not thinking about what he's saying.

Matt's eyes go wide, and he looks around.

"It's more like a clinic, but keep your voice down. If

anybody hears you talking about that..." he starts, but then he seems to think better of what he's saying and clams up.

"Matt, what is going on?" I try to sound as calming as possible, but my voice sounds frantic in my ears.

"It's not... It's not what you think," Matt says. He is staring at his feet and looking miserable.

"Since I don't know what I think, and I'm not even sure what 'it' you are talking about, that seems self-evident."

"We can talk more after dinner, but now, you just need to play dumb and be amiable. You're going to meet Art. It's Art's lab. It's Art's solar panels. Art's pretty much taken over this community. You need to stay off his radar."

"You don't know this dude," Russ stabs a thumb in my direction. "He's not the stay-off-the-radar type."

"Thanks for the vote of confidence, Russ," I glower. I can stay off the radar. Sure, I end up in the middle of a lot of weird stuff, but that isn't my fault. Is it?

"I just call 'em like I see 'em."

Matt looks absolutely miserable as he turns toward the door to the community hall. "Let's go."

We follow him into the hall. There are twenty people present, give or take. Pamela and Winnie are absent; it seems to be mostly men, and no children are here.

"Dude, there's no chicks," Russ whispers to me.

I'm about to scold him, but then I realize that he's commenting on how weird it is, not trying to be a chauvinist.

"Yeah," I mutter, "I noticed that. How very old-fashioned."

"I was thinking 'cult-like.' I told you, dude."

"Yeah, you might have been onto something."

Everyone is milling about, eating what looks like tiny sausages wrapped in biscuit dough and sipping on mugs of an almost black-looking liquid. A three-piece string band is playing a bluegrass tune that I don't recognize. Matt guides us over to a large punch bowl and pours out three mugs of the blackish liquid. He hands one each to Russ and me. Matt takes a small, polite sip and then holds the mug like a prop. It smells sweet but with a funk to it. I take a closer sniff.

"Let's see. Elderberry, botrytis, and am I getting a little whiff of brettanomyces?" I say, doing a terrible French accent.

"This is Petersen's wine I was telling you about."

"Smells like Tetrachloroethylene," Russ leans over and whispers to me. "Don't drink this shit, man."

If Russ is saying don't drink it, it can't be good.

"That's the good stuff!" Says an older gentleman. He speaks with a slight lisp. He has wild gray hair that billows cloud-like around his head, like a mad scientist. He is wearing black and purple-stained overalls and is missing one of his front upper teeth.

"And this," Matt says in a tired tone, "is Petersen."

"Hola dude, I'm Russ," Russ raises his mug in a toast. However, he notably doesn't drink the concoction.

"Good t'meetcha!" Petersen responds, clinking mugs with Russ. He proceeds to chug down half of his mug. A little blackish-purple rivulet dribbles down his chin, winding a zig-zag between his gray whiskers. "But it'd be Mr. Gortenheimer, Petersen Gortenheimer, at your service!"

"Good to meet you, Mr. Gortenheimer. Miles Ward," I clink my glass, too. I reflexively almost take a sip, but then I remember Russ' warning and feign a sip instead. The concoction smells sickly sweet but with a slightly nauseating chemical odor hiding in it, like volatile antifreeze.

"Just call me Petersen, everybody does!"

"Petersen, if you don't mind the interruption," a deep voice says from my left. I turn to face the voice. It is the man I saw watching us from the hill, the man I heard Matt address as 'Art'.

"O'course not, Art." With a tip of his mug, Petersen bows away from the conversation and vanishes to speak to some of the other men. I note that the little groups of people drift away as Art approaches us.

"Mr. Miles Ward," Art stares through his tiny spectacles, unblinking, into my eyes. There's something familiar about the way he's looking at me. It's the same mesmerism trick John Hale has tried on me a few times. Now I can see it coming, and I avert my eyes.

Art is probably in his sixties, but he's still pretty large. He has ditched the overalls and flannel and is now dressed in a dapper but antiquated-looking suit. He has a felt hat on his bald pate and tiny round spectacles perched on the end of his nose. I'm reminded of the guy on the oatmeal box if only he were a nineteenth-century mesmerist.

"Mr. Art..." I say. "You have me at a loss."

"Doctor Arturus Grable," he holds out his hand, and I shake it. He has a strong grip, and he continues to try to make eye contact, but I avoid his gaze.

"What'cha a doctor of, dude?" Russ says. "I'm Russ, by the way."

Art raises his eyebrows, and his face falls into a displeased grimace. There is something about Russ that he doesn't seem to like. Russ can be an acquired taste, it's true, but this is more than that.

"I hold a PhD in parapsychology, and I have an MD as well."

"You are a parapsychiatrist?" I conclude skeptically.

"Precisely."

"Parapsychiatry is not a real thing, is it, dude?" Russ asks, quirking an eyebrow skeptically.

"A growing field, to be sure," Art looks at Russ like he is looking at an annoying fly.

"What landed you out here, in the backside of nowhere?" Russ continues to seem oblivious to Art's growing displeasure.

"I found that most of society is too ignorant and judgmental for my tastes. Science has not explained the world to my satisfaction. Here, I can pursue my studies without the grind and distraction of city life. No television. No internet. The brainwashing of society does not reach us here."

"Oh, man, do I get that. Television is like brain rot in a cathode tube, man," Russ waves his hands emphatically, spilling his mug of wine in the process. "Oh, shit, sorry about that."

"It is no problem. I'm sure that Ms. Fontaine would be happy to clean it up," as Art speaks, one of the three women present appears with a mop and begins to clean up Russ' mistake. Russ and I exchange an alarmed look, and I think he mouths the word 'cult' at me. "And I am sure Mr. Petersen is happy to refill your beverage."

"No," Russ shakes his head and puts his mug on a nearby table. "I'm all full up, thanks anyway, Art. What was I saying? Oh, yeah, TV is cathode tube brain rot, man."

"No one uses CRTs anymore," I mumble.

"You know what I mean, man. But Art, I mean, why here? This is more than getting away from society, am I right?"

Art is about to continue when someone jangles a triangle that is hanging in one corner.

"Soup's on!" The man calls out in a colloquial holler.

"If you two would care to join me at my table," Art motions toward a large table at the front of the room. He begins leading us toward the table. I take the opportunity while his back is turned to slide my gazing crystal out of my pocket. I use it to make a quick scan of the room and the auras of the people here.

Art's aura looks like any human aura might, though it looks

slightly icky, with putrid yellow-green streaks running through it. Aside from Russ, everyone else in the room has what I can only describe as a purple-black slime seeming to coat their auras like oil floating on top of a puddle.

It is rare that I look at an aura and know exactly what I am seeing, and this is one of those rare moments. The purple-black slime has the exact same color and oily viscosity as the elderberry wine. Different auras have different amounts of taint on them. Matt has only a little bit of the film. Petersen's aura is almost completely enveloped by it. I'm not certain what effect it has, but I can feel in my gut that there is nothing wholesome or good about this.

I look down at the concoction in my mug with the crystal and discover something horrifying–it has its own aura. It's all shades of oozy purple-black, but it shifts ebbs and flows. If I didn't know better, I'd say that the elderberry wine was sentient. Maybe that's assuming too much, but I'm inclined to believe that it at least has moods. This is a very unsettling thought.

I casually slide my gazing crystal back into my pocket and follow Art and Russ to the table. I set my mug of viscous black liquid down on the table and leave it untouched.

Dinner mostly consists of Art interrogating me about my work, asking my opinions on various bits of magical phenomena, and me trying to answer as vaguely and uselessly as possible. Everything about Art gives me the creeps. He knows more about me than one might casually know. I play up the angle that I am doing more faking it than making it. Truth though it might be, he doesn't seem to accept this framing.

We are served an array of roasted and creamed vegetables, home-baked bread, and smoked slabs of meat. I surreptitiously examine them with my gazing crystal. It all seems fine, no purple-black coating there. Russ sees me doing this and asks a pointed question to keep attention off of me. It doesn't work. Art definitely notices me examining the food but does nothing more than give me a slight smirk. We finish the meal and sit back in our chairs.

"Your name has come up more than a few times in my circles, Mr. Ward," Art folds his hands on the table before him.

"Miles, please, call me Miles. Mr. Ward was my grandfather."

Russ shakes his head at this. It's one of my fall-back jokes, and he clearly thinks it is tired.

"Magical corporate security. Mr. Ward," Art pauses dramatically, "excuse me, Miles."

"That's where the money is. Draw some little squiggles on some doorframes and get paid!"

"Do you subscribe to the Biltmore Principle, or are you more of a Sendintiary Post Realist?"

"I have no idea what you are talking about," I say. It's true. I think he's just making things up. I'm pretty sure 'Sendintiary' isn't even a word.

"Ah," he says. He looks at me, squinting as if trying to ascertain if I'm messing with him or if I'm really that incompetent. From the resigned little sigh he gives, I suspect I've finally lived up to his lowest expectations.

"What about you, dude?" Russ asks. "Do you subscribe to Biltmore's belief that magic is an act of individual will imposed on reality? You know that the greater the intent, the greater the effect? Or do you believe the Sendintia Prophecy, how magic is a cyclical product of chaos, no different than something like earthquakes or the weather?"

Art turns from me to Russ with a smile.

"There is more below the surface than I would have expected, Mr...Russ, was it?" he says obsequiously.

I'm pretty sure I've just been dismissed.

"Well?" Russ persists.

"I think untested theories will generally lead to poor outcomes, and it is only through the evolution of scientific study that we find the truth. There is ample evidence to suggest that Biltmore was a bumbling idiot, and while there is some observable legitimacy to the Sendintian theory, it is, at best, incomplete and untested. What's your opinion?"

"I think, man, that lots of people have used hypothesis and science as a rationalization to do bad shit. But to pursue cruelty in the name of research is the lowest calling of man. Science needs to be performed with a moral filter. I've been there, dude," Russ staring Art down.

Art's forehead crinkles and the wrinkles and crevices around his mouth tighten into a forced smile. Russ has struck a nerve.

Art turns and stands. He raises his earthenware mug off the table. I note that I never saw it filled with elderberry wine. Art clinks his mug with a spoon, and the room falls silent as everyone turns their attention to him.

Nothing is abnormal about this scene, but everyone is too quick to fall quiet and a little too focused on Art. There is something subtle but unsettling about the room's easy compliance.

"I would like to propose a toast!" Art exclaims. "To our esteemed visitors. You may not know this, but we have a celebrity in our midst."

I feel a little red in the cheeks. While the whole Devora debacle has not yet blown over, I am surprised that word has gotten out here in the backwoods.

"Miles Ward, a security consultant to the stars. He's worked for Walt Carmichael, a renowned trillionaire, and Jim Devora, a famous movie producer."

Uncomfortable, I scan the array of non-plussed faces in the

room, finally landing on Russ'. He is straight-backed and wide-eyed with discomfort.

“To our guests!” Art raises his mug in a toast. Everyone in the room raises their mugs as well. Russ raises his fork; I reluctantly follow suit with my still-full mug of elderberry wine.

“Praise thee, oh lord, in evening!” They chant in unison and quaff down the remainder of their elderberry wine. Art, Russ, and I do not drink from our mugs. Russ raises his fork as if he were drinking from it in an uncharacteristically sassy fashion. Art gives us an appraising look, obviously taking note of the fact that we refuse to drink.

After the toast, Art places his mug back on the table.

“Now, if you will excuse me, I have some matters to which I must attend,” Art says. He holds his hand out to shake mine, and I reluctantly accept. His hand feels cold and clammy, and his grip is like a vice. He attempts to make direct eye contact with me again, but I do not meet his gaze.

He turns to Russ and holds out his hand.

“No thanks, dude," Russ says, holding his elbow toward Art. "Elbow bump?"

Art looks taken aback. He stares at Russ's elbow for a while. After a long pause, Russ shrugs and lowers his elbow. "Suit yourself, dude."

Then Art turns on his heels and leaves without another word.

“I've worked with shitheels like that before, no bueno,” Russ mutters to me as Art leaves.

“There’s something in the wine,” I say.

“That's not wine, dude; that shit will make you go blind and crazy before it kills you.”

"You sure?"

"Organic chemist, remember? Yeah, just smelling that crap is bad for you."

"We should get out of here."

We sit quietly for a few minutes after Art leaves. With his departure, the tone of the room shifts slightly. There seems to be more conversation, and it gets a little louder. The band starts playing again, and everyone seems to be enjoying themselves more. It feels like an office where the boss has just left.

"I think this is our moment," Russ says.

I nod, and we both rise to leave.

Matt moves across the room and intercepts us near the door.

"Be careful," Matt speaks in a quiet voice, trying not to draw attention.

"What's going on?" I ask Matt.

Matt shakes his head, "Not here. Not now. I'll come by the yurt later."

Matt glances furtively over his shoulder at the room. I see his gaze fall onto Petersen, watching us suspiciously from the corner. He holds a mug of his 'wine' in two hands, clutched right below his nose, like a goblin protecting his most precious treasure.

Russ follows me as I leave the community hall.

Once we are outside, sufficiently far away not to be overheard, Russ leans close to me to speak.

"Something fucked up is going on here, dude," he says in a low voice. "This is bigger than you and that portal. Some real dark shit is going on. I got that itch in my bones."

"Yeah, I picked up on that. Doctor Arturus Grable even sounds like a comic book supervillain. I'm convinced the gate is linked to whatever Art is doing at that laboratory, or whatever it is."

"Agreed, dude, agreed."

"I can't believe I am saying this, but I'd feel much better if Magdalena was here."

"Fight fire with fire sort of thing?" Russ asks.

"Yeah, something like that."

"Those that play with fire, man, always get burned."

"Her skills would be useful if Dr. Art decided to go all mad scientist on us."

"What do you mean 'if,' dude?"

"I mean when. Just once, I would like to have a nice weekend without some monster-filled nightmare. Is it just me? Do I attract this kind of crap?"

"Dude, there has always been fucked up shit in the world. You're just seein' it more now."

"I wonder why that is," I say distractedly.

"Because now you are looking for it."

I shrug. "Maybe."

"So what's next?"

"I think we get in a car, drive back down to town, and call for help. Yeah, maybe the police won't be useful, but Magdalena sure would be, though last I knew, she was stuck in France or something. Some more of Jeff's special concoction could come in handy. Seeing if Emily can find more on Doctor Creepenstein there, too," I speed walk over the barren ground toward the car, Russ falls in step with me.

"That works, dude."

The sun has sunk low in the sky, and gray light filters through the trees. We stomp through the dusty sunset to my car and climb in. It's weird to me to call this my car. This is not a car I would have bought. Though she gave it to me, it is very much Magdalena's car.

I press the starter button. Nothing happens. I press it again. Nothing. I make sure that the car is in park and that I am depressing the brake pedal. I press the button and again, nothing.

"I can't stand it. I know you planned it..." I mutter.

“Huh?”

“Listen, all y’all, it’s a sabotage,” I conclude.

“Sure, dude,” Russ’s forehead crinkles as he glowers at me.

"While I am surprised to discover that the car has been disabled, I’m more surprised that I am surprised than anything. In hindsight, we should have seen this coming."

"Probably shoulda."

I pop the hood, and we get out of the car. Under the hood is a mess of smashed metal and plastic, cut wires, and tubes. It looks like someone has taken a sledgehammer to the electric motor.

"This is a hack job; whoever did this didn't have any plans for driving the car out of here afterward and didn't want it repaired, man," Russ says after a careful examination.

I look over the mess. I am not much of a mechanic, but I concur; there is no possibility of fixing this; it's been wrecked.

"We should check out the trunk, dude," Russ’ tone is worried.

"We got our bags out of the trunk," I say, looking at him incredulously. How would the trunk help us?

"The secret lock box in the trunk?" It's dark, but in the dim light from the community hall, I can see his eyes bugged out at me.

"Oh, right. How did I forget that?"

"Listen, dude, I've been sitting on these for a while, but we need you at full capacity," Russ says as he reaches into his coat pockets and brings out two cans of cold-brewed black coffee.

"I'm staying off the coffee," I say. "Doctor's orders."

"Can I be honest with you, dude? You're a fucking mess. Meth head, gotta meth, man. Drink up, doctor's Orders!" he thrusts both cans at me.

"I'm not a meth head," I say petulantly.

"Okay, stimulant addict gotta stimulate. It's pretty obvious that you use caffeine to self-medicate for something. You are spacy and inattentive without it, and we need you in the here and now, dude. Your doctor would rather you have a couple of sips of coffee than end up dissected in some weird ass mountain cult lab."

"Fine," I am secretly thankful that he's giving me the excuse. I take the two cans of coffee from him. I pop one open and chug it down. The caffeine can't possibly be hitting my system this fast, but I suddenly feel whole again. It's like a piece of me was missing that has suddenly been replaced. It feels like magic, true magic...but it's probably psychosomatic.

"All right, dude, what's next."

"Let's try to search the car for a way into that lockbox. I'll start in the trunk. You start in the main cabin of the car."

I pop the trunk and walk to the back while Russ searches the car. My stomach immediately lurches when I look inside the trunk. The secret compartment is unlocked and standing open. Inside, there is a large foam block with custom cutouts for several weapons, each of them empty.

"Well shit Russ, I don't think we need to search."

Russ comes around to the back and looks in the trunk.

"Well, dude, that's no good. It looks like there were two pistols, a submachine gun, and a broken-down rifle in there."

"You seem to know a lot about this stuff," I cast a sideways look at him.

Russ shrugs, "So now we got some cultists with an assassin's armory."

"We have to get out of here."

“We could try to hike out.”

“Yeah, it would take us all night just to get back to a paved road. That’s if we don’t get lost or hunted down by some psycho in the dark.”

“There’s the community phone.”

I nod, and we walk briskly across the open circle to the community telephone mounted on the store's wall.

We get to the phone, and Russ picks it up.

“Dead?” I guess out loud.

He nods as he hangs it back up.

“Well, what now?” I ask. My voice sounds calm in my ears, but inside, I am feeling anything but. Our little weekend of self-discovery has quickly turned into a nightmare.

“Well, if I were Art, I'd expect us to try to get out of dodge. So I think we do what they don't expect us to do,” Russ twirls the hairs on the end of his beard.

"What is that?"

"Go investigate that lab and figure out what they are up to, man. Who knows, maybe we find something that gets us out of here."

“I'm not sure that staggering around in the dark, on the side of a mountain, with a cult that says ‘Praise the lord of night’ is the best plan.”

“What are you thinking?”

“I'm thinking we go back to the yurt, hole up for the night, and get out of here at first light.”

“On foot?”

“Maybe Matt can get us a car?”

“Do we trust Matt?” he asks.

“More than I trust the rest of these people.”

With a brief nod of acknowledgment, Russ and I walk furtively back up the trail to the yurt. Weird has gotten very dangerous in a hurry.

CHAPTER 18

Back at the yurt, Russ quickly checks the leaf threaded through the zipper tab.

"It looks good," he says.

"I'm getting paranoid," I compare the state of the zipper to the photo on my phone. Nothing seems to have been disturbed. I notice with disappointment that my phone is down to under a quarter of its battery life again. We slip into the yurt and zip the door closed behind us. Russ ties the door shut from the inside. It isn't exactly secure, but it would slow someone down trying to get in.

We sit down on the bed. I'm suddenly aware that I haven't bathed since yesterday, and I've been hiking all over a mountainside, sweating, nervous, pungent sweat.

"Man, I could use a shower," I mutter.

Russ sniffs his armpits and laughs, "Yeah, you and me both, brother!"

We both laugh. It's a nice reprieve from the anxiety and stress.

"I'm not going to be able to sleep tonight."

"Yeah, dude, I'm not sure sleep is in the cards for either of us."

We sit for a while longer in silence. I pull my phone out and look at it. The battery is all but dead.

"How much battery do you have?" he asks.

"Like twenty percent. I'm going to turn it off and save it for when we get somewhere with service."

Russ gives me a double thumbs-up and a goofy grin. I don't know how he seems so damn calm through all this. It's almost like he's having fun.

I get up and pace. Russ picks up his book and starts reading.

"How are you so calm?" I ask, sounding more impatient than I intended.

"What's to worry about, man? We are here, and that is the only reality we have; stressing out about it isn't going to change our situation, just our perspective," he nods sagely.

"I guess."

"Also, I am meso-dosing shrooms and macro-dosing cannabis."

"Great," I murmur. I sit back down on the bed and wait for Russ to be done reading.

"Want a cookie?" Russ says. "Calm your nerves."

"Are those your cannabis macro-doses?"

"Sure are."

"I'll pass."

I find myself falling into a sort of trance, half awake and half asleep, mind drifting but not quite dreaming. My perception of time becomes flat. An eternity later, or only an instant, Russ' hand is on my shoulder.

"Dude!" He hisses.

"Wha? What's going on?" I sit upright with a start.

"Nothing, it's all good. I finished reading," he says.

"And?"

"And I'm like, totally positive this William Baros guy wrote that Phantasmagoricon. It's got the same voice, some of the same phrasing and shit. Heck, the Phantasmagoricon could almost be his Silmarillion for this book, you know?" Russ pats the old book in his hands.

"No, I don't know."

"Tolkien?"

"The Hobbit, Lord of the Rings, yeah, I'm familiar," my nerves are taut, and I am feeling more annoyed by this conversation than is probably reasonable..

"Right, but he had this whole rambling set of stories and notes and stuff that he wrote for himself to keep all his back story straight, like a reference. Later, his family published it as the Silmarillion. It's got some cool stuff in it, but it's sprawling and confusing.

"Sprawling and confusing compared to The Lord of the Rings?" I ask incredulously.

"Yeah, man."

"Ugh, pass."

"Anyway, the Phantasmagoricon feels a lot like that; like a bunch of background notes sort of jammed together, with this book being more of his final, public-facing work."

"How public-facing are we talking, though?"

"Like three hundred copies published. They are numbered and in high demand. I found it in a thrift store for thirty cents, if you can believe it, dude."

"High demand?" I ask.

"You know, among a certain discriminating clientele."

"Dreamwalkers."

"That's right, The Big Ds. That came out wrong. But yeah, man, Dreamwalkers."

"He was really into dreams, this Baros guy?"

"His whole jam is about the collective self, which can only be actualized in dreams. He says that this world is fixed, but it is your dream self that has the capacity for true change. Only through awakening your dream self can you see the whole of reality, the oneness of the universe, self-actualization, and all that. Through that oneness, we can seek the collective consciousness, our only true path to immortality, and the ability to willfully transition spheres–the bubbles we were talking about. This is his refrain, not mine, man. It's not a new tune, though he put some kind of objectivist riffs in it."

"That sounds pretty out there. He sounds a little focused on finding his own immortality. Certainly, Baros wasn't the kind of guy who would kill himself."

As I say 'Certainly, Baros' aloud, it triggers something for me. Russ is about to respond when I hold up a finger. He raises his eyebrows, and I bite my lip, thinking.

"Certainly Baros. Circe Baros. That's what Lorelei Redbrook called Circe at the Lantern. That's why it sounded so familiar."

"Wait, you think Circe is William Baros?" he asks, holding up his book to one of the first pages, where a blurry black and white photo of a man with a goatee, glasses, and a turtleneck sweater stares at me. It's too grainy to really identify much else about him. "Doesn't look a thing like Circe to me. Maybe she's his kid?"

"I don't know, but it is too much to be a coincidence. When Redbrook said the name, she was clearly trying to tell Circe something, and Circe did not like it. Also, I thought Circe was supposed to be really old."

"Well, you know, it was you that told me the Hizarin inherit names from their master; maybe she's not that old, just, you know, putting on airs."

"How many followers did William Baros have in this suicide pact?" I ask.

“Like a thousand.”

"A thousand is a lot of willing sacrifices...” I say, and then we sit in silence for a while.

“I know some shit about magic; that's a lot. What could you do with that kind of sacrifice?” Russ asks, breaking the silence.

“Almost anything. It would be a powerful magical catalyst if you had that many *un*willing participants. But *willing*? Yeah. It doesn’t answer exactly what Circe is or how, but that could explain who Circe is.”

“She’s a monster,” Russ says.

“Not exactly news.”

Our conversation is interrupted by the distant report of a firearm. We glance at each other, alarmed. Russ grabs his backpack and starts to hoist it onto his back.

“Might be nothing,” I say hopefully.

Russ quirks a single eyebrow at me skeptically.

“Okay, probably not nothing.”

We sit on the foot of the bed next to each other in silence. My ears strain to hear something, anything. I can only assume Russ is doing the same. There is an occasional creak of a tree or rustle of leaves, but nothing identifiable as a threat.

We sit quietly until it becomes maddening, and I just want to scream so that there is something to hear, but I don’t.

“This is driving me crazy,” I whisper.

“I'm sorry, what's driving you crazy?” Russ whispers back.

“Sitting here and listening for people coming after that gunshot?" I ask incredulously.

“Oh! Right man, sorry, I kinda zoned out there.”

"Russ, come on, man!" I scold him. He's about to respond when we hear the loud crack of a stick breaking outside. We both freeze.

“Shit,” we hear a muttered curse in the darkness outside. “Miles!”

We sit silently without responding.

A familiar voice says in a hushed cry, “It’s Matt.”

Right, Matt said he would stop by.

Russ and I exchange glances, and he nods toward the door. He takes a small folding shovel out of his backpack and starts extending it. I slide off the bed and make my way to the door, which I slowly untie. I stand to one side and unzip a couple of inches of the door flap. I can hear footsteps on the wooden platform the yurt is raised on. Peeking out, I see Matt. He looks sweaty and wane.

I turn and nod to Russ. He moves to the other side of the door, ready to swing the small metal shovel if Matt does anything weird. Matt comes through. He doesn’t look great.

“Are you okay?” I ask.

“Yeah,” he huffs, “I had to go off the trail. Art has people watching the path up here.”

“What’s going on?”

“You shouldn’t have gone snooping around. I told you to stay away from that bridge,” Matt puts his hands on his knees and leans forward to catch his breath.

“That's not an answer, buddy,” Russ responds crossly, lowering the shovel.

Matt shudders a little like he has a whole-body tremor. Then, as if in a trance, he recites:

“He wore his mask of morning.
And served the coming light.
He removed his mask at midday.
To take away man’s sight.
He donned the mask of gloaming.
To hide his mirthless spite.
He wore his mask tenebrous.

To call forth eternal night.
He has as many names.
as masks upon his faces,
Visages in number equaled.
By man's many disgraces."

A riddle. I hate riddles.

"You could have just said, 'I don't know!'" I throw my hands in the air.

Then Matt begins to shudder and convulse. He falls to the ground, writhing silently.

"Matt!" I exclaim and leap forward to him.

"Shit!" Russ yells and slings his backpack to the floor next to Matt.

I kneel next to him; his convulsions are becoming more violent. I think the archaic term is 'the rigors.' A thin trickle of blood drips down his face from his nose. But as I lean forward, I see it isn't blood at all; it's a thick, viscous, purple-black liquid. I lean over and hold his shoulders so that his thrashing doesn't cause him to hit his head on anything. I am so close, I can smell it—the sickly sweet smell of the elderberry wine.

Russ is by me with a first aid kit. He feels Matt's forehead.

"He's burning up!" Russ declares and gets a chemical ice pack from the kit. He activates it and places it on Matt's head. I continue to hold Matt's shoulders to restrain his thrashing, but I'm not successful. The strength of his involuntary muscle spasms is intense.

After a moment, he stops thrashing and goes still.

Russ takes out an electric thermometer and runs it across Matt's forehead.

"His temp is like a hundred and four," he says, "he needs medical attention."

"The only doctor nearby that I know of is Doctor Arturus Grable," I mutter.

“I’m pretty sure he knows what’s wrong, but I don’t think he’s gonna fix it!”

“What was that riddle? Mask of the morning and all that? I mean, it’s about the sun, right?”

“Not so sure,” Russ says.

“Morning, midday, gloaming, eternal night; what else could it be?”

“That is if it is a riddle. Which, who knows, man, it might just be a poem. Maybe some sort of chant or prayer? Anyway, if it is a riddle, the obvious thing is never the answer.”

“I hate riddles,” I grumble.

"I thought you loved that shit, puzzles and locks and all that."

"Love puzzles, hate riddles."

Matt has fallen into a state of unconsciousness. His breath is shallow but regular. The trickle of liquid from his nose has abated. I feel his forehead. He is still burning up.

“What should we do?” Russ asks.

I think for a moment. There is no way we are going to make it off this mountain tonight, especially if there are people watching the paths. And there is no way we are going to get Matt off this mountain without a car.

I take out my gazing crystal and look at Matt’s aura. It looks much like it did last night–a normal aura with a haze of something gross and oily around it. But now, little tendrils of the oiliness are boring into Matt’s aura, specifically around his head.

“This is a magical ailment. I don’t think there is a medical cure. We need to find out what is affecting him and stop it,” I say.

“I mean, it's the wine dude. Duh.”

"Okay, yes, but what is that, and how do we undo it?"

"Art’s secret laboratory,” Russ says, “that’s where we look.”

"That seems like the most dangerous place we could go, but I agree that if we want to help Matt and all these people, that's the obvious place to go. It's also probably the last place they will expect us."

"I don't know about that," Russ says.

"What do you mean?"

"You are getting a bit of, you know, a public reputation, dude. He seems to know it, too; you aren't known for being a cut-and-run guy."

"That's only because I have bad luck with the direction I run in."

"Sure thing, but still, it might be exactly what he expects you to do."

"What about the portal, the vortex? I think this is related. What if we close that?"

Russ nods and thinks momentarily, "Maybe, man, maybe. But whatever we do, I don't wanna split up."

We sit in silence for a minute and think. There is obviously something about the alleged elderberry wine that is affecting the people of Stanyon's Hollow. It is magical. It seems unimaginably improbable that the vortex is not related in some way. But I see nothing magically tying the liquid to the vortex. There doesn't seem to be any mystic link. So, closing the portal might not change anything.

"We need more information," I say in a low voice. "I think the lab is the best place to get it."

"Okay, dude," Russ says back quietly. "How are we gonna do that?"

"Matt said there are guards on the path, so we can't go that way."

"And crashing our way through the woods will send us off a cliff, get us lost, and probably attract attention. I have an idea. But dude, you aren't going to like it," Russ grimaces at me.

"Oh?"

"From the topo-map, I'm pretty sure that the ravine, you know, where the bridge is? I'm pretty sure that if we head south through that ravine, it brings us around to the back of the grove the lab is in."

I look at him questioningly. "So, you want us to rappel down into a ravine in the dark and then crawl our way up to the lab? In the dark."

"'Want' is an awfully strong word. I'm just saying I think we could get there unobserved that way."

"We could also plummet to our deaths that way."

"Truth, truth. Any other ideas?" Russ says.

I go through other possibilities. All of them involve a confrontation with groups of armed men in the dark on their turf. I don't love any of our options.

"We can't Dreamwalk out for help. What about going into the vortex? Magdalena used something like that and ended up in southern France," I offer earnestly.

"Suicide, man. Maybe worse. What your friend did was pass through something built for that purpose to points linked, a kind of shortcut. This is just a giant tear in reality. It's like jumping into a black hole and hoping for the best, dude."

"Then into the ravine it is." I hate this plan. I'm almost more comfortable with the idea of jumping into the vortex into the vast unknown outside of reality. Almost.

Russ nods.

Russ rifles through his bag and produces a spool of climbing rope.

I look at him slack-jawed, "Why'd you bring that?"

"You never know, man, you never know," he says and starts

rearranging stuff in his backpack. I see Flashlights, a little food, rope, and some other essentials.

I slide Matt to a side of the yurt and put a pillow under his head. I rearrange the ice pack on his head and try to make him as comfortable as I can.

“Winnie,” Matt whispers almost inaudibly, “get my girls out.”

“Matt?” I say, but he is unresponsive. “Goddamnit.”

I rifle through his pockets and find a set of keys. There is a key to an American-made vehicle and more keys that are probably to his house.

“Do you remember what the lock on the gate was like?” I ask, noting a couple of padlock keys on his keychain.

“Hmm, there was a combination lock and two keyed locks if I recall, dude.”

“All right, this might be a key to one of those. I also have Matt’s car key, but I don’t know which car it is down there.”

Russ looks at the keys, “That’s a truck key. Chevy, not the original key, a copy.”

“How can you tell?”

“I used to be a Chevy man myself.”

“Oh,” I say.

"What, you think I drove a Volkswagen van or something?" Russ says with a snort.

"No!" after a second, I correct myself. "Well, yeah, actually, I did."

“All right, you ready?” he shoulders the backpack.

“No, but it doesn’t seem like waiting will improve things.”

We slip out the front of the yurt and zip the door shut behind us. As we start down the path, I can see the occasional glint of a distant flashlight through the trees. We wind our way downhill. About the time we get to the fork where the path to the bridge splits off, we hear voices in the darkness. I can’t tell what they are saying, muffled by trees and the night air, but I know they are not far from us.

As I step over a rock, a sudden wave of vertigo washes over me. I stumble and stagger briefly on a rock, barely catching myself on my hands and knees.

"You okay, Miles?" A familiar but unexpected voice says. There is a ragged edge of barely controlled panic in the tone. I push myself to my knees and turn to look up at Alistair standing over me, where Russ was an instant before.

"Shit, I am getting tired of this," I say as I take his hand and let him help me up.

"Tired? Miles? Tired? We are being chased through the woods by rednecks with guns and flashlights. How about 'terrified'?"

"Alistair, take a deep breath. What I am about to tell you will sound crazy, but you have to believe me."

"Miles, what could be crazier than this?"

"Well, I keep having flashes where I am with different people. I was up here with Russ till just a second ago; before that, it was Genevieve and my dead brother."

"Okay, you are right, that is crazier. Miles, please, man, I am freaking out enough; if this is some joke, it's not funny."

"It's not; come on, let's move and talk," I say as I start the path again. "Listen, can you tell me what has happened over the last day or so? I want to know if things have gone differently."

"Okay, okay," he says in a barely audible whisper. "Um, you wanted to go to where you grew up. You asked if I'd come along. I said sure. Jon was pissed, and you promised him that nothing weird would happen. You promised him, Miles! I am not going to see him again. I am not going to see the kids again. He was right, he was right."

"Alistair, I'm sorry, I really am. But what happened in the last day or so?"

"Um, we went to a really weird dinner. We saw the ruins of the house you grew up in. You wanted to go further into the woods, but I wanted to head back. We checked out some solar panels and ran into that Art guy. He gave me the creeps."

"So we didn't go to the cabin or see the vortex? The lab?" I ask.

"I don't know what you are talking about. Then, after dinner, we came up here and went to bed, and your friend Matt woke us up. Then he had an episode. My guess is an overdose of something in that wine. There were gunshots; then you led us out into the woods."

"Do you have rope in your backpack?" I ask.

"Rope? No, Miles, I don't have any fucking rope. I have granola bars and binoculars for looking at birds, Miles!" Alistair is frantic.

We turn the last corner, and I can see the bridge supports up ahead in the moonlight. As we approach, I startle when I see a ghostly figure leaning against one of the posts.

"Jesus, what are you doing here?" I ask Hank. "You scared the hell out of me."

"I have been asking myself the same question, Miles! What the hell are we doing here?" Alistair demands frantically.

"No, sorry, Alistair, not you...Hank."

"Who?"

"My..." I think about this: Alistair is a therapist who used to work at the State Mental Hospital. What's he going to think about Hank? "Never mind."

"You're going to be fine," Hank says in a calm tone.

"I don't know, I'm so scared my hands won't stop shaking," I reply.

"Miles, listen..."

“Mine too. I find it almost reassuring that you're scared, too. This is all too much. Way too much!” Alistair's voice shakes wildly with terror.

"Alistair, I'm sorry you got dragged into this. I'm really sorry. I don't understand what's happening, but I want you to know that I would never drag you into this stuff intentionally; I wouldn't even call you if I thought this was possible. I didn't call you...I called Russ. Well, sort of, the details aren't important," I try to explain.

"Miles!"

"Who is Russ?" Alistair asks incredulously. That's right, Alistair has never met Russ.

"Um, this old hippy that I know."

"Miles, you are not helping my state of calm!” Alistair stabs a finger at me violently

"Miles! Can you hear me?"

"Why am I responsible for your state of calm? You are not the one rocketing around between realities and seeing ghosts!" I rant. Alistair's frenetic energy is contagious.

"Oh, for fucks sake! This is getting so old. Miles Ward poops his drawers! Nah, nah, nah nah, coffee tastes like dirt water!" Hank begins howling and jumping around in circles with his hands in the air, wagging his tongue like some sort of cartoon character. I didn't know he had a tongue.

"Hank! Can you shut up? I am trying to have a conversation here!" I yell, turning to yell at Hank. I turn back and see Alistair blinking at me, slightly ashen-faced. "Sorry about that."

"No, no, it's great, it's perfect. I'm going to die on a mountain because I trusted someone who my dependable, wise, insightful husband said was unstable. I'd say this is the worst night of my life, but it will likely be the last night of my life..." Alistair continues rambling to himself, but I can't follow what he says because Hank shoves his silicon face right in mine.

"You can hear me," he says very loudly and slowly, like an American tourist trying to get directions from someone who only speaks Mandarin.

"Unfortunately," I mutter back. Alistair is still having a nervous breakdown in the background.

"You need to step back and to your left."

"Whatever, if you'll stop harassing me, fine," I step back and to my left.

"Left a little more. Yeah, right there. Now, wait for it..."

In the distance, I hear the loud report of a firearm echoing up the mountain; as it fades into the night, I feel that swimming sense of vertigo, like I am about to fall and vomit again. The world swims and then comes back into focus.

"Oh? Sweet, dude, can he help us out in any way?" Russ is asking me, but I have no context for what he's asking. He's standing by the bridge, holding a rope and fastening it to one of the bridge's supports.

"Russ!" I say, overjoyed. "You're back!"

"Um, never left, dude."

"Told you."

"How?"

"There are these–I don't know, it is hard to explain–these squishy places that grow and float around. When you step into one, everything changes. Took me a bit to figure it out. I just had you step back out of it."

"Interesting," I say out loud. "Let me know if you see or feel another of these squishy places."

"I'll try," Hank looks annoyed.

"Let me know when you are done talking to your ghost. No rush. It's not like an armed cult is hunting us or anything," Russ quips.

"Okay, fine. I am back. I was just in a dream, timeline, universe, fuck, I don't know, whatever, where I was with Alistair, and he was not cut out for this. Hank found a way to guide me out of it."

"Um, cool?"

"I'm curious. What has happened over the last few minutes?" I ask. I want to know what happens when I am 'away'.

"Um, well, we walked up here, and I explained this knot." Russ holds up the rope in his hands. "And then you said yer dude Hank was here, and I said sweet. I think that's it. So can he?"

"Can he what?"

"Can he help out in any way?"

"Can I help out in any way?" Hank asks, in sync with Russ. *"Jinx, you owe me one of those cookies."*

"Well, can you?" I ask.

"Yes, but you have to listen, I have something important to tell you."

"Okay, Hank, what is it?"

There is a long pause, and then Hank slaps his face with the palm of his hand.

"Ugh! Never mind! That is so annoying. Um, I can tell you that there are four people up by the vortex, all with guns. There are another six on the trail behind you, but they are just sitting there waiting."

I relay that to Russ.

"Can we trust the apparition in your head?"

I shrug, "I don't know."

"Hurtful, man."

"Okay, do you want to rappel down first or second?" Russ asks.

"Is that a trick question?"

"Have you ever done this before?"

"Nope," I say.

“Okay, then you go first, and I can belay you, then I will come down second. I’ve done this a couple of times. Well, not exactly this. I’ve rappelled before, but I’ve never slid down a rope into a ravine in the pitch black before.”

“That is reassuring.”

“Yup, y’all are going to die.”

“Not helping, Hank!”

"The location is ironic. But don't worry, once you hit the ground, it's not so bad."

That was dark. Russ ties one end of the rope in an intricate web around my pelvis. He has to loop it between my legs, and he's moving fast.

"Woah, not on the first date, buddy," I say as he brushes me.

"Grow up, dude."

"*Yeah, grow up, dude. Then you might actually get dates.*"

The middle of the rope is looped around the wooden post, and the far end is tied off to it.

“So, the loop around the post will add friction to slow you down. I’ll hold this end and lower you. When you get to the bottom, I will tie this end around me, and you will tension the rope and lower me from the bottom.”

He holds up sections of the rope and pantomimes what he means. It’s hard to make out in the faint light of a gibbous moon, but I get the overall idea. When he demonstrates, it doesn’t seem nearly as crazy as I originally thought.

“Okay, let’s do this,” I say.

He pulls the slack on the rope so there is light tension on my end, and I start to lower myself off the edge. No sooner than I clear the precipice do I rethink everything I just concluded. This is totally insane. I am feeling woozy with panic. Part of me wants to scramble back over the top, clutch onto Russ's leg, and beg him not to make me go. But I have to do this; this is our best way out.

Inch by inch, I start to climb down the side of the ravine.

"Nope, don't put your foot there. It looks loose."

As I climb, Hank directs me where to place my hands and feet. At first, I find it annoying, but as I get used to it, it turns out to be helpful. I don't know how long it takes me to get to the bottom, but it's not a short climb.

"Okay," I call as loudly as I dare back up the cliff, "I made it."

I'm standing on a large flat rock at the bottom of the gorge. A trickle of water, too thin to be called a creek, flows around the rock.

"I think you are standing on the exact spot that my body shattered on," Hank says dourly.

I feel a sudden wave of panic and anxiety, "Really not helping, Hank."

I pull all the slack down to my side and almost immediately feel Russ' weight on the line. I hold on and lean back to support him.

"You can lower me faster," he whispers down.

I release the slack at a quicker rate, and before long, I can see his silhouette on the cliff wall. Where I crawled down, gripping and scrabbling like a desperate wildebeest that inexplicably found itself at the top of a tree, Russ confidently bounds down backward. In a moment, he's untying the rope from his waist.

"Groovy."

CHAPTER 19

Russ quickly pulls one end of the rope to slide the whole thing down from the post it was wrapped over up top, leaving no sign we were there. He has it coiled up in his backpack in less time than it took me to extricate myself from my makeshift harness. He then pulls out two flashlights and hands one to me. He flicks his on, and I see it has a red bulb or maybe a red film over the end. The light should carry less in the darkness. I flick mine on and discover that it, too, casts a red light.

"Smart thinking," I say.

"He is really prepared," Hank says admiringly. *"I honestly didn't think the stoner had it in him."*

"Me neither."

"Hmm?" Russ looks over his shoulder.

"Nothing, Hank's just being...Hank."

"Whatever that means, dude," Russ turns and starts southward through the ravine.

It's slow going, even with flashlights. There are large rocks and boulders that we have to climb. There are pools of water to be leaped over or skirted around. We quickly fall into a silent progression up the ravine. After maybe two hours of crawling up the gorge, the walls have shortened, and the climb up appears more manageable. Russ climbs out to check. He moves slowly, and once, some rocks slide beneath his feet and crash into the water below. We sit in the darkness, holding our breath for ten minutes, waiting for a sign someone heard us. Eventually, he finishes scaling the wall. It is thankfully much lower here than it was at the bridge, and while falling would still be catastrophic, it would not be fatal. At the top, he pops his head up over the edge for a moment before climbing slowly back down to me.

“We’re at the edge of the field with the solar panels. We are probably two hundred yards straight to the grove, but it’s probably another quarter mile following the ravine. I’m guessing another half hour to forty-five minutes in the ravine gets us there or just a few minutes across the field. But the field would leave us in easy sight of anyone watching.”

"You are pretty spry for a guy your age," I muse.

"Namaste, man, fifty minutes of yoga every morning," Russ makes a little bow that I can barely see in the muted red light.

I am exhausted, and the idea of spending another half hour or more climbing over rocks does not appeal to me. On the other hand, getting sniped while walking across a field doesn’t sound all that pleasant, either.

“I guess we take the ravine,” I groan.

I feel a little woozy and put my hand to my head. I've felt this feeling before; every time, I suddenly have a different companion. Russ puts a hand on my shoulder.

“Are you okay, dude?”

“Yeah,” I say, “fine. You're still Russ?”

“Yeah, man. Still me. Do you need a minute to rest?”

"I had that feeling I get whenever that thing happens. But it doesn't seem like anything has changed this time."

"Maybe you are just tired," Russ says, a hint of concern in his voice.

“Yeah, it could just be that,” I wonder."You haven't felt anything weird at all? Nothing has been off for you?" I ask. It seems so strange that reality could be shifting, and I am the only one who notices it. "Unless..."

"Unless, what?" Russ murmurs in the darkness.

"Well, my Hizarin neighbor, Magdalena, does this thing where she can, like, I don't know, bend time. Only she says she looks into all the possible futures, learns from the outcomes, and essentially picks the one she wants. Kind of. No one else seems to notice when she does, but I can. Do you think it's related?"

"I mean, it seems reasonable. Like I said, I think you are feeling it because of your connection to Hank, making you, like, a conduit for energy flowing into the universe through that hole. Or any hole. You are like ground zero for this shit. So if she is poking a hole into all these other probabilities, and you are nearby, it's going to, you know, like flow over you on its way to her. Stretching the metaphorical rubber band, but not enough to launch you, so you, like, you feel the tension," Russ explains.

"I am not certain I follow, but okay."

"Probably not theory time, man; we should move."

“Okay, let’s keep our eyes open, though.”

“Always a solid plan, man," Russ says with his signature slow, drawn-out syllables.

He starts up the creek bed. I fall in line behind him.

After another forty minutes, we come to a second branch of the creek. The pine trees become thick on the bank, and we are cast in deep, dark shadows. If not for our flashlights, we wouldn’t be able to progress forward at all.

"I think this should be a good spot to get out of this creekbed and reassess," Russ whispers.

He starts to climb up. It isn't much of a climb anymore—maybe eight feet of rocky soil to the ground level above. I start to follow Russ up, but I have another wave of vertigo and fall, sliding back down to the bottom of the creek bed with a moan.

"Ugh," I grunt and roll over onto my back. Suddenly, a warm weight is on top of me, a body pressing down. I start to panic and thrash. Before I can let out a scream, a hand is held down over my mouth, and I recognize the perfume. I recognize the silhouette. "Can I kiss you?" Genevieve asks.

"Is this the best time?" I reply. "Or place?"

A week ago, this would not have bothered me. I don't understand what is happening, but kissing my ex in an alternate universe where we apparently didn't break up feels wrong.

She leans in and gives me a long and intimate kiss.

"Ooh la la."

Behind her back, I flip Hank off.

"That was a no," I say. "I'm sorry, but this just doesn't feel right."

"In case this goes very badly," her tone sounds hurt. "I want to say 'I love you.'"

I suddenly feel very uncomfortable, and I'm sure she can feel my whole body go stiff beneath her.

"Oh, shit, man! No, she didn't!"

I feel flush in my face. Hell, I feel flush all over.

"I...Um...That is... This is awkward, but oh, shit, how do I say this? I don't know you. I am from another universe, and we broke up. I don't know what is going on, but..." I stammer out almost incoherently.

"Fuck off, Miles," she says and pushes herself off of me. She charges up the hill ahead of me.

"You are a real smooth operator, bro."

"Shut up," I say as I climb out of the creek bed.

Genevieve is moving low and slow through the grove of trees around the laboratory building. I follow at her pace. I use my fingers over the flashlight to cover all but a sliver of red light to guide me from stepping onto large branches or other noisy obstacles. Her flashlight doesn't have the red film, but mine still does. Hmm, another piece of data.

As I am stepping over a branch, there is a distant report of gunfire, and a wave of vertigo flashes over me. I trip and fall to one knee. Genevieve turns to look at me, but it isn't Genevieve. There is a more masculine-looking silhouette, but I can't make out who it is in the darkness. I don't have time to react before there is another report and another wave of vertigo, and I can see the leering face of John Hale standing above me. I wonder why I can see his features in the darkness, but then I realize the entire forest is ablaze.

"What's keeping you, slow-poke? Let's move it," Hale holds his hand out to help me up. I stare at the proffered hand blankly. "Problem?"

Hale is glowering down at me. Then his head turns as I hear another gunshot, closer now, and another wave of vertigo tears over me. This rapid succession of changes is taking a toll, and my stomach churns.

"I think I am going to throw up," I mewl. I don't quite finish before I am hunched over, retching.

"Woah, dude, you didn't drink that thermos of tea in my bag, did you?" Russ asks me.

"It's good to be back," I say. "I am going to stay down here for a second in case it happens again."

"What happens again?"

"I did the switch thing a bunch of times in a row, every time there was a gunshot."

"Dude, I didn't hear any gunshots," Russ hisses at me.

"Great," I say, pushing myself to my feet. "Well, it seems to have stopped for now. Let's move, shall we?"

The laboratory building is dark, and the grove is eerily silent. The only sounds I can hear are the occasional crunch from Russ' steps and my own breathing echoing loudly in my head.

Russ moves quickly across the open space to the rear wall of the barn. I follow suit, and we both press our backs against the outside of the building. Russ skirts to a window and peers in. It is pitch-black inside; no signs of light or movement.

"Can you watch the front while I try to find a way in?" Russ whispers.

"Sure," I say.

"Try the skylight."

"Hank says, 'try the skylight,'" I repeat, confused by this turn of events.

"Yeah, I'll keep that in mind," he whispers skeptically.

"Okay, I'll hoot like an owl if I see anything," I say, giving a little "whoo whoo" as a demonstration.

"Whatever floats your boat."

"You could try something more subtle, like blowing an air horn."

Maybe if I ignore him, he'll go away, I think to myself.

"Fat chance of that, buddy."

Right, he hears my inner monologue.

"Dialogue."

"You're more like a heckler than a participant," I whisper aloud.

"You have to stop that, you're freaking me out," Russ whispers back.

I grunt. "Keeping watch now." I skulk toward the front of the building.

In the dark, behind a tree in the front of the building, I crouch. I turn my flashlight off, and my eyes strain against the darkness. At first, I think my eyes are playing tricks on me as I see little motes of light appear and vanish in my vision. After a moment, I think it might be fireflies in the field.

"Not fireflies."

"Flashlights," I mutter. Somewhere on the far side of the field, people are searching around with flashlights. My guess is they went to the yurt and discovered we were gone. I wonder what happened to Matt. I hope he's okay. Whatever is going on, he seems like he's not a bad guy.

I go back to the building and look for Russ, but I can't find him anywhere. I crouch down by the rear of the building and scratch my head. "Where the heck did he go?" I mutter to myself.

My question is answered: about ten feet away from me, the back door to the building swings open, and Russ comes out. "Doors aren't locked, man."

"Well, that seems short-sighted," I mutter.

"Or they know something we don't."

"Seems likely. I can see flashlights out there in the darkness. I think they are searching for us. They are still far away, but I don't think we have infinite time."

I can see his face briefly lit up by the backlighting of his watch.

"We only have about three hours until sunrise," he says.

"Let's hurry."

He ducks through the door, and I follow close behind, then slowly and quietly close the door.

This large, barn-like space consists mostly of one big room. Curtains hang from a metal runner on scaffolding, creating two separate exam spaces. Two doors on the far wall lead into some unknown space beyond. Russ makes his way to the door near the rear of the building and peeks in with his flashlight. I peek into the other door.

“Supply closet, dude,” he whispers.

“Office,” I say. I scan the room with the red-lens flashlight. A large desk takes up most of the room, with a laptop and a big office chair behind it. There is a three-tiered bookshelf against one wall. The bottom two shelves are crammed with books, but the top shelf seems reserved for plaques and trophies. A filing cabinet sits in one corner, pressed against the wall by an old, worn couch. Next to the door, there is a small end table with an electric coffee maker and some mugs.

This room has no other doors and no windows. Russ joins me, and we both duck into the little office.

"You get the desk, I'll get the bookshelf," I whisper.

He walks over to the desk and immediately starts going through the drawers. I move to the bookshelf and scan the titles with my flashlight. There are several medical texts, including a complete set of the DSM. The bottom shelf is devoted to texts on the occult. I recognize several titles, including my favorite, Traditions of Magic. There are also a few other works on mythology and cryptozoology on the shelf.

Stacked on top of the other books is a very old-looking journal. It’s hard to tell what color the cover is in the red-tinged light, but it is definitely old. I take it off the shelf and sit on the couch with it in my lap. I gingerly open the pages. It is a handwritten journal. The rough-edged pages jut out, many of them loose. Additional pages have been added in by simply shoving scraps of paper between the journal pages.

It is hard to read with a red flashlight. The penmanship is excellent but very stylized. It is in English, but the dialect is archaic, and it reads like an old Civil War letter. This is probably from the eighteenth or maybe early nineteenth century.

I skim through it as fast as I can under the circumstances. It is the diary of a trapper. Each entry is written as a letter to the author's family. The author, however, never lists their own name, and the letters are all addressed to Annabelle, with no family name listed. The relationship between the author and Annabelle doesn't seem to be romantic. The tone makes me think of a grown daughter or a younger sister.

As I turn a page in the middle, a piece of paper falls out and slides under the couch. I crouch down to retrieve it, and I notice something odd about the floor as I do.

Carefully and quietly, I slide the couch to one side and shine my light on the floor beneath it. The paper that fell out of the journal sits on top of a large, hinged panel on the floor.

“A trap door,” I whisper.

“Woah, cool!” Russ whispers back, coming to my side. “That's so Young Frankenstein, man.”

"Huh?"

"Walk this way!" He says, shuffling around in a circle. "No? The bit with the spinning fireplace? No? Oh man, classic Mel Brooks, dude. You gotta check it out."

"Okay," I say. I still don't understand why he doesn't seem to be taking this more seriously. "What did you find?"

“Some papers and stuff, but not much of it is in English, dude. Hungarian, I think, but only 'cause of the Hungarian diploma above the desk,” Russ points to a framed document hanging above the desk.

I pick up the paper on the floor. It has a poem written on it:

He wore his mask of mourning
And served the coming light.
He removed his mask at midday
To take away man's sight.
He donned the mask of gloaming
To hide his mirthless spite.
Adorned his mask tenebrous

To call forth eternal night.
He has as many names
as masks upon his faces,
Visages in number equaled
By all of man's disgraces.

“Well, now I'm even more creeped out,” I hand the slip of paper to Russ.

"This wasn't about the sun, dude; it was mourning," he says, drawing out the 'u' sound in the word, "not morning. I think this is some kind of funerary prayer."

“What do you think is down there?” I motion to the trap door.

“If we are lucky, it's just storage.”

“You think that's likely?”

“Nope.”

I don't want to open the trap door. On the one hand, we might find something horrible down there, like a nightmare crypt or secret shrine to a dark and ancient god. But also, if I am being honest with myself, I will be very disappointed if it's just old file boxes or a sump to manage excess rainwater.

“What did you find in the desk?” I ask more to stall our trap door opening than anything.

“Like I said, a bunch of shit I couldn't read, man. Looks like logs. There's lots of dates and times.”

“It would be so much easier if every dark sorcerer kept an English manifesto on their desk.”

“Yeah, though, are we dealing with a dark sorcerer or a mad scientist?”

“I'm not sure I see the distinction.”

“Good point, brother, good point,” he says.

Reluctantly, I lean over and yank the trap door open. Russ seems about to say something more but is cut short as a musty, slightly sweet odor wafts up from the darkness below.

"It smells like the elderberry wine," I gag a bit.

"VOCs and BO, Bro."

Our whispers to each other are interrupted by a loud clang, followed by a moaning sound echoing up from down below.

I jump, "Jesus!"

"I don't think that is the wine he was turning water into," He shines a light down and looks in. I glance down from the other side of the opening. A ladder leads down about ten feet to a concrete floor below. He twists the flashlight around to maximize the lit space. The walls of the space below seem to match the walls of the office we are in. It might go farther back, but we cannot see underneath us into the rest of the space.

Russ crouches on one side of the opening and dips his head to peek in. As his light shines back into the space below, I hear something or someone cry out. There is more metallic clanking.

"There are cages and people in the cages," he whispers before he stands up. "You first, dude."

I get a brief glimpse of his face in the red light of the flashlight. He has a wide-eyed, wild look; he is terrified. I realize now that all his goofing around is his way of coping with his abject terror. I can't blame him. I'm about to wet my pants myself.

"If we go down there, we are stuck between a rock and a hard place. One of us should stay up here."

"It's a good point," Russ says. "Ro-sham-bo you for it?"

"Huh? What, fine," I say. Neither of us wants to go down there, but both of us feel compelled by curiosity–or maybe it is, as Russ has accused us, a hero complex. We are playing ro-sham-bo. I haven't done this in decades.

What kind of guy is Russ? Rock is hard, crushing. Scissors are devious and slicing. Paper is passive and covering. Russ is a paper guy. So if I want to win, I play scissors. Shit, am I a scissors-guy? I just learned something about myself. However, Russ is more terrified than I am. I should be the one to go in, so I should play rock. He probably thinks the same way and knows I am a scissors-guy. So he's going to play rock, but then he'd know I was going to play rock, so he'd play paper. So I should play...

"Are we going to do this or just stand here?" Russ asks with a quirked eyebrow.

"Right."

"Ro. Sham. Bo," we chant together. I have a long moment of indecision on what to play. I'm too far into my own head. I debate between all three a thousand times as my fist descends to my palm the last time, and my two fingers fire out almost by reflex into scissors. Shit! I am a scissors-guy. I hate scissors-guys!

Russ sits there holding a closed fist.

"I knew you were a scissors-guy, dude!" He exclaims a little too loudly.

I feel frustrated and disappointed, even though this was the outcome I was trying for.

"You win," I say, my frustration sounding authentic. "Slide the couch in front of the door, maybe?"

While I begin to climb down, I can hear the faint scuffing as Russ slides the couch in front of the door. It isn't going to hold anyone for very long, but it's something.

The room below is a large concrete bunker. The ceiling above is also made of concrete and covered with sound-dampening baffles. There are four large iron cages against the far wall. From the rough and drippy-looking joints, these were all hand-welded. The bars are not quite parallel, and the seams are all a little rough. The artisan who manufactured these was not a professional.

Inside three of the cages are people—emaciated, sickly

people. It might be the red light of our flashlights, but their skin has an unnatural-looking hue; it doesn't reflect the light quite how I would expect.

There is a large industrial-looking switch on the wall next to me. I lean over and throw it.

Cah-chunk!

Rows of halogen lights blaze on. The sudden light briefly blinds me, and the howls of terror from the inhabitants of three of the cages deafen me.

I look at each of them in turn. There are two men and one woman. It is hard to tell their ages; their faces look young, lacking in wrinkles and sun damage, but their eyes look sunken and dead. Their skin is pale with a slightly purplish hue. Their veins are all varicose, dark, and standing out of their skin. Each is wearing an identical light blue cloth gown–similar to a medical gown, but closed in the back and floor-length. The woman's gown is too long and drags by about an inch.

"Russ," I hiss, "can you come down here?"

The room smells overpoweringly sweet, musky, and sickly. It smells like everything unpleasant about that elderberry wine, layered with the smell of urine and feces.

Russ climbs down the ladder and comes to stand next to me. "Fartballs, man, what in the nine hells is going on down here?"

"Mad science meets dark sorcery?"

The fourth cage is empty, its door standing open. It looks unused.

There is a small cart against one wall and a refrigerator beside it. The cart holds several medical tools: scalpels, forceps, some sort of probe or prong, and a number of large syringes. Russ walks over to the fridge and opens it. There is a light inside. Over Russ's shoulder, I can see some vials of black liquid inside the refrigerator. Russ reaches in and takes one out. He looks at it, then unstops it and smells it.

"Eww," she says, "I think this is the secret ingredient in the elderberry wine. They are labeled with date, time, sample number, and specimen number. Dude, this is their blood!"

He motions to the three people in cages. None of them are acting like people. Their behavior seems more like the most far-gone Fetch I've encountered.

"The elderberry wine is made with blood?" I say in revulsion. "Glad we didn't drink it."

"I'm not sure it's blood anymore, not in the most technical sense. But I think it was harvested from them."

I take out my gazing crystal and quickly examine their auras. I can't see their human auras through the murky, oily, black-purple filth surrounding them. It's like the people in the common hall at dinner, but whatever it is has completely enveloped everything except the area around their face. In their aura, around each face, there is a halo-like disc of a sickly brassy orange, with lines of blackish purple that form a pattern. Each of the patterns is unique, and can only be described as a face, but not a human face.

I stare in horror at the auras of these three people. I've never seen anything like this; its implication is horrifying and nightmarish. I didn't think I could see something more revolting than the destroyed wreckage of an aura created by a Fetch, but I was wrong. Something is infecting and feeding on these people. That something is sentient and alive. The most terrible thing about the strange alien faces worn by these people's auras was that all three were smiling.

"Masks," I stammer, "their auras are all wearing masks. Nightmare, alien masks."

"Do you think that is what the poem or whatever was referring to?"

"Yeah, I do,"

A clanging sound from above punctuates my sentence. It's distant and muffled, but with all the soundproofing down here, that's not surprising.

"The front door!" Russ says and starts for the ladder.

"We should try to find another way out. We are cut off that way."

"There's no other way out!" Russ says, eyes wide with panic.

"We don't know who they are, how many, or what they are armed with. We should try to escape or hide."

Russ looks up the ladder, then back at me, "Okay."

He pulls himself halfway up the ladder and pulls the trap door shut.

"There's a latch," he says as he locks the trap door from the inside. I can hear them trying the office door.

I look around the room. We are in a concrete box. There are no vents, and the walls are bare. The only thing that could even move is the little refrigerator. I quickly slide it away from the wall. There is a small grate behind it!

I kneel and shine my light through the grate. It's about two feet square, and the space beyond goes about eight inches before opening into what appears to be another room.

Russ kneels next to me. He produces a multi-tool from his bag and starts taking screws out of the grate. I take my pocket knife out and do the same on the other side.

"This is going to be a tight squeeze," Russ says as we take the grate away.

"You go first, and I can help push, then I'll follow, and you can pull," I whisper back.

He shoves his backpack through. It is a tight squeeze, and he has to rock it and twist it to get it through, but it finally slides in. Then I toss my shoulder bag through. He slides his head in and maneuvers an arm through. I'm on my knees and push on his hips to help him pass. It's a struggle that gets more frantic when I hear the trap door above us rattling against its latch.

With a final grunting shove, he suddenly moves through the hole, accompanied by a chorus of tearing cloth. I don't have time to stop and think. I shove both my arms through and wriggle my head in. I can feel him grip my wrists as he yanks. I am surprised at how strong he is. Fifty minutes of yoga a morning, I might have to try that. I exhale to make myself as small as possible. With some dragging, scraping, and bruising down my sides, I get through.

I quickly swing my legs around, reach back in, and grab the grate that covered the opening. I turn it at a diagonal angle and slide it in the hole with us. I grab the base of the small refrigerator and, with some struggling, pull it back against the wall.

Beyond the refrigerator, I can hear a pounding, hacking sound.

"They are breaking through the trap door," Russ whispers.

I roll over onto my back, out of breath. By the red glow of Russ's flashlight, I see the room we are in now for the first time. It's another concrete box, but it has a large water heater. The ceiling is choked with long flowing mats of cobwebs. They are thick and obscure the rest of the room, reflecting the red light back at us. We crawl across the floor. It is dirty and smells bad. I put my hand down, and something sticks to it in small dots—rat feces.

In the other room, I can hear the trap door cave in with a crash. The crash is echoed by a moaning cry from the three caged people. Their cry is animalistic and, while vocal, gives no indication of language.

"There's a door," Russ whispers. I look to where his light is shining, and sure enough, a short flight of concrete steps leads up to a heavy door. It doesn't have a handle, but it does have a deadbolt.

We stay low and move across the fetid floor beneath the mire of cobwebs. Russ reaches the door first and throws the deadbolt open; we rush out of the room and into a small concrete stairway that leads up to the outside.

Dashing up, we find ourselves at the back of the large barn-like building. Not thirty feet away is the creek bed that brought us here. We charge through the downed branches and underbrush. It sounds deafening, and I'm certain we will be heard. My expectations are not disappointed as I hear cries from the other side of the building. As we both leap over the edge ten feet down onto a soft sandbar in the creekbed, I can hear crashing footfalls behind us.

"This is not good!" I hiss at Russ.

His flashlight is off now, and it's pitch black. Our faces are only inches apart; otherwise, I wouldn't be able to see his expression at all. He nods, raises a finger to his lips to indicate silence, and then points. I turn my head to follow where he is pointing.

The embankment has eroded, exposing the roots of a large tree on the bank above. The roots overhang the creek bed and create a dark den.

I put a hand on Russ's shoulder to avoid losing him in the darkness and follow him as he moves toward the roots. We press up into the space below the tree, which is much deeper than I expected, and we are both plunged completely into darkness.

We are much closer together than I was ever hoping to get with Russ. Both of us are rank with stale sweat and body odor. The only other sense I am aware of is the pounding of my heart and the gasping of my breath echoing inside my head. It is deafening and feels like the entire world can hear each breath.

I try to relax, slow my heart rate, and get my respiration under control. But the quieter my breathing gets, the louder my heart hammers inside my chest. I push down the urge to break free from this hiding spot and run frantically into the night.

We wait for an eternity, though it's probably only a minute before we can see light flitting back and forth between the tree's roots. Someone is down in the creek with a flashlight searching for us. Our hiding spot is deep enough into the embankment that I can't hear their footsteps or see the light directly.

I can hear muffled voices talking, but I can only make out occasional words: "somewhere," "down," "up there," and "forever." There are at least three distinct voices, but I can't tell how many total.

I can feel Russ shifting his body a little bit. He probably feels as cramped, claustrophobic, and impatient as I do. I put what I hope is a reassuring hand on his shoulder. Though I'm certainly not assured, myself.

CHAPTER 20

The flashlight is getting closer and closer. We can now clearly see a beam shining on the lowest roots in front of us. I can feel Russ's body tense next to me.

Suddenly, there is a distant report of gunfire. Not a single shot, but a long series of shots, each about two seconds apart. They are rhythmic and staccato. I tense for the waves of vertigo to come, but they don't.

"Shit!" I hear a voice much closer to us than I am comfortable with.

"This way!" another, higher voice farther away declares.

The light vanishes from view, and we hear distant yelling and shouting, but I cannot determine what is being said.

There is a cacophony of chaotic gunfire, behind which the rhythmic, staccato drone of weapon fire picks back up. The entropic symphony of battle slowly fades until three last rhythmic shots echo unchallenged through the night.

The world is silent except for Russ's breathing and my heart's jackhammer. Russ and I are pressed closely together in the dirty space beneath the roots.

I sit in silence, my ears straining to pick up any sign that our pursuers have returned. I imagine Russ is doing the same. I don't know how long we are there. Eventually, my nerves can't take it anymore. I feel like I am going to crawl out of my skin and scream into the night sky.

"I think they are gone," I whisper.

"Yeah, what the hell was that?"

"It sounded like they got into a firefight."

"With who?" Russ whispers, his breath is right in my ear.

"Maybe Matt woke up?"

"Maybe," he sounds skeptical.

"What do you think we should do now?"

"I don't know. At this point, I think our best bet is to wait until the morning and try to make our way down the creek bed to civilization."

"But they might come back and search here, so maybe we should move now," I conclude.

"Yeah, probably."

"I am going to crawl out. You stay put in case anyone is out there, and I'll let you know if it is clear," I say.

He's so close I can feel him nod even though I can't see it.

I slide backward out between the roots and try to move onto the sandbar as quietly as I can. I didn't realize until now that my legs and one of my arms had fallen asleep while cramped beneath the stump. I stagger noisily through the water.

I stop stone still and listen carefully. The night is silent—eerily silent. I can hear no insects or birds, no vague distant crunch of leaves. The whole world is frozen.

"Clear," I whisper.

Russ comes crawling his way out next to me. He tugs my arm, and we stagger downstream. The creek should lead us downhill, away from Stanyon's Hollow and eventually toward civilization.

We make our way in the blackness for a couple hundred yards before we dare to turn on our flashlights. Once we have them on, Russ climbs up out of the shallow ravine and back into the forest. I follow here we can make slightly better time.

“We were leaving some pretty big tracks in the sand and mud down there. We should be harder to track up here,” Russ whispers to me.

After an hour of following the embankment downhill, we come to a large tree with a recess on one side.

“We need rest,” Russ mutters.

“Agreed.”

We crawl down into the hollow of the tree and lay back. I sit there silently next to Russ, keeping an ear out for signs of being followed. I have no intention of falling asleep, but at some point, wakefulness fades to black.

I am awoken by a sudden wave of vertigo and a need to vomit. Thankfully, I don't really have anything to heave up. Sunlight brushes across my face like a warm and comforting feather. I shift my head slightly and realize there is a body pressed up against mine. Cuddling with Russ isn't exactly what I had planned for the weekend. The form next to me starts.

“Sorry, I fell asleep,” a feminine voice mutters, but it isn't Genevieves. My body goes rigid.

I look down at the mousy brown hair that is pressed in my face.

"Emily?" I say as I recognize my friend.

"Yeah, yeah. I am fine. Thankfully, none of those God of the Mourning cultists found us this morning," she says. "Get it?"

Do I try to explain this whole thing to Emily? So far, Russ is the only person who has believed me about the whole reality/time-switching thing. I also don't have any idea how long it will last.

"Do you believe in alternate realities?" I ask.

"Weird question for first thing in the morning, but sure. I mean, in an infinite universe, all possible things, by definition, must occur."

"Okay. This sounds nuts, I get it, but I don't remember coming here with you, I came here with Russ, but every now and again, I like, I don't know, shift realities. Suddenly, I'm here with Genevieve, then I'm here with Russ, then Alistair, then like, maybe people I don't even know, then one time I am dead, and I'm here with my brother and..."

"Slow down, slow down, Miles," she says, putting her hand very intimately on the side of my face. "It's probably just a dream."

"It's not. Wait. Are we, like, involved?"

She looks at me, a little shocked; then she gives me a friendly slap on the face. "Get over yourself, Ward."

"Oh," I say, taken aback. “I'm sorry. It's just been a weird couple of days, and I don't know what's what anymore. I misunderstood."

Emily pushes back from me and crosses her arms. She purses her lips pensively.

"Anyway," I begin, but she cuts me off with a single finger raised in my face.

"I am thinking," she says.

"Okay."

"Okay, if you are from another reality, jumping timelines, where is my Miles? In your timeline?"

"I'm not sure timeline is the right word, but we can go with it. I don't know, exactly. Maybe?"

"So, it might be that all possible Miles Wards are sort of slipping through different timelines."

"I guess so. But then that would mean, from what Russ said, I will theoretically never truly get back. But I might manage to get somewhere close to where I left. But it was just a theory," I say.

"And I might never get my Miles back," she says. "So what is causing it?"

"I don't know. It seems random. Sometimes, the shifts are hours apart. Sometimes it's seconds."

"Time magic... I have only met or heard of one chronomancer in my life," she says.

"Magdalena," we both conclude at the same time.

"Last I knew, she was trapped in Europe, though. And she's not that powerful. Is she?" I probe.

"Well, we know that there is a vortex causing a bleed in reality. Maybe messing with time near that thing could cause what you are experiencing?"

"Russ said that because of my connection with Hank, I was like ground zero for the energy coming through the vortex. And it is weird that no one seems to notice this stuff but me, just like with Magdalena's time-bending, so maybe that's it. Maybe there is another chronomancer."

"Interesting," she says and gets her familiar pouty-lip look of contemplation. "But it's not just any vortex. There was that one outside of Sedona, and nothing like this happened there. Of course, it was a tiny fraction of the size."

"I've never been to Sedona, but I did encounter a small one in Portland, and it wasn't like this."

"Then there is something special about you and this vortex, which probably makes sense; you grew up here. So we need to close it, and in order to do that..." Emily begins to say, but she is cut off as a wave of vertigo passes over me, and I am suddenly alone in the woods.

"Shit."

I scan the woods thoroughly, "Is anybody here? Russ? Genevieve? Emily? Hank?"

There is no answer. Where the hell is Hank?

The forest around me is a deep and ancient wood. The trees here are massive. If this area has been logged, it was a century ago. I see no signs of civilization anywhere. Ten yards or so away is the shallow creek bed we traversed alongside last night. Beyond it are trees in every direction, trees and leaves and underbrush.

I stop to relieve myself behind a tree. I am completely alone, so I don't know why I seek privacy. Part of me worries that, at any second, I could suddenly find myself surrounded by a live camera crew; this whole thing is getting too weird.

Once I've finished my business, I hop down to the trickle that passes for a creek. Last night, I got covered in mud, sticks, leaves, cobwebs, and even more disgusting things. I rinse myself off as best I can and then douse my hands and arms with hand sanitizer from my bag before winding my way downhill, using the creek bed as a guide. I stop once to eat a lonely, very mashed toaster pastry that I find in my bag. Russ had packed all sorts of food in his bag, but of course, I suddenly find myself alone. Is this what the Hierophant's prophecy was hinting at?

After my makeshift breakfast, I continue downhill. Hours pass, and there are still no signs of people, animals, or anything except trees, rocks, and moss. The sun is high in the sky as I climb over a large rocky outcropping.

Finally, below, I see a modest house. A large pickup truck and a smaller SUV are parked in front of it. A curl of smoke rises from a metal stovepipe coming out of the roof. The house is painted off-white and has a red-shingled roof. There is a garden in the back, and I can see a row of greenhouses down the hill.

“What do you think?” I ask no one in particular. "It's secluded, and who knows who lives inside, but it's pretty far away from Stanyon’s Hollow. It is probably a drug dealer; look at those greenhouses, but that's better than a cultist. I need a ride, so I guess I am going in.”

I climb the rocky outcropping and slide my way down the hill through fallen leaves and sticks to the flat the house is built on. I walk up to the front door. There is no doorbell, so I knock, step back from the stoop, and put my hands in my pockets. I try to put on a pitiful and non-threatening look, which shouldn’t be too hard, considering I crawled through the mud all night and slept under a tree.

In my peripheral vision, I see a figure in an upstairs window looking out between curtains. The figure's features are too obscure for me to make anything out. A few minutes later, the door opens, and a man answers.

He looks young–I’d guess in his mid-to-late twenties. His eyes are bloodshot and gummy. He’s wearing a white sleeveless undershirt and jeans. He has dark blond hair, grown out into a mullet, complemented by a fuzzy mustache. I notice his jeans are still unbuttoned, suggesting he got dressed hastily. He is arranged with one hand behind the door and one hand out on the doorframe, in a forward-leaning posture.

“You look lost,” he says.

“Yeah, I was camping and got turned around. I’ve been staggering in the woods all night until I saw the smoke from your chimney,” I say. It’s not really a lie, but it is a little deceptive. I don’t want to give any more information until I know who this guy is.

He looks past me to my right and left, “You alone?"

“Um, yeah. Sort of," I stutter. I don't like lying, but I am not sure what the truth is. "I was with someone, but we got separated."

He looks me up and down, considering for a moment. Finally, he nods and opens the door completely. He has a pistol in his hand. I start a little when I see it.

"Sorry," he says, "living up here, when a stranger comes unannounced to the door, well, you can't be too careful." He slides the pistol into a holster attached to a belt hanging on a hook next to the door.

"I understand," I say. Honestly, I do. If I had Art for a neighbor, I'd probably answer the door armed as well.

"Come on in. We'll get you cleaned up and give you a ride," he says.

There's no guarantee this guy is on the level, but if he meant me harm, I think he'd have done that by now.

"I'm Brent," the young man introduces himself.

"Michael," I lie. I feel churning discomfort in my gut as I do, but with the week I've had, I am feeling extra paranoid.

Brent leads me in but stops to put on his gun belt. He notices his pants are unbuttoned and flushes a little in the cheeks as he quickly buttons them up.

"You caught me with my pants down," he chuckles.

"Yeah, sorry about that. Like I said, I've been lost all night."

"This have anything to do with all the gunfire I heard last night? Sounded like there was a war going on at that commune up the road," he says, going to the stove and putting the heat on beneath a kettle.

"I don't know what that was about. I heard it, and it was more of an incentive for me to run away. I didn't do any shooting, if that's what you're asking. Do you have a phone? Do you get cell service?" I ask, changing the topic quickly.

"We have a phone, but the lines went down yesterday–probably a downed tree or something. Don't get cell service this far up the mountain."

I look around the house. It has a largely open floor plan,

with only a few rooms on the first floor. The place has an overwhelming smell of marijuana. This mystery is solved when I glance around a corner and see half the room is filled with cannabis flowers hanging from strings to dry.

"There's a bathroom through that door if you want to get cleaned up," he indicates, pointing to a door on the far side of the room.

"Thank you," I say.

"You want some coffee? I make it like motor oil," he chuckles.

"Yes, please."

He has a very meticulous process. He measures his water temperature, then measures the grounds, two giant scoops per cup. He puts the grounds into a little metal filter over one cup and pours the water in carefully. He lets it sit for a bit until a crust forms, then breaks it with a spoon and swirls the water and grounds around before pulling the filter away and letting all of the coffee drip in.

He hands me the first mug and then repeats the process for himself.

"I like it black," he says as he concocts the second mug, "but there's cream in the fridge and sugar in the cupboard there, if you like."

"A work of art like this? I'll take it black," I say, sipping the coffee. It's rich, dark and nutty. It's bitter, as coffee is, but there is a hint of sweetness. He must get some very gourmet beans. It's an amazing cup. A paranoid part of me says I shouldn't accept a cup of coffee from a stranger under the circumstances. But this is a kindred spirit. This is a man who loves his coffee. He brews each cup with the care and consideration of an artist. I don't know much else about this man, but I know, deep down, that if this man were going to poison someone, it wouldn't be through their coffee.

“This is very good,” I cup the mug close to my face and feel its warmth.

“Thanks. I did this trip to Costa Rica a while back, one of these things where you go work on a coffee plantation for three weeks. It was life-changing. I’ll never drink coffee from a paper cup again.”

“What do you do up here?” I ask.

He motions with his head to the drying cannabis flowers.

“It’s a rough way to make a living these days. I have a little edible brand. Got a niche market. It does me okay. Combined my favorite things: pot, coffee, and chocolate. I make the best double mocha brownie this side of the Rockies.”

“They make them better on the other side?”

He laughs, “No, probably not, but it just sounds better that way.”

I take my time finishing the coffee. Brent is the kind of guy who can sit in silence and not be uncomfortable. Once I have savored every drop, I excuse myself to shower.

As I head to the bathroom, I have a moment of worry. Depending on the kindness of strangers right now feels very vulnerable.

"Relax, Miles," I mutter to myself.

I let the water run for a minute to heat up and quickly glance through his medicine cabinet. You'd think I would have learned my lesson by now, but I tell myself this isn't being nosy; this is being prepared. One toothbrush is in the holder, but another is in a case in the cabinet, along with a bottle of ibuprofen, an albuterol inhaler, and an array of antacids and herbal hangover remedies.

The bathroom is tidy and clean but not suspiciously spotless. A light women’s bathrobe hangs inside the small towel closet. My conclusion is that Brent lives alone but has a regular girlfriend. I also think Brent likes to party a bit, which fits with his career.

I shower quickly and rinse all the mud from my hair and body. Then I look at my filthy clothes, repulsed to put them back on. There is no option, so I start to get dressed until I am startled by a knock at the door.

"I have an old flannel and some jeans I was going to get rid of anyway if you want something a little cleaner," Brent says from outside.

"Um, yes, thank you!" I say and open the door a crack. He hands me a plastic bag with some old clothes. They are well-worn and a bit baggy on me, but at least they are clean.

"You can keep 'em," Brent says as I return to the kitchen in clean clothes, with my muddy clothes stuffed into the plastic bag. "Like I said, those were in my pile to go to the thrift store anyway."

"You are a lifesaver, Brent, thanks."

He has brewed another mug of coffee, which he hands to me.

“This is a highland Peruvian. Arabica, of course. It’s grown by this woman-led co-op. It’s so good,” he says as I sip it. This one is a little more full-bodied, less bitter, and has an amazing flavor.

“Thank you, this is phenomenal.”

He nods.

“Where do y'all need a ride to?”

“Whatever the nearest town is."

He considers for a minute.

"Well, that'd be Covelo, but that won't do you much good. I was going to go to Willits tomorrow, but I can give you a ride all the way there today if that’d help.”

“I mean, that would be great. But you don’t need to go out of your way on my behalf.”

"No, like I said, I have to go anyway, and if I left you in Covelo, you'd just have to hitch your way to somewhere else anyway."

"Well, thank you, Brent. That is very kind of you," I cup the warm coffee mug between my hands and take a deep inhalation of the steam. Brent, while not necessarily the kind of person I'd hang with on my own, seems like a decent guy. We...I am in imminent danger, and it doesn't feel right to take advantage of his largess without mentioning this.

"Hey, Brent," I say, "there is something I need to tell you."

"What's up, Mike? Or do you prefer Michael?"

"Um," I stammer. Right, I said my name was Michael. "Michael, please."

"Sorry. What's up, Michael?"

"So, I was staying at Stanyon's Hollow in an AwayFrom-Home, and things got weird. Scary. I ended up running into the woods. I don't want to drag you into this without letting you know."

He gets a grim look on his face, "I reckoned. Damn Hollow folks. Not surprised. They're an off bunch, but I ain't scared of them."

"It sounds like you have some history with them."

"Shit, everybody on this mountain has some history with them. Been up there since I can remember; my dad says it used to be this hippy-peaceful commune. People went up there to smoke pot and get away from the city. But they aren't like that anymore. Now, it's some kind of cult. You hear stories, moonlit orgies and human sacrifices and all that."

"Have you ever seen anything weird up there?" I ask.

"I mean, I haven't seen any orgies or sacrifices myself. But they are a weird bunch. I couldn't tell you why exactly; you just get a sense when talking to them. They keep giving me this wine if you could call it that. Putrid stuff. Smells like death eating a cracker."

"Do you have any here?"

"Nope, I dump that crap out every time I get it," he eyes me suspiciously. "Why'd you want it?"

"To be blunt, I'd be suspicious of you if you didn't dump it. I don't think it is just wine."

He nods, "Wouldn't put it past a cult of devil worshippers to drug their wine."

"I don't think it's the devil they worship," I mutter.

"Satan's in his labors, not in his name," Brent says sagely. "That's what my grandpa always said. I think it's true."

I nod. I see what he's getting at there. Evil can be done under any banner.

"You hungry? I already ate, but I could cook you up some eggs or something before we hit the road."

On the one hand, I'm pretty hungry. All I've had today is a toaster pastry and probably too much coffee. On the other hand, I want to get the hell out of here. My stomach growls loudly in protest to my train of thought.

"Breakfast would be great," I nod. "Thank you, Brent."

"Of course. Some grub, and then we can get you to a phone. Maybe the Sheriff will finally do something about those goddamn cultists."

Brent starts cooking. He has been nothing but hospitable and hasn't said or done anything to make me suspicious of him, but that doesn't mean I am not suspicious. While his back is turned, I take my gazing crystal out and give his aura a once-over.

He has a normal human aura, a mesh of colors ebbing and flowing around him. There is no purple muck or indication that he's been controlled or magically influenced in any way.

It only takes Brent a minute to whip up some eggs, bacon,

and toast. I gratefully scarf it down while Brent tells me about himself. He was born and raised here in the mountains and went to school in Covelo. His parents moved to Florida five years ago, and he's lived here ever since. He grows pot and sells edibles. He has a girlfriend in Willits and spends a lot of time there.

After eating, I gather my things, and Brent guides me to his truck. I note he doesn't lock his door behind him, which is probably pretty common up here, but coming from a city, I cannot imagine it.

His truck is one of those huge machines with running boards that slide out when you open the doors. I have to literally climb up into the cab. I clamber into the front passenger seat and buckle up.

Brent drives his giant truck a little too fast on the winding dirt roads, at least for my comfort. A plume of dust follows in our wake as we bounce and rattle over potholes and rocks. Soon, we come to a closed gate. This isn't the big iron-and-wood barrier in front of Stanyon's Hollow; this one is more of a reminder that this is private property—a wood and steel frame holding up a sheet of corrugated metal roofing. On the outside, a hand-painted sign reads 'Private Property: No Trespassing'.

Brent hops out, opens a combination padlock, and swings the gate open. Then he drives the truck through and jumps back out to close it. He returns to the truck and tears off down the dirt road before his door swings shut. He is so fluid and quick doing this that it is like he's tying his shoes. A hundred feet past the gate, his little dirt drive joins the slightly larger gravel road. Occasionally, I see more 'no-trespassing' signs tacked to trees.

Suddenly, Brent slams on the brakes, and we slide to a halt on the gravel road.

"Shit, fucking shit bags," Brent says.

The road curves sharp to our right from here, but he points across the hill. I can see the road curve back out from behind the hillside and a stand of trees. It's probably a hundred yards as the crow flies, but it could be a quarter mile or more by road. There is a parked truck barring the road and a half-dozen men with rifles and shotguns standing beside it.

"What are we going to do?" I ask.

"You get in the back and stay down. I'll deal with them," Brent says.

He pulls the pistol off his belt and arms it, then slides it into a door pocket with his left hand. He then reaches into the glove box in front of me and takes out a hat and another pistol. The hat is a green trucker's cap with a mesh back. He pulls it onto his head. It has the Knights of Saint George logo on it. He arms the other pistol and puts it on the console between us.

"Knights of Saint George?" I ask as I climb into the back seat.

"Heard of us?" He asks.

"Yeah, I've met a few members," I say vaguely.

"Chapter two-fourteen," he says matter-of-factly.

"You ever deal with any actual monsters?"

He looks over his shoulder grimly at me.

"There was something out there once," Brent looks up the mountainside briefly. "I don't know that we did more than chase it away. But once you seen something like that, well, the world ain't the place it was when we were kids, you know?"

"It's the same place; it's just that there are fewer shadows to hide in," I murmur.

"Mmm," he grunts. "Anyhow, keep your head down, and I'll talk us out of here."

"If you are going to talk, why do you need the guns?" I ask.

"In case they aren't in a talking mood."

Brent roars down the gravel road, slides around a corner,

and approaches the blockade like he isn't going to stop. At the last second, he slams on the brakes, spraying dust and rock in a cloud onto the men standing in front of the truck. I hunker down farther behind the seat before the dust clears. My view of what is happening is completely obscured.

I can hear the motor of Brent's window as he rolls it down.

"Get the fuck out of my way," Brent hollers.

"We are looking for a city guy who came up here and stole from us."

"Well, I'm not some city dude, and I didn't steal from you, so get the fuck out of my way."

"We are going to search your truck, Mr. Corden."

"The fuck you are, you ain't no cops. Now get outta my way, or I'll get you outta my way!" Brent says, getting angry. I am not sure if his tact is the one that I would take, but I am not really in a position to back-seat coach him.

"Don't step up on me, bro!" Brent declares.

Brent moves suddenly and begins firing out the window rapidly. He fires off several rounds and then throws the door open. There is a pause as he grabs the pistol out of the door, followed by a deafening din as he unloads it.

I am surprised to hear no reports of return fire from the half-dozen armed men. I stay huddled behind the seat in silence for a moment.

"Jesus fucking christ," Brent declares.

I sit up and gaze through the front window of Brent's truck. The men are all lying on the ground. Their truck, parked perpendicular across the road, is spattered with a purplish-black liquid. Pools of the liquid congeal on the ground around the bodies.

Brent says, "I'm gonna move their truck. Could you help me get 'em out of the road?"

"Remind me not to mess with you, Brent. Was shooting them all necessary?" I ask.

"They were going to let us through. There's a moment where you decide if you will be a victim. My daddy didn't raise no victim."

I open the back door of the truck and slide carefully to the ground. After a rough landing on the dusty road, I start walking toward the men's bodies on the ground. Brent steps over one to climb into their truck when suddenly a hand grabs his leg.

"Shit!" Brent exclaims.

Somewhere, someone shrieks like a terrified child. It definitely isn't me, though.

Brent staggers back, kicking as all six men begin to push themselves to their feet. Their clothes are doused in the purple, black liquid. The sickly sweet smell of the elderberry wine becomes overpowering on the breeze.

My terror is punctuated by Brent firing three more rounds into one of them. The man staggers backward into their truck and then lurches forward. Brent drops one pistol, yanks the other from where it is tucked in his belt, and fires another shot. Their truck window explodes into a rain of safety glass. The men, now visibly quite dead but still moving, seem quite unperturbed by the bullets. I am using the term 'men' loosely because zombies seem more appropriate now. Two of them converge on Brent and drag him to the ground, screaming. I leap into the passenger side door of Brent's truck and begin struggling to get to the driver's seat.

Unlike zombies in most horror movies, these men aren't staggering and moaning. They move quickly and are organized. Brent is pinned to the ground and struggling. I am stuck with a choice. I can try to drive away and get help, or I can stay and try to free him. I don't like my odds on the latter, but I can't just leave him. I don't know what to do. I quickly lock the doors and look through the cab for something to help. There is a box of ammunition in the glove box, but both of Brent's pistols are with him, not that they helped him much–and he was an excellent shot. I take my pocket knife out and look at it. That's not going to help.

I look forward, thinking about ramming the truck in front of me, but they have Brent pinned against it. I'll run him over if I drive this truck forward. I could try to drive away in reverse, but on this narrow road, I know I will just go over the cliff.

Shit.

I'm not letting Brent die for trying to help me. I take my knife and put a small cut on my arm so that I can use the blood to activate my warding runes. I climb out of the truck with my hands up. Hopefully, we will have more opportunities to escape.

I am quickly and silently thrown to the ground. My face is pressed into the gravel as a rope is bound around my hands, elbows, knees, and legs.

"Someone's spent some time at a BDSM club," I mutter. They seem unshaken by my quip.

"I'm gonna kill you fuckers!" Brent chimes in. "Let us go!"

Soon, I find myself face down in the bed of a truck. I can feel Brent on one side of me. A boot clunks down in the truck bed right next to my face. The sickly smell of the elderberry wine is strong in my nose. I can see a thin trickle of that familiar, purple-black liquid dripping down the boot.

"Well, this is a fine mess you've gotten yourself into," Hank whispers.

"Nice of you to show up. Can you help me get out of here?"

"Shit, if I could, we'd be out right now," Brent replies.

"I'm afraid I don't have hands, feet, or a face. Well, I do, but

they are not here, they are in Napa. Even then, it's just a big lump of silicone."

"What the hell did you want–a robot body?"

"Huh?" Brent grunts.

"Ignore me. I'm just talking to my imaginary friend."

"Be quiet, little piggies," a gruff voice says above us. There is a bit of a gurgle in the voice like he's half choking on a throatful of mucus.

"A robot body would be cool, but that won't help you right now."

"Well, if I get out of here alive, I'll get you a robot body, then maybe you'll be useful in a situation like this."

"Good luck," Hank says wistfully.

"I said shut up," the gruff and gurgling voice says above me. This is followed by a boot to my head, which leaves me reeling and seeing stars. Another boot follows, and it seems like a really good idea to go to sleep.

CHAPTER 21

Blackness. Warmth. I feel like voices are beckoning me to come home, relax, and let go of my burden. They close around me, trying to tell me something important, but I can't quite make out what. Whatever they are telling me, it's comforting, and I'm happy.

Wait, what burden? I'm not burdened. Well, there is this crushing feeling of weight in my chest. There is this cold roughness on my face. Cold all around me. My head hurts. My body hurts everywhere. No, no, I am feeling burdened.

My eyes flutter open. I am laying face down on a cold, slightly damp concrete floor. It is pitch black, and I cannot see anything. I hear breathing, multiple people breathing in the darkness.

"Um, hello?" I mutter quietly.

I hear some unintelligible moans from my right.

"Miles, dude, you're awake," Russ whispers.

"Yeah," I say.

I try to move, and I realize that my hands and feet are

numb and tingly. There are ropes tied tightly around my limbs, cutting off circulation. I can't move or rollover.

"We are in the shit," Brent's voice mumbles. His voice has a little lisp like he's talking through frog lips.

"Where are we?"

"The basement below the barn? With the cages?" Russ's voice sounds hoarse and dry.

I imagine the small concrete box and the three caged people with weird masks on their auras.

"How long was I out?" I mutter.

"A while. They dosed us all, dude," Russ says.

"I been trying to slip these ropes, but it isn't working," Brent chimes in.

"I've tried everything I can think of," Russ says.

"I can't even feel my fingers, let alone use them," I groan. "I think we should wait for an opportunity."

We sit for what seems like days in the darkness. Periodically, one of us gets the energy and urge to escape our bonds, but it's a pointless struggle. The blood flow to my extremities is so impeded that I can barely move anything but my head.

Eventually, the trap door opens with a clang. When I was last here, they busted it in. But then it occurs to me that I am probably in a different reality now since Russ is back. There is motion as people come and silently lift Brent and take him away. He screams, curses, and threatens as he's taken up the ladder out of the room.

A few minutes later, they come for me. I go limp and silent in the hope that maybe they will say or do something to give me an advantage if they think I am unconscious. It doesn't seem to work. They work wordlessly to drag me bodily up the ladder. I am manhandled and slammed into the walls; my long-term health and safety are clearly not of concern. My already battered body has even more scrapes and bruises by the time I am hefted onto the concrete floor of the office above. Soon, I find myself outside, with a pole shoved between my bound hands and feet. I reflect on the Hanged Man card that the Hierophant left me. I'm living the picture out almost exactly. Creepy.

Four robed figures lift the pole, two on either end and begin carrying me out of the grove and across the field. I imagine my wrists and ankles would hurt if they weren't too numb to feel anything but intense pressure. I'm sure they are bruised and cut at this point. I look around, upside down and sideways. I can see a group carrying another figure on a pole ahead. That must be Brent.

I sway and bump as I am carried. My face is dragged through branches and grasses and over rocks. It takes a while craning my neck before I see another group bearing a burden behind us. That must be Russ.

These silent sentinels carry us for a long time, but I know our path. It winds up the hill, turning away from the yurt and toward the suspension bridge over the ravine.

Are they going to dump us off the suspension bridge?

"No, you know what they are going to do."

"The vortex," I whisper.

"Righty-oh bro-migo,"

"The mask of the mourning, the mask at midday, the mask of the evening, and the mask of night. They've got three in the basement. They will summon the fourth mask."

"You're the expert here."

"Why do they need three of us? Wouldn't they need just one to be the host?"

"Again, you're the expert here."

"They need a sacrifice to invoke the summoning. One to host...whatever they are summoning."

"And?"

"And they need the ballast to go into the vortex so that something can come out," I whisper. I know I can have this conversation with Hank entirely in my head, but for some reason, I find it more comforting to vocalize. It feels more like a real conversation.

"So, I have a plan," Hank's voice sounds hesitant.

I can see the suspension bridge up ahead. Panic begins to swell in my chest. I start thrashing against my bonds.

"Miles, you have to calm down and listen to me."

"What?" I hiss.

"I can't do anything here, but if you go through the looking glass, I can help you."

The group carrying Brent begins to chant as they cross the bridge.

"The looking glass? You mean the vortex?"

"Yeah, you need to not be the host or the sacrifice. You need to be the ballast."

"Why?"

"This is where you do your work. That's where I do my work. I can protect you there. I can help you."

My pallbearers begin their way across the suspension bridge. They begin to chant as they place their first foot on the bridge. Their chant is an eerie and almost inhuman-sounding dirge. It isn't in English; I am not sure it is in any language, at least not spoken in this reality. I sway wildly from side to side with the bridge itself.

We are halfway across the bridge when I hear the group behind us begin chanting. The three groups chanting is very loud and distracting.

"And then what?" I whisper.

But either Hank doesn't respond, or I can't hear him over the creaking bridge and chanting cultists.

The procession continues up the path through the forest. I'm all but dragged up a short ridge and then down into the large bowl-shaped valley. As we crest the far side, I know we are closing in on the small cabin. The panic has gone. I'm calm, and my mind is clear.

In my mind, I can feel the vortex–like a whirlpool–trying to suck me in. It is cold, uncaring, and hungry. I feel malice surrounding me. I am carried up the stairs into the cabin and unceremoniously dropped onto the floor. I cannot see the vortex, but I can feel its ominous presence. A dozen or so pairs of legs are silhouetted in the cabin, and many people are crowded on the stairs. I hear Russ drop onto the floor next to me.

I crane my head over to see him. I can barely make him out in the gloom, but he nods at me and whispers, "It's been good riding with you, amigo; see you on the other side."

If I had said that, it would have been filled with snark and sarcasm, but somehow, Russ comes off as sincere. I whisper, "We aren't to the end of the trail yet, Sundance."

"I woulda pegged you as Sundance, man."

"Okay, whatever," I'm annoyed with the nuance. "You're Butch, is that better?"

I crane my head in the other direction to see Brent, but he seems to be asleep. I suspect they drugged him to silence his constant cursing.

The cultists around us continue to chant, building to a crescendo. Just when it seems like they will all go hoarse from screaming their invocation, they stop suddenly.

The silence is jarring. Then, it is broken by footfalls on the steps to the cabin.

“Miles Ward, Russell Russo, you return,” Art’s now familiar voice says from behind me.

“Despite our best efforts,” I quip.

“Yes, yes, I should not have been so surprised by your resourcefulness. But I was.”

“So, this is a marry, fuck, kill situation, right? Or should I say, host, banish, sacrifice?”

“Very insightful. Yes, Mr. Ward, that is correct. One of you will wear the mask of night, allowing our lord to return to this world, so that we may bask in his glory. One of you must take his place in pandemonium, and sadly, one of you must wear the mask of mourning and be sacrificed to pave his way home in blood,” Art says. He doesn’t sound at all sad about that last part.

"Is this the part where I ask you questions about your evil scheme?" I ask.

"Evil is a matter of perspective, and in order to advance, sacrifices must be made; sometimes figurative, sometimes literal."

"Why us? Why now?" I demand.

"Oh, forgive me. This is not our first attempt; sadly, it will probably not be our last. This ceremony is, well, something of a work in progress."

“The people in the basement, those were your previous hosts?" I ask.

"Yes, and while they weren't successes, they did prove...useful," he says.

"Their blood, you used it to make the wine which lets you, what, mind control people that drink it?"

"They are touched by the Lord in the Mourning, and their blood is his blood. Those that drink it have become one with him."

I see. So he's trying to summon this Lord in the Mourning character, but it hasn't worked completely. The hosts have a little bit of...well, whatever it is, in them, but it has yet to escape the Dreamtime. The open vortex allows the connection between the hosts and whatever parasitic spirit Art is trying to summon to maintain. Art spreads the Lord's influence through wine made from the victims' blood. Gross.

"So, do you have a plan for which of us gets sacrificed? Or is this up for negotiation?"

"I did have a plan, Miles, but I am curious what you are negotiating for?"

"Well," I say, "I was hoping you'd just sacrifice me and get it over with. I don't want to be the host, and I don't really want to go into...whatever that is. Just kill me and get it over with."

I jerk my head toward the vortex. This is a ploy. Hank says I should go into the vortex. I think I have Art figured out a little, and reverse psychology is going to be the easy thing.

"I am afraid you, Mr. Ward, don't get out of this that easily. You are not worthy of our Lord in the Mourning. All those sigils on your body make you an unacceptable host. I wish you to suffer the most, as you are the greatest thorn I've had thrust in my side. So, an eternity in Pandemonium, well, that is the greatest suffering there can be."

That sounded personal.

"Why, what did I do this time?" I ask.

"Lorelei Redbrook was a friend of mine."

"Do all egomaniacal lunatics know each other? Do you go on theme cruises together or something?" I force a chuckle. "Come on, you can tell me. Is there a secret handshake?"

I get kicked in the stomach for my troubles.

"The time is upon us! Brothers! Sisters! Let the ceremony begin!" Art calls out. The figures that have been standing silent and motionless around us begin chanting. I struggle to twist my head as two of them, still chanting, drag Russ to the center of the room. Four pairs of hands lift me bodily from the floor and carry me over the black disk of the vortex.

I continue to crane my head around.

Art stands at the small summoning circle beside the vortex, and Brent lies motionless. Art pulls a large knife from its sheath and begins chanting.

“He wore his mask of mourning.
And served the coming light.
He removed his mask at midday.
To take away man’s sight.
He donned the mask of gloaming.
To hide his mirthless spite.
He wore his mask tenebrous.
To call forth eternal night.
He has as many names.
As masks upon his faces.
Visages in number equaled.
By man’s many disgraces.”

"You know," I quip, "This is a lot less ceremony than I was hoping for."

Art lowers his knife to Brent’s throat. "Behold the mask of mourning!"

“No! Stop!” I scream. For some reason, I’m surprised. He threatened murder so casually that it seemed like a joke or a bluff. I didn’t expect him to kill Brent immediately. Hell I didn’t expect him to kill Brent at all; I was going to stall, make a plan, save Brent, save everybody. That’s what I do. Right?

Time seems to slow as Art's knife gets closer and closer to Brent’s throat. I keep screaming and struggling as four robed figures lift me into the air. I know there is nothing I can do, but I try anyway. The inevitability of that moment is clear to me, and I can’t watch. I close my eyes while I continue to thrash and scream. Somewhere in the distant recesses of my brain, like a television show playing in a next-door apartment, I can hear Russ screaming, too.

"Behold! The mask at midday!"

I am falling. Then cold. And hot. Pain, pleasure, roughness, softness, prickling, itching, bright, dark, loud, quiet, all the other sensations ever experienced by man, and some perhaps unimagined, wash over my body as I plunge into the deep, dark pool of the vortex.

CHAPTER 22

Vertigo, existential, eternal, endless vertigo. My senses stretch out to the ends of the universe, and there is only one thing I know: I do not fit into it. I can feel the tidbits, thoughts, and perspectives that makeup Miles Ward beginning to drift apart, disseminating into the chaotic void of forever, and part of me wants to scream and fight this dissolution. Another part of me is relieved. I can let go of the burden of being me and just become everything. Between those two desires drifts my reality, a sense of wrongness and loss that defies definition—a swirling loss of intention.

Life is a brief, ephemeral blip. It seems so important in its instant, but from the perspective of eternity, it is just a spark–an ember that flares in the night and fades into a cloud of other embers. There are countless other embers and fires, each one a star in the night sky that, too, flares and fades unnoticed. What does it mean? Nothing. If it means nothing, then what is the point?

If there is no point, if nothing has meaning, then any instant, any life, any story is as important as any other. If nothing has meaning, then everything has meaning. The point of life is life. We have this brief moment to experience joy, happiness, pain, and sorrow together. I will not put down my burden so easily. No, there is still more life to live. Others are depending on me so that they can live their lives.

"I will not go quietly into oblivion!" I try to scream. But I have no voice. I am not sure if I have a body. I am not entirely sure what 'me' is at the moment, but not going quietly is a start.

Miles, I am Miles, and I have to save my friend Russ from being possessed by The Lord In the Mourning. Okay, let's start there. Russ taught me how to deal with this current problem. What was it Russ said? Build context? Contextualize? What is the first thing I can think of? It's hard. It's round. It's shiny. It's cold. It's a table. Why a table? I don't know, it's a table.

I'm sitting at a table.

A round table, small and metal.

It's one of those obnoxious folding cafe tables they put on the street in front of restaurants to make them seem more European or something. All they really do is make me trip and spill my coffee when I am walking and looking at my phone. I focus on the table, make it real, and give it details. I've seen this table somewhere before.

Bits of gum are on the sidewalk below me. They've turned gray with dirt, looking like asphalt zits. One is stuck to my shoe. My shoe is canvas, high-topped, and unlaced. My jeans are maybe a little dirtier than I am proud of. These are good details; these feel real and like me.

The chair I am sitting in is a folding metal chair. It is aluminum-colored and matches the table.

This is good. Context.

It's sunny and warm. I like the sun. The light bathes the back of my neck like a warm blanket or a lover's caress.

There is a wine glass in front of me. There is a small gerbil or hamster in the wine glass.

That's weird. I didn't put that there. Did I? I don't much care for wine or rodents. I don't want it to be a wine glass. I like that dark, hot, brown liquid. It tastes kind of like smoke and dirt but a little sweet. There is some old legend about it making goats dance. Coffee, that's it, coffee.

I close my eyes and try to imagine that I have a cup of coffee instead of a gerbil in a wine glass. I imagine the smell and taste of the coffee in my mouth. The feel of hot, smooth ceramic in my hand. I open my eyes, nothing has changed. I guess I am stuck with a gerbil in a wine glass. What is my unconscious trying to tell me?

I can hear traffic in the background. An old, wood-paneled Studebaker rolls by, drawn by two large Clydesdale horses. That is also strange.

I look across the table at my companion. He is talking, but I can't understand what he's saying. His jeans and T-shirt are muddy. I think he's a handsome-looking guy for someone made out of rubber. He squints his glass eyes at me.

"Miles, do you hear me?" My companion says.

"Huh?" I look up and down the street. I notice a light pole overhead, but instead of a bulb, the fixture holds a pineapple.

"Something is wrong here," I say as two human-sized ragdolls walk by hand in hand.

"Yeah, man. You are doing an okay job of pulling it together, but you have to do it a lot faster. It is coming."

"What is coming?" I have a sense of urgency, but I cannot remember why.

"Focus, Miles. I know this is hard. You were thrown into a vortex, and now you are...here."

"Right, where is 'here' exactly?"

"Heaven, Hell, the Dreamtime, the Outside–I don't know,

bro. Pick your poison, pick your metaphor," Hank seems impatient.

Right, Hank. I remember Hank.

"You're Hank."

"Glad you're catching up, buddy. Through the vortex. Summoning ritual, they will make your friend the host of something."

"Russ!" I am starting to piece things together. "Right, sorry, I got lost."

"The fact that you've got anything speaks volumes, but you'll need more. It's right on us."

"What's is?" I ask.

Hank points over my shoulder, "That."

I have a sudden panicked feeling right in the pit of my stomach. Stomach isn't the right word; it is more existential than that. It's a blend of every sight, sound, feeling, smell–and myriad other sensations–all mixed together into an overwhelming experience. Dread. The most literal existential dread.

I slowly turn.

There behind me, blotting out the skyline, are long purple-black tendrils that ebb and flow and wind around each other in a shapeless, formless mass. Each tendril extends and contracts, grows, and retracts in a maddening lack of pattern. At the end of every hideous, loathsome tendril is a yellow, disc-shaped mask, each a contorted parody of a grinning human rictus. Each is its own horrifying nightmare, the sight of which would destroy my mind, but I'm pretty sure that already happened. That's what the gerbil in my wine glass keeps whispering, anyway.

"What the hell is that?" I ask aloud, not expecting an answer. I don't know what I'm looking at, but I know I saw it in the auras of those three people in the cages below Art's laboratory.

"I don't know what you call it. A 'lost god' could be one way of putting it," Hank says.

"What does that mean?"

"It was something from your reality that got banished out here, and it wants back in."

"Jesus Christ," I say.

"I'm no expert, but I don't think so."

The mass of black tendrils writhes down the city streets toward us. Everything it touches turns to ash and floats away, leaving nothing but the cacophonous tapestry of the universe behind it.

"It's coming right for us!" I exclaim.

"Yeah, and I don't think it will stop until it gets you; it has to touch you to trade places with you," Hank puts his hands on the table and grimaces.

I think for a second.

"What if you traded places with me? Could you go out?"

"Yeah," Hank says, "maybe. But then I'd be leaving you here with it. And the only body I have out there is an inanimate chunk of silicone that wouldn't do me much good."

"Let's skip that plan. Do you have something?"

"Yeah, but it might not work." Hank stands up and weaves his fingers together like he's cracking his knuckles, but there is only the faint squeak of rubber on rubber.

Hank lowers his hands down to his sides and then raises them suddenly and dramatically.

Huge slabs of black stone rise from the ground and unfold around the lost god, like slats in a Jacobs ladder, encasing it in a giant black box. Then, another forms around it, and two more above it. I've seen this before; this happened when Circe got trapped—the Donjon.

“That was you?” I ask incredulously as I watch the black tower rise into the sky. As it finishes forming, the bottommost block with the lost god in it settles into the ground with a rumbling thud.

“Yeah, I built this for you, Miles,” Hank says, motioning up at the tower.

“What? Why? I don’t understand.”

“All the things you didn’t want, all the things that hurt you, I made a place to lock them away forever.”

“What are you?” I ask, suddenly terrified of this creature I think of as Hank.

Hank shrugs, “Do you really want to know?”

"Um, yeah. I think so, anyway."

"I've been trying to tell you for a long time, but you never listen."

"Huh? I've asked you a thousand times. You always have some snarky quip."

"No," he says, "I tell you, and you don't hear me. You filter me out like, I don't know. Then I get frustrated and make a snarky quip, and suddenly, you hear me."

"No, I don't," I say, but deep down, I know he's right.

"I don't think it is your fault, though," Hank says with a solemn nod. "Now that I think about it, it's my fault."

"What do you mean?"

"Well, early on, I locked a lot of the bad stuff away for you so you wouldn't have to be hurt by it. I think all the stuff you won't hear. Can’t hear. It requires that you heard the bad stuff first. You never got to process or feel it, so you weren't prepared for what came later," he says softly.

"I don't understand. What do you mean, ‘locked away?’"

"Memories, emotions, all that hurt and pain. In those early days, there was a lot. I locked it all away. I have some bad news, too."

"What's the bad news, Hank? What did you do?"

"It's all in there," he says, pointing at the enormous black tower above us.

"Why is that bad news?"

"I don't think it's strong enough. That lost god is smashing and thrashing, and I don't know how long the tower will last. When it breaks, everything trapped away, every bad thought, memory, or spell I ever protected you from will come flooding out when it breaks free."

“Can’t you fight it?”

“I’m a lover, not a fighter,” Hank says.

I think for a moment. I have an idea.

“Follow me. I think I know where we can get a fighter,” I tell Hank, and I start running toward the black tower. I glance back, and Hank is following along behind me. I notice over his shoulder that the gerbil in the glass takes the opportunity to climb out and slink away into a storm drain.

We tear into the black tower, and I bound up the stairs two at a time until I reach a door with ‘Circe’ scrawled on it in childish, crayon-like markings.

“William Baros!” I shout as I pound on the door.

There is a long silence. I wonder for a second if Circe is dead, but then I hear her voice croak from the other side. She doesn't sound well.

“Getting warmer, Miles, but not quite there. It was Redbrook’s little slip, wasn’t it?”

Oh, right. Russ said that William Baros was into some collective consciousness thing.

"You are the collective consciousness of Baros and his followers. You became one...what, like, hive mind?" I blurt out as fast as the theory comes to my mind.

"Almost there. Don't worry, you'll join us soon, and then it will all be clear. What’s your question, Miles?”

“I figured out how to free you. If I do, can you kill a god?”

“You're cute, but you’re not a god," Circe growls.

"No, I mean there is a, I don't know, a lost god? A dead god? Something here is trying to get back into reality. It benefits us both if we stop it.

There is a long silence. I wonder if Circe has decided to ignore me completely.

"Fine, but once I'm done, you owe me. You owe me *big*."

Below us, the stones of the Donjon pulse and writhe as if great pressure is building beneath them. From those writhing stones, I feel something–not in my body, but a clawing at my soul, an emotion that sears into me like a branding iron deep into the flesh. Hatred and deep, existential loathing. The force locked inside those stones will crush me like a bug and then pour its way into reality. I don't know what happens then, but it is not good.

I'd rather take my chances with Circe.

“Deal,” I say. “Hank, let her out.”

“You sure about this, bro?” Hank asks.

“You have a better idea?”

“Okay, but I want to hear the incantation first,” he crosses his arms on his chest.

“What incantation?”

“You know, the North Wind, the South Wind, all that?”

“What are you talking about?” I am so confused.

“Circe said it when she demanded that you release her? North Wind? South Wind? You don’t remember?” Hank asks incredulously.

“Now that you mention it, it sounds familiar,” I groan.

“What is the matter with you two? Just let me out!” Circe screams from within her cage.

“You two?” I ask. “You can hear him too?”

“Everyone can hear his braying! Now, do you want me to

do this, or do you want to debate about Miles' crappy memory?"

"And," Hank adds, "promise not to murder Miles for trapping you; he had nothing to do with it, it was all me. He came to free you the moment he found out–I want that on the record."

"Pfft, fine. I promise not to murder Miles," Circe puts a pointedly strong emphasis on 'murder.' It doesn't give me the warm-and-fuzzies.

Hank shrugs his rubber shoulders and sneers petulantly, "Okay, but I want to hear some good beseeching first. I liked the sound of that. I don't get beseeched enough, you know."

"Seriously, Hank?" I exclaim, "You are the worst. Fine. By the cold powers of the north wind, I beseech you, oh mighty Hank, who knows and sees all, release Circe. By the warmth of the south wind, hot like the gas I pass when I walk by your effigy at night, I beseech you, mighty Hank, release Circe."

"Hey now," Hank interrupts.

"And by the east and west winds, and the smoggy south by south-west winds and tradewinds or whatever those RVs are called, by the windbag that you are, Hank, I beseech you, can we please just get on with it?"

"You suck," Hank claps his hands together with the dull slap of rubber on rubber. For a mannequin, he can really be a drama llama.

The door swings open.

I can see Circe's silhouette in the deep, recessed shadows of the cell she is trapped in. I'm pretty sure she is stark naked, but it's too dark to see much. As she steps forward, armor forms around her, and a giant sword forms on her back. By the time she's out the door of her cell, she looks like a female warrior you'd find air-brushed on the side of a seventies van. It's probably my imagination, but I swear I can hear a heavy-metal guitar solo echoing faintly in her wake.

A yellow-masked tendril bursts from between the stones below us as if on cue. With a fluid motion, Circe draws her sword and cleaves it in half. Viscous purple-black rain splatters on us, filling the tower with that familiar, sickly-sweet smell.

"Buckle up., the seams are bursting. It's all coming out now," Hank says resignedly.

"All of it? All of what?" I ask.

"Like I said, all the unwanted emotions, memories, and magic I've ever trapped for you. Everything."

"Magic?" I exclaim. "What the heck does that mean?"

"Oh, don't sweat it; it doesn't have any form or function or anything," Hank says dismissively. "All long forgotten. It won't do anything. Hopefully. Maybe. Well, it will certainly do something, just probably not to you."

"What does 'probably' mean?"

"It might turn into a giant uncontrolled vortex of power, ripping everything apart."

I am about to ask another question, but I am interrupted when the immense black tower explodes in a ball of viscous darkness, with little motes of light scattering down the street like shattered glass. Hank and I are flung from where we stand, plummeting through nothingness. Looking up at Hank above me and the shattering tower behind him, I am reminded of the Tower card that the Hierophant sent me. The Hierophant's prophecy is a magical way of giving me the middle finger. It never made sense until the moment had passed, and then it was suddenly clear. One big, existential "I told you so."

Circe leaps between the falling pieces of debris, growing wings as she goes, and then swoops down to catch Hank and me. Her grip is firm and warm, and she smells spicy and sweet–not the sick, cloying sweet of the elderberry wine, but an enticing smell that conjures up primal thoughts.

"Down, boy," Hank snaps at me as Circe drops us onto a large, flat section of earth below the tower.

“The Masked,” Circe spits at the amorphous thing above us, “pitiful.”

"You know this thing?" I ask.

Circe responds, but I can’t pay attention as emotions suddenly overcome me. Sadness, anger, regret, humiliation, and a flood of thoughts and memories come pouring into me from the shattered tower. None of them are good.

I clearly remember my parents fighting. Oh god, how they fought. They didn't agree on anything. My mom wanted to leave Stanyon's Hollow, but my dad didn't. My dad thought my mom was having an affair, but my mom said she wasn't—the screaming night after night.

I remember playing with my brother on the bridge. I remember the terror of almost falling off, the elation of him pulling me back up, and the confusion, horror, despair, and guilt of discovering that he had plunged to his death on the other side.

I remember the day we found my mother at the cabin in the woods. The blood. The magic circle. The strange floating black disc, then tiny compared to the inky pit of despair it has become. My mother's sacrifice to try to bring her lost child back. I remember crying for days. My father packed our things in the middle of the night, and we left the only home I had ever known.

"She summoned me back, but I didn't have a body," Hank’s voice is soft.

"So you were bound to the closest thing to it–your twin."

"You."

"Oh. Shit."

"For a long time, I couldn't talk; I just watched. Everything you built in there, I built out here. It started small, with scratches on the ground, but I added on and added on. Every time you made a new ward, I replicated it. I used it to help you. Then you made me a body, and I could connect with you—a bit. And you started sending me things to trap, so I did: magic and emotions you didn't want to deal with," Hank explains.

"But as long as we are connected, that vortex can't close."

"Yes. And it grows, tearing a little bigger every time something passes through it. Which, lately–with these Lord in the Mourning guys–is a lot. I tried to tell you, but you didn't want to hear it. You block me out. It's like you started putting stuff you didn't want into that tower yourself."

"Yeah, I remember now," I say. And I do–every one of the thousand warnings Hank has tried to give me over the years that I ignored. If they were too hard to hear–if they required me to acknowledge that he was the ghost of my dead brother or that my mother had killed herself to try to save him–I blocked them out. He also tried telling me that Genevieve had betrayed me, that she had revealed everything about me to someone after we broke up, and I took no notice.

"I hate to break up your reverie, but I don't think we have time to dig into this right now." Hank shakes me by the shoulder.

"Yeah, I," I don't know what to say. It's a lot. I'm overwhelmed.

"You're overwhelmed because you never had to do this before. But you will have to shove that aside, push it down Miles. We need to move."

I shudder and turn back to watch Circe and the Lord in the Mourning, which Circe called the Masked, fight. I am impressed. Circe seems to be holding her own, splitting, morphing. Each time one version of her gets smashed beneath a giant tendril, three more split off and attack. While there is an inexhaustible supply of Circe, there is also an inexhaustible supply of tendrils. They seem to be in a stalemate.

A swirling mass of energy is building where the Donjon, the great black tower, stood crumbling. If heat existed here, it would be white hot. I feel certain that if I touch that torrent of energy, I will be undone–the motes of whatever composes me spread evenly across existence. The ball of energy grows and begins to envelop the Lord in the Mourning, burning through its tendrils.

“That’s a lot of magical energy,” I say, slack-jawed and stunned.

“Yeah, a lot of people have tried really hard to kill you with magic,” Hank nods with certainty. “It’s the price for being so obnoxious.”

“I’m not obnoxious. I'm persistent.”

"I've heard it both ways," Hank says with a shrug.

“If you locked up all my bad memories and fears, how come I still have bad memories and fears?” I ask. It's been bugging me since he first mentioned it.

“Oh, well, I stopped doing it once you were an adult. I just wanted to protect you from the most hurtful stuff: your brother dying, your mother dying. Some stuff slipped through the cracks. Then you started shoving stuff in there on your own. I had to keep building it bigger and bigger to accommodate all of your baggage.”

“You said my ‘brother dying’ like that was someone else. Aren't you my brother?”

Hank shrugs, “I think I am, but who knows? Maybe I am. Maybe I am your memories of him, trapped here forever. Maybe I am a spirit that our mother summoned and forced into a Hank-like shape."

"You don't know what you are?" I ask.

“Do you know what you are?”

“I...I guess we all have an idea, but no, none of us knows for sure.”

“You have got to get out of here,” Hank points to the ball of impending doom. "All that energy is going to tear everything apart."

I look over, and Circe has changed tactics. She is driving the Lord in the Mourning back into the torrent of energy, which grows as it consumes the lost god’s tendrils.

"It's getting bigger."

"Like wildfire. Oh, yeah, that fire demon is in there too. That can't be helping," Hank whistles appreciatively at the growing plasmic ball.

"So we have to get out of the vortex."

"You have to get out of the vortex. I belong here. I don't have a body out there."

"But if you stay in here, the connection between us keeps the vortex open."

"So we sever the connection."

"Or you come through the vortex. You do have a body."

"You want me to live for eternity inside an inanimate silicone body in your apartment? Sounds like hell."

I pause for a moment. This is hard. "As much shit as you give me, Hank, I don't think I can do this without you."

"You came in without anything going out. You can leave still; things are still unbalanced. The Lord in the Mourning hasn't left yet."

"How is that balance? We've been here forever."

"That's not how time works," Hank says.

"Ugh, I don't want to think about how time works. Okay, so I can go back out, but something would have to come in for you to leave?"

"That's right," he says.

"And if our connection is severed, the vortex closes?" I ask.

Hank shrugs, "Your guess is as good as mine."

“Okay, how do I get through the vortex? It’s way up there," I say, pointing up where the vortex spirals high above us, like an inky black sun. "How do I get there? I can’t fly.”

“Time and space are things you impose on the universe. You just have to be there.”

“That is infuriatingly fortune-cookie of you,” I scold.

Hank motions over at the battle. Circe is flagging. Fewer Circes are fighting each second. Two Circe copies inscribe a huge circle in light around The Lord in the Mourning, trying to hold it down while the rapidly growing column of wild, magical energy consumes it.

“Go, Miles!” Circe yells.

“What about you?” I ask.

“I’ll just open a vortex out of here when you’re gone!”

That's right, she can do that somehow. It violates every rule of the universe as I understand it, but she seems able to step in and out of the Dreamtime at will. I close my eyes, focus on the vortex, and on the feeling I had when I came through. I play the experience in reverse; I imagine Russ lying bound on the floor. I click my heels together. “There’s no place like home, there’s no place like home.”

“You’re an idiot,” Hank whispers.

Suddenly, I feel a rush as if I am falling sideways. I am violently ejected from the vortex and tumble across the floor, knocking the wind out of me.

I look up, blinking and half-dazed. Art is standing above me, looking down at me incredulously. I am lying on the ground under him, his legs straddling mine. His hands are raised above his head, splayed in a complicated ritual hand sign.

“What the...?” He starts to say.

I swing my foot up hard into his groin. He lurches forward with a squeak. I put my foot into Art's stomach, grab his flailing arms, rock back, and let go, vaulting him over my head into the vortex.

"Come on, Hank, there's your ballast," I mutter, pushing myself to my knees. I look around the small one-roomed cabin. Half a dozen men in robes are staring at me, shocked. Brent's body is on the floor in a pool of blood. Russ is bound and gagged on the plywood bed to my right. The robed figures lurch toward me. Out of the frying pan, into the...well, not the fire, but maybe the microwave.

My derailed thought process is interrupted by a wave of vertigo, nausea, and deja vu. I feel like I have been here, sick and dizzy, staring at all these cowled figures in the darkness a thousand times before—a million.

The first robed cultist seems to explode in front of me, a rain of that viscous black-purple splattering across the wall. I glance over and see that it is now Genevieve who is bound and gagged on the bed.

Then, that sense of deja vu and another cultist explodes before me. It is Alistair bound and gagged on the bed. Then another and another, and it is Emily. The sense of deja vu and vertigo makes me feel weak in my knees and like I am going to vomit. Now, some famous actor is bound on the bed. You know, that guy in that movie that I can't think of the title of in a moment like this. It doesn't matter. I'm struck by wave upon wave of deja vu. The world spins around me. I only get glimpses as a burst of rapid-fire cycles through many versions of reality, many bound faces on the bed, in an instant, and I fall to the ground, overcome by vertigo, deja vu, and nausea. This is getting too fucking weird. There is only one person I know of that makes me feel like this.

Magdalena.

I curl up on the floor and hope this sensation will pass. I feel a strange tension in my arms and legs. A growing pressure, like I have fishhooks in my skin, pulling in different directions. Just when the pressure feels too great, there is a snapping sensation, as if the fishing lines all broke at once. The vertigo and deja vu subside, though the ruckus of gunfire does not.

I push myself to my hands and knees and scuttle over to the bed and find Russ is back, tied and gagged. I kneel and begin loosening his ropes and pulling the gag away.

"Duuude!" He exclaims. The world is chaos, with exploding cultists everywhere and violent reports of gunfire outside. Some of the cultists are producing guns from under their robes and discharging them out the door and windows of the cabin. The reports are deafening as they echo between the bare wooden walls. The floor is slick with the horrifying purple-black ooze they call blood or maybe elderberry wine.

Russ and I huddle in a corner and cover our faces until the eruption of violence ceases.

I look up. A dozen bodies crowd the floor of the cabin, including poor Brent's. The smell of death and that sweet chemical odor permeates the room. I glance over toward the vortex. It is gone. So either Hank found a way to sever our connection, or he came out when Art went in. Hopefully, the latter.

I glance nervously at Russ, as it's possible the Masked, Lord in the Mourning, or whatever, possessed him before the vortex closed. I pat my pockets, looking for my gazing crystal, but I don't seem to have it. I make a mental note to check on that later.

Russ and I stagger outside. We flinch at the loud snap of a lone report of a firearm. There is a litter of bodies on the ground. Seven or eight of Art's minions lay in heaps, oozing purple-black ichor from numerous holes torn through their bodies. The purple-black ooze is spattered across trees, slicks the cabin's porch, and coats the leaves.

Magdalena is standing ten yards away in a pink tracksuit spattered with stinking slime, hair held up in two springy, curly pigtails. She has the enormous pistol I am used to seeing her carry in one hand and a submachine gun in the other. She also has two smaller sidearms strapped to her waist.

"Hey, brah," Magdalena says as she shoots one of the prone figures in the head without looking. "Thought you could use some help."

Ten yards behind her is Allen, holding a rifle. He is wearing camo BDUs and his Knights of Saint George truckers cap.

"The Cavalry has arrived!" Allen hoots. "Whoo-eee! They just kept getting back up. I was gettin' nervous there for a minute."

I look around at the charnel mess around us and try not to wretch.

"These friends of yours?" Russ asks suspiciously.

"Russ, this is Magdalena and Allen. This is Russ," I say by way of a short introduction.

"Oh," says Russ flatly, eyes narrowed skeptically.

"I know who he is," Magdalena says with a coy smile, returning her attention to the bodies.

CHAPTER 23

MAGDALENA SNAPS a pair of latex gloves on and begins carefully arranging the robed corpses.

“What are you doing?”

“Suicide pact,” she says. She takes a folded piece of paper and tucks it carefully into the pockets of each. “Cultists and their manifestos, am I right?”

I am horrified by the implications of the fact that she has prepared a cult manifesto.

“Why are you here?” Russ asks as she walks up beside me.

“Just continuing to fulfill a contract,” Magdalena carefully tucks another piece of paper into the pocket of a corpse.

“This was a contract?” I ask, looking around at all of the bodies. I don’t believe that. It’s too coincidental.

“What?" Magdalena says, confused. Then she sees me staring at the bodies and says in a tone dripping with scorn, "No, of course not!"

“What was your contract?” Russ' eyes narrow suspiciously.

“You know what? No stipulation in the contract says I can’t

tell you. It'll be easier if I tell you. My contract is to keep Miles Ward alive."

"Well, that raises a lot of questions," Russ says, quirking an eyebrow in surprise.

"Does it?" Magdalena asks innocently.

"Like, who hired you?" Russ asks.

"Oh, there is a stipulation in the contract that I can't tell you that."

"It was John Hale," I say on a hunch.

Magdalena shrugs suggestively and doesn't refute what I've said. I take it as passive confirmation.

"Why would he hire the Hizarin to keep you alive? Doesn't he hate you?" Russ asks.

"I think he does, but I know something that he wants to know. Plus, he's said a few times that he finds me useful, as a distraction if nothing else."

"How did you find us?" Russ looks tired, old, and worn.

Magdalena rolls her eyes and sneers, "You old people are dumb. There was a GPS tracker in the car. Duh."

I dramatically slap my forehead with my hand. I should have been suspicious about that. It wasn't the cultists that got the guns out of the trunk; it was Magdalena.

"I needed a way to follow you. Giving you a trackable car seemed like a good plan. So here we are."

"Here we are," says Russ, pointedly surveying the litter of dead bodies.

"But how did you get here?" I rub my temples and close my eyes.

"We drove in Allen's truck and then hiked in, duh."

"No, I mean, you were in France. How did you get to California?"

"Oh," Magdalena scoffs. "That's easy."

"No," Allen shakes his head vehemently. "Easy isn't a word I'd use for international travel."

"I called in some favors," Magdalena shrugs and continues bustling around, carefully arranging bodies.

"We got smuggled back in a Syzmek delivery plane, and she bribed the customs people to look the other way," Allen's head shakes as if he doesn't believe the story himself.

"He's making it sound so dramatic!" Magdalena shakes her head.

"' Here is my green card,' she said while she handed them this big-ol stack of cash," Allen throws his hands up in the air.

Magdalena shrugs, "I tried like ten thousand different lines. That one worked best."

Magdalena continues her grim endeavor. I look around and shake my head at the carnage.

“We need to call the police. This has got to be reported,” I rub my bleary eyes. My hands hurt. My arms hurt. My whole body hurts like I’ve been kicked, beaten, dragged over rocks and through briars.

“Yeah, that sounds like a good idea. 'Hello, police, I was walking in the woods, and I found a cult, sacrifice, suicide pact, you know, coincidentally.' I'm sure no questions will be asked,” Magdalena retorts.

“Can we not stand around here? It’s...really creepy,” Russ scratches his arms and rubs his scalp anxiously.

“Yeah,” I say and start walking back to the path. Russ follows close behind me. Magdalena begins to make a physical effort to cover our tracks and lags behind us.

When we get to the path, I go down the back route to Matt’s house. If I can help it, I never want to cross that bridge again. Allen falls far back on the path and watches our rear. Magdalena slides a few yards ahead of Russ and me as we stumble down the rough dirt path and make our way down the mountainside. Soon, I recognize that we're getting close to Matt's house, and something occurred to me.

"We should get those people out of the basement," I sigh. It feels like the right thing to do, but I don't want to do it. Secretly, I am hoping that someone will talk me out of it.

"Do you think closing the vortex undid whatever was done to them?" Russ asks.

"Does it matter?"

"No, I guess not. Either way, if we leave them locked in that basement, they will all starve to death long before anyone finds them," Russ concludes.

We arrive at Matt's house. I turn toward the house.

"What are you doing?"

"We should check on Matt, Pamela, and Winnie, right?"

"I guess," Russ says skeptically, "What if they are still under the influence of...whatever that is."

"Circe called it the Masked."

"Circe?" Magdalena perks up. "You talked to Circe."

"Yeah, I left her fighting the lost god, Lord in the Mourning, Masked, whatever it was."

"Good, I have some questions for her," Magdalena says.

"How did you free her?" Russ asks.

"I don't know; I guess Hank had her trapped, so I asked, and he let her go."

"You're ghost-bro had her trapped..." Russ looks at me through narrowed eyes.

"Yes. No. I don't know. I will explain what I know later," I walk up the front stoop to Matt's house and knock on the door. There is a long, quiet moment. We hear a single indistinct sound, like a door closing. I notice a curtain move in an upstairs window.

A moment later, the front door opens a crack. I can see Pamela's eyes peek out.

"Yes?" She says timidly.

"Hi Pamela, we came to check on you, Winnie, and Matt," I say as calmly as I can.

"Who are you?" She asks. There is no glimmer of recognition in her eyes.

"I'm Miles? This is Russ? We had dinner with you a couple of nights ago?"

"I'm sorry, I don't remember you. Please leave."

I turn and look at Russ and shrug. I turn to look at Magdalena, but she's vanished.

"All right," I say, and we turn to walk down the stairs.

We are halfway across the clearing to the path when Pamela calls out to us.

"Wait," she says.

We stop and turn.

"Can you help? Matt is really sick, and I don't know what's wrong."

"Yes," I say.

"Can we come inside?" Russ asks.

Pamela pauses for a moment to consider and then nods. We walk back over to the house and up the stairs. Pamela leads us inside. I can see Winnie peeking out from a door upstairs, but she closes it when she sees me looking. We follow Pamela up the wooden staircase and across the loft to the second door, which she opens and lets us in. It is a small room with a queen-sized bed covered by a hand-made quilt. Matt is lying on top of the quilt, wrapped in blankets. He is sweating and shaking terribly.

"He staggered in last night, drenched in sweat. His skin was purple. He crawled up here, muttering incoherently, and collapsed on the bed. I've tried to get him to drink water and keep him warm, but he just sits there shaking," Pamela explains.

I grimace and look around the room. Crystal prisms are hanging in the window. In the daylight, they would spread little rainbows around the room. One is cut very similarly to my gazing crystal. It may work. I take it down from its fishing line hanger.

"What are you doing?" Pamela asks, looking confused.

"Trust me," is all I can think to say.

I gaze through the crystal at Matt. It takes some moving and adjusting before I can get it to unfocus my vision enough to work. Purple-black tendrils cling to him, still digging into his aura. The tendrils look like moss straining to cling to a rock in an intense gale-force wind. I turn and scan Pamela's aura. It doesn't look healthy; it looks pale and diminished, but there are no signs of the tendrils.

"There is a little bit of the Masked clinging to him," I say.

"What do we do?" Russ asks.

"I learned a banishing ritual from Magdalena. I think I remember it."

"Where is Magdalena?"

I shrug.

"Who is Magdalena?" Pamela asks.

"A friend of ours, she was with us, but I guess she isn't much of a talker. I am going to try a kind of exorcism if that's okay with you?"

Pamela nods weakly, "Whatever gets my husband back."

I look down at my side to where my courier bag normally hangs. But I realize it was taken from me when I was knocked out earlier today. Was that today? I have no idea how long it has been now. I look around the room.

"Do you have any chalk? Some salt would also be good and..." I try to remember the ritual. "And a cup of coffee?"

"The ritual requires coffee?" Russ asks.

“No, I require coffee. I can do the ritual with just some chalk and salt.”

Pamela bustles off downstairs.

"And blood," I mutter, looking at my scraped and beaten arms.

“Do you think this will work?” Russ inquires.

“It won’t hurt.”

He nods. His eyes look half-lidded and bloodshot. He looks as tired as I am, which is absolutely exhausted.

Pamela returns with a canister of salt and a box of children’s chalk.

“Help me move him into the middle of the floor,” I say.

Russ, Pamela, and I all take part of the blanket under him and gently transfer Matt to the floor. I wrap the blanket around him to take as little space as possible. Then, I pour salt into a circle around him. I carefully inscribe the runes for the banishing spell inside the circle of salt. This part I remember very well; the part I am hesitant about is the chant.

“I hate this part,” I say, cutting a small wound on the outside of my arm. I carefully smear blood into the runes.

“I hope I get this next part right,” I begin what I remember of the chant.

I chant for a minute but don’t feel anything happening.

“You’re doing it wrong; you have some of the syllables reversed, and you’re missing an entire phrase,” Magdalena’s voice corrects me from the bedroom door.

She joins me and begins chanting; once she goes through the chant one full time, I remember it, and I start chanting in chorus with her. I motion for Russ and Pamela to do the same.

I guide them by pointing so that we are each standing at one of the cardinal points around the circle, chanting.

It takes only about five minutes, and then the chant

concludes. I step back, feeling far more drained than I should be.

"That's doing it," Magdalena says, gazing down at Matt. "Whatever was on him is getting sucked back to where it came from."

"I wonder why it clung to him and not everyone else," I say.

Magdalena shrugs, "At least it is coming off him. It had completely consumed the others. The only cure for them was a lead vaccination, if you know what I mean."

Pamela takes a step back, eyes wide in horror.

"You need to work on your bedside manner," Russ says.

"That's what she said," Magdalena says humorously, turning and walking toward the stairs.

"That doesn't even make any sense!" Russ calls after her.

I take my improvised gazing crystal and check Matt's aura. I don't distrust Magdalena's diagnosis, but I verify it.

Matt's aura now has that slightly faded or washed-out feel that Pamela's does, but the purple-black tendrils are gone. I suspect that without the Masked feeding on them, they will recover in time. I sneak a peek at Russ's aura while I have the crystal up. He looks like the same old Russ. I sigh a sigh of relief.

"He should be fine after a while," I say.

"Thank you," Pamela says. She looks like she's on the verge of a breakdown.

"We need to go get help. Some bad, bad stuff happened up here last night."

Pamela nods, but tears are streaming down her face.

"Pamela, I know this is tough, but you need to be strong, okay? You gotta stay here and watch Winnie and Matt while we get help. Can you do that?" Russ asks in a calm and sympathetic voice.

"Yes, yes, I can do that," Pamela says weakly.

"Okay, we will be back soon, with help."

Pamela nods.

Russ and I let ourselves out. Allen is standing sentinel on the front deck. Magdalena is crouched at the edge of the clearing, head cocked to one side. She reminds me of an over-eager hunting dog. Once we are clear of the house and out of earshot, Russ stops.

"Dude, there's other people up here, families, people who weren't up at the cabin, we should check on them too," Russ says.

"What are you thinking?"

"I'm wondering if one of us shouldn't go looking."

"Is splitting up a good idea?" I ask. I'm pretty sure it is a terrible idea.

"We stay in pairs. Allen can go with me. You go down to the cages with Magdalena. It will be fine. Art's dead. The vortex is sealed. What could go wrong?"

Allen gives us a silent thumbs up without breaking his vigilant scanning of the tree line.

I groan. "Oh man, why'd you have to ask that?"

"Dude," he sounds exasperated.

"Okay, fine, I'll get those people and figure out how to get help. You see if you can find others. Be careful. Magdalena?" I say, turning back to where Magdalena was crouched, but she is nowhere to be seen. "Dammit."

I get to the trail and start walking. There is no sign of Magdalena. Where did she vanish to?

My internal question is answered as she pushes herself out from behind a tree and falls in line with me. I jump at her sudden appearance.

"You scared the hell out of me!" I say.

"Could be worse, I could have scared the hell back into you. Or you back into hell?"

"Touche."

"Where to next, boss?" Magdalena asks.

"We need to go save some people from a basement," I say. "Follow me."

"Lead on, boss."

"Please don't call me that."

"*Lo tienes, jefe,*" Magdalena says, grinning.

I groan and roll my eyes.

We make our way down the path to the community center. The entire walk is without a sign of another living soul. We walk by the community center, whose front doors stand wide open. The little row of buildings suddenly reminds me of an Old West ghost town. The trudge out to the secret laboratory takes far longer than I want it to. The front doors here also stand open. I guess they were so focused on dragging us up to the cabin that they didn't bother to close anything behind them. I lead Magdalena through the open door of the office. The worn old couch sits against a wall to one side, shoved out of the way and forgotten. The trap door is exposed next to one end of the room but has been closed.

I grab the ring on top and pull it open. I quickly climb down the ladder with Magdalena close behind me.

I can barely make out the three figures in the cages in the gloom. They are all lying on the ground, inert.

"Are they dead?" Magdalena asks, flicking on a flashlight.

"I don't know. It doesn't look like they are breathing," I say, frozen at the base of the ladder. The smell in the room is overwhelming and noxious. Death, rot, decay, and the sickly sweet smell of the elderberry wine are heavy in the air.

Magdalena moves quietly across the room, her face a stony mask of disinterest. She is so hardened for someone so young that I pity her. She strides to the bodies without hesitation or concern, kneeling and unflinchingly examining them.

"They're all dead. They've been dead for a while."

"They were alive earlier today!" I say.

Magdalena shakes her head. "Maybe they were moving, but they weren't alive. These people have been dead for quite a while. Let's get out of here."

I stand frozen in place, staring at the bodies on the floor. They were alive last time I was here. Weren't they? Were they just zombies? They seemed alive; sick, maybe, but alive. Now they are gone.

"Miles," Magdalena says in a soft tone that I am not used to from her. She places a hand on my shoulder, "Come on, there's nothing we can do here."

Magdalena gently guides me to the ladder, and we climb back to the surface.

CHAPTER 24

I WALK OUT of the barn into the dawn light and Magdalena closes the doors behind us. I start when I see a tall figure in the shadow of a tree, leaning against it with arms crossed. It's Circe in a black leather bodysuit. It has no sleeves and a large diamond cut-out in the center of the chest. It clings to her body in a way that no actual garment could, like it was painted on. Her long black hair is hanging down around her shoulders. Her yellowy-brown eyes seem to almost glow in the shadows.

"I kept the Masked off of you. You escaped. You owe me," she grins coyly.

"What do you want from me, Circe?"

"Join me, Miles, and become immortal with me. Become one with me."

"Um, thanks for the invite. I think I'll pass, though."

"You owe me, Miles," she hisses. "I will get what I want, one way or another. This is the easiest and least painful way for everyone."

"I'm not much of a joiner, sorry."

"Fine, Miles. Then we do this your way. But remember, when it is all over, and you come groveling to me, I tried to play nice."

A wave of disorientation and deja vu sweeps over me. My brain snaps suddenly out of it as sharp pain erupts in both of my arms.

I blink, confused by what is happening. A half dozen throwing knives are stuck into the ground and trees in a circle around Circe, blood dripping off their blades onto little paper tabs hanging from the knives' ends. There are sigils drawn onto each tab of paper. I've got several small cuts through my clothing. Two on my left arm, three on my right, two on my left thigh, and one on my right. Magdalena is suddenly next to me, leveling an enormous pistol at Circe.

Circe is only just reacting as I catch on. She was caught almost as off guard as I was. The knives and their little paper sigils make up an inclusive boundary, binding Circe to the spot. Magdalena used my blood to activate them, cutting me when she threw them. It is clever, efficient, and ruthless. I can see the light around Circe dim ever so slightly as she tries to shadow-jump away, but it doesn't work. Magdalena must have rigged up some special trick just for Circe.

"You know shooting me won't work, right?" Circe snarls at Magdalena.

"This one's got your name on it," Magdalena quips back with no small dose of teenage snark. "A little bit of dragon scale was left after the Lamia job."

"It would take more than a 'little bit' of dragon scale."

I sense something beneath Circe's usual confident swagger, something I've never observed in her before: doubt.

"Magdalena, wait!" I blurt out and step in between Circe and Magdalena.

"My knight in shining armor!" Circe says in a trilling falsetto that makes me consider stepping aside and letting Magdalena shoot her.

"Get out of the way, Miles. She's going to kill you. I can't let that happen," Magdalena says flatly.

"You trapped her; we have time to figure something else out," I say, raising my hand and slowly pushing the barrel of her enormous gun toward the ground.

"That isn't going to hold her long," Magdalena says. "Morgan always said, if it came down to it with Circe, that I had to make it quick and thorough. No partial measures."

"The plot thickens," Circe says from behind me. "And she's right; this little cage won't last long, it is already starting to weaken. What she's wrong about is that I am not going to kill you."

"You want to absorb me into your collective consciousness or whatever? I got that. Hard pass."

"Something like that."

"Why do you care? Why me? Honestly, this is a lot of trouble to go through."

"A girl can't be interested in spending eternity with a boy anymore?"

"Please," Magdalena says with a sneer.

"You're some kind of amalgamation of what, hundreds of people?" I say. "I just don't think it'd work out."

"Tens of thousands, I would guess. I stopped counting after a few hundred."

Tens of thousands? That's a big number; magically, that's a tremendous amount of power. I stammer for a second, collecting my thoughts.

"Tens of thousands of people, and you are this focused on just one guy. One guy who is, if I am being self-aware, a loser."

"She just wants to know who the Blethspah Amah is,"

Magdalena says. "You know, that one thing that makes you valuable to every magical being around."

Why is this a mystery? This isn't a secret that I've been particularly good at hiding. It would take very little to piece together that it is Jeff.

"You are wondering why it has to come from you, why nobody else can figure it out?" Magdalena says. Apparently, my poker face is pretty bad. "It seems obvious, and people just don't see it."

"Magic," I say.

"A dragon's word. The dragon told you," Circe growls, "That secret is hidden. Only you and those you reveal it to will ever know. But you haven't been very subtle about the fact that you know."

"What if it is me?"

Magdalena snorts.

"Oh, Miles..." Circe grins. I can feel my cheeks flush from the dismissive tone.

Who have I told? I guess Genevieve knows, and obviously, Jeff. I don't think I told anyone else. Who knows who Jeff told, though? Emily.

"Oh, you didn't keep it a secret," Circe says, getting a wicked grin on her face.

"Oh, Miles..." Magdalena sighs with disappointment.

"No!" I protest, "I haven't told a soul."

I can tell I am not fooling anyone.

"Maggie, you should have taken the shot when you had the chance," Circe quips.

"Next time," Magdalena's tone is eerily devoid of emotion.

Circe gives a dismissive shrug and says, "I'll tell Emily you said 'hi.' See you around, Tiger."

"It's not Emily!" I shout, "I didn't tell Emily, I swear. That would put her in danger, and I wouldn't do that again."

All of that is true; I didn't tell her, Jeff did. I also wouldn't have dragged her into this. Circe pauses.

I feel wave upon wave of deja vu wash over me as I stare at Circe, her beautiful face twisting quizzically. Magdalena is using her power, but to what purpose, I don't know.

"I told John Hale," I blurt out. "He was blackmailing me. I'd go to prison if I didn't tell him."

Circe quirks an eyebrow. "Well, now. That complicates things." She steps back, and black, inky shadows envelop her. Then, she vanishes into the darkness.

"Why didn't you shoot her?" I turn back to Magdalena. My voice is raised, but it isn't really her I'm upset with. "You used your power, I could feel it."

Magdalena shoves me lightly with her left arm, "I tried, you jackass; I could have stopped her if you hadn't jumped in the way. By the time I had a shot again, it was too late. I tried a thousand different ways, and the only way I could get her was by shooting through you."

"You shot me?"

"Only to test a hypothesis."

Oh my god, what if Circe goes after Emily anyway? "We have to go. What if she goes after Emily!"

"She's already wherever she is going. We can't beat her. In the best-case scenario, we are hours away," Magdalena says reasonably. "Why would you tell Hale, of all people, who the Blethspah Amah is? Did you wear your stupid hat today?"

"What?" I shake my head. "I didn't. I made that up so she wouldn't go after Emily."

Magdalena's face splits into a grin, "Miles, you are a better liar than I give you credit for. You had me fooled."

"I'd like to try to call Emily and warn her. I think I saw a landline in the community hall."

"It's been cut," Magdalena's voice sounds quite certain.

I raise an eyebrow at her. How does she know that exactly?

"I cut it, standard procedure, control communications."

I think back to the dead bodies littered around that cabin out in the woods. If Russ and I were the victims and Arturus Grable and his followers were the monsters, what does that make Magdalena? At the end of the day, who's the bigger menace, the monster or the monster slayer? This is at the core of the Greek hero legends. Heroes are great people to have around when a giant, slavering beast is eating your village. But once that's done, you better lock up your children and hide your valuables.

"So what do we do?" I sigh, assessing Magdalena. Then I mutter, "My hero."

"That's better! First, we find your friend and Allen, cover our tracks, and get out of here as fast as possible," Magdalena says, moving toward the field with the large array of solar panels.

I fall in behind her. Once we get out into the field, I notice that the sun is just cresting from behind the mountains to the west, and though it is late morning, it is just beginning to get light. Magdalena moves at a brisk and sure-footed pace. I stumble and curse behind her as I step in gopher holes, and my legs are stabbed by familiar thistle and briar.

Back at the community center, we poke through all the buildings, looking for anyone hiding, but no one is there.

"We should wait here for them," I lean against a wall.

Magdalena huffs and crouches down in the lee of one of the buildings. We sit in near silence for an unendurable length of time.

Eventually, Russ and Allen come stumping down a path from the west.

"Anything?" Magdalena slides out of her crouch.

"All quiet," Allen drawls.

"Some inhabited houses, but not a lot, dude. And not a super friendly reception," Russ shakes his head sadly.

"Nobody we found wanted our help. I think we should bug out of here," Allen seems less emotional and more pragmatic.

"How about back at the lab?" Russ asks.

"I think anyone left alive has fled or is hiding," I shake my head.

"With that vortex closed, the hosts are no longer viable," Magdalena says.

"With that, can we dust off," Allen drawls, "please?"

"Agreed," Magdalena runs to the road, her pigtails bouncing as she goes. I look at my pant legs and socks, which are filled with burrs and stickers. I can feel a thousand stinging jabs in my calves. Magdalena's pink tracksuit seems burr free. Ugh, I hate magic.

"Should we go back and check on Pamela?" Russ asks with concern.

"At this point, additional contact is ill-advised. I am fairly certain they are safe and will recover. We are doing them no good by staying around," Magdalena says coldly. It's like she has put on her stone-cold, bad-ass mask and is impervious to emotion.

"Well..." I begin.

"No, she's right. Seems like they didn't remember you. If we just fuck off, everyone is safer when this all comes toppling down," Allen says.

"But..." I begin to protest.

"Miles," Allen interrupts, "do you need another Devora situation on your record?"

Allen, Magdalena, and I were all part of a heist at movie producer Jim Devora's Napa home. It went sideways, but I was the only person found on the scene. The only reason I am not in prison now is that John Hale bailed me out. I hate John Hale.

Now, I am being blackmailed to help Hale and his mysterious benefactors at Syzmek Industries.

"No," I say with a sigh.

"Then let's go," Magdalena begins marching up the road.

"Dude," Russ says.

"No, Russ, let's go. I think they are right," I hang my head as I follow Magdalena.

Russ doesn't seem convinced. He sits there for a moment, considering. "Well, dude, if you say so."

Russ gets up with a shrug and begins to follow the group. As we pass the parking area, I point at Magdalena's car.

"What about your car?" I ask incredulously.

"Not my car," she quips without looking back.

"Okay, what about my car?" I ask.

“Brah, you don't want that thing. It's stolen merchandise."

"What?" I sputter.

"You don't think I would ever own a car that is traceable back to me, do you? Not a chance."

I fall behind Russ, sputtering and cursing. He shrugs at me hopelessly.

When we reach the other side of the community center, Magdalena pulls something out of her pocket. It looks like an old-fashioned walkie-talkie. She fiddles with it, then holds it high above her right shoulder and dramatically presses a button.

I'm not sure if it is the concussive force of the explosion or simply all of us reactively leaping for cover simultaneously, but Russ, Allen, and I all find ourselves shocked and sprawled on the ground. I glance back and see that Magdalena's car is now a pillar of fire—bits of glass and metal rain down from the sky.

I look at Magdalena, who sneers at us with a disgusted teenage grimace, "Why are you all crawling on the ground? Someone lose a contact?"

Allen gets up and begins dusting himself off. I am close behind him. We help Russ to his feet.

"Shit, Mags," Allen says, "you could give us a little warning."

"I told you we had to cover our tracks."

"You didn't say blow them up!" As I say it, I realize I am yelling.

She shrugs and resumes walking.

"I mean, dude," is all Russ can add.

Magdalena leads us a hundred yards down the main road in silence. I start to say something at one point, but she hushes me with a single finger and points at her ear. I resume silence. She turns right and climbs up a short embankment.

"Get your stuff," she says, motioning over the embankment. We climb up, and discover that my bags and Russ' backpack are there, along with a couple of small, military-style bags that must be Magdalena and Allen's. We grab our gear.

"You gathered all our stuff?" I ask.

"It was that or burn it," Allen grimaces toward Magdalena.

"I see."

"Okay, we'll hike out from here. Allen's truck is parked at the bottom of the mountain in a turn-out-thingy," Magdalena says.

"It's an old skid road," Allen corrects.

Magdalena shrugs, "It's a shitty dirt road, off a slightly larger shitty dirt road, off a normal-sized shitty dirt road. I don't care what it's called. It's a little turn-out-thingy."

"Right," Allen says, looking surprisingly cowed by Magdalena's snark.

"Can I proceed with the plan? Unless someone else has any other trivia they would like to share?"

I look at Russ. He's wearing filthy torn jeans and a similarly filthy gray shirt. His orange gnome hat is gone, and his long ponytail is matted with twigs and burs. His face is streaked with dirt, dried snot, and tears. He looks like hell.

I look at Allen. He's wearing camo BDUs and a military-style pack. He has a rifle cradled in one arm, with a knife and pistol on his belt. His face is painted camouflage. Middle-aged but fit, Allen looks every bit the paramilitary survivalist.

Then I turn to Magdalena, dressed like she's on Real Housewives of School of the Americas, in a spattered and stained but still bright-pink tracksuit. She carries a huge pistol casually in her left hand. She is otherwise bristling with extra weapons and armaments, not that she seems to have needed them.

I look down at myself. My canvas Chuck Taylors are so encrusted in mud and filth that it looks like I am wearing shoes made of dirt. My baggy jeans are layered with burrs, twigs, and streaks of dirt. I try not to think about the crust of dried ichor ground into them. My second-hand flannel is so torn up that it looks more like a tattered shawl, and my t-shirt is soiled to illegibility.

I take the group in, and I start laughing. I can't stop. Tears come to my eyes. I can barely stay standing.

"What's so funny?" Magdalena demands, but I can't catch enough breath to point out the ridiculousness of our little band. I keep laughing.

Soon, Russ and Allen start laughing, too. It is good to break the tension. A moment later, I push myself to stand, gasping for air and wiping tears of mirth from my eyes.

"Are you all done yet?" Magdalena says in disgust.

"Yeah, sorry, it's just. I don't know. Look at us!" I gasp.

"We're a sad lot, for sure," Allen says.

"Hey, does the air pressure feel funny to you?" Russ begins to turn in a circle, scanning the forest around us.

"Yeah," I say. The hair on the back of my neck starts rising on end, and my whole body feels warm and cold. Russ' eyes are locked on something over my shoulder, his jaw slack. I turn and look.

At first, I think the mountain's shadow is moving toward us in the setting sun. I then realize the shadow is coming from the southeast, the wrong direction. Besides, it isn't even midday yet. Then, the shadow breaks through the line of trees; they bend and break before its mass. Wood is cracking and splintering like toothpicks in a hurricane. The form is almost on us, and it looks familiar. I saw it in the Dreamtime. Writhing black tendrils, mouths, and eyes everywhere, it shifts, twists, and darts in a way that defies natural movement. Circe called it the Masked, and the cultists called it Lord of the Mourning. It is not supposed to be here. It was trapped outside. We closed the vortex and kept it out. Didn't we? Or maybe that's how it came through; maybe when that connection, that rubberband, as Russ called it, snapped, this Masked thing grabbed the thread and followed me back out. Is this my fault?

I glance at Russ and Allen, who are frozen, mouths agape and eyes wide. I grab them both by the shoulders and try to drag them, but they are too rigid. Not paralyzed, but hard and cold like stone.

Magdalena is on my other side, held rigid midstep. Her face unmoving in a mirthless smirk.

"Run!" I yell at them. "Run!" But they don't run. They don't move. The air is stagnant, and there is no sound except a faint, distant buzzing.

I turn and sprint down the road. The surface is hard, too hard. I can feel every step in my knees and back in a way that makes no sense. Running won't save me, though. The Masked is closing in on me fast. There is a sickly sweet chemical smell and a prickling sensation in the air. I don't dare look back, but I can feel its presence enclose me like a cloud of mustard gas. The black tendrils wrap around me and scoop me up, enveloping me in soft blackness like a velvet sheet. I am violently lifted and dragged off into the afternoon sun. Someone is screaming a long, sustained, ululating scream. It's probably me, but I am too terrified to be certain.

CHAPTER 25

IT'S BLACK. It's silent. I'm floating in velvety darkness. A queasy, motion-sick feeling roils in my stomach, and mortal terror arcs through my limbs.

"Tell me," a voice says. It sounds like thunder, an earthquake, a tornado, and a volcano fighting a battle that none of them can win, but everyone else loses.

What does this voice want to know? I'm an open book.

"When I was fourteen, I stole a bottle from a liquor store. I was trying to show off to the other kids; it was just a little pint of blackberry brandy. I only put a tiny bit on my tongue, but it tasted so foul I couldn't drink it; the other kids drank it all. One kid, I don't remember his name, got sick and threw up, and we all left him there. I remember he got in a lot of trouble, but he didn't tell on the rest of us; I always felt kind of guilty about that. And then, when I was fifteen..." I ramble, I am still trying to figure out what I am saying. There is something in the timbre of the voice that has disconnected my mouth from my brain; I'd tell this voice anything it wanted to make the terror end.

"No. Tell me about the others, about my kindred."

"Kindred, kindred, relations, family, you um," I stammer. How the hell should I know about it's family? Isn't it a lost god or something? I don't know any gods. I do know a dragon, though. Is it a dragon? "Do you mean dragons? You want to know about other dragons?"

"**Vulgar. Yes. Go on,**" the voice says. I can't tell if the voice is in my head or if it simply resonates throughout the universe. Is this a dragon in its true form? When not disguised as a human or a giant lizard, it's a primordial force of nature, and it's cranky.

"Um, I don't know a lot. Goldsmith is a dragon. He lives in a house on a mountain, surrounded by stuff. I think Walt Carmichael is one. Most of them got killed off by the Knights of Saint George. I am sorry, I don't know much," I stammer.

"**As if it were in the power of your kind to do anything to me. The Aurous and the Carmine. Yes. You protect their secrets. Tell me more of them**."

Their secrets? Is this yet another being who wants to know about Jeff? It would be nice if, for once, I was being put in mortal danger of my own accord.

"Wait, you were dead, outside, in the Dreamtime. But if the Knights didn't do it, who did?"

"You will answer my questions, or I will unmake you."

"Well, then, I won't be able to answer any of your questions."

"I can remake you."

"Well, aren't you quite the drama llama?" I say. I search my brain for the filter that keeps me from mouthing off to godlike beings. Apparently, like an affordable restaurant in Napa, it's the first to close up shop and skip town when things take a turn.

People talk about existential dread and existential horror,

but we rarely talk about existential regret. No words can describe being picked apart molecule by molecule, feeling every last thread of your existence meticulously unwoven—the horror of true oblivion encroaching on you. No one talks about how much it hurts, not in the sense of your nervous system or corporeal pain, but seeing every bit of your life flaked away, in knowing how small, simple, insignificant, and meaningless you were. Then, the empty bleakness of the void. It is almost a relief, no longer needing to care, the burden of struggling to live removed.

Then, nothing.

The horror is compounded by the simplicity and ease with which everything you ever knew is put back together again. There is a humbling brevity to seeing how little it takes to undo and then redo your existence completely. This is what the Masked does to me. They save my regrets for last so that they are fresh in my mind and seem larger and more real than the rest of me.

"Okay!" I yell. "You made your point."

I am usually good at compartmentalizing, but you can't put something like that away. I don't ever want to go through that again.

"Tell me."

The Masked wants to know what I know about dragons. That's not a lot. There are few left. Most were killed by Saint George hundreds of years ago. Killed, or now I wonder if it isn't, maybe banished. Could a human kill an entity like this? Having just been erased from existence and remade by one, I have doubts. What else do I know? I know Goldsmith, the weird old hoarding hermit, is a dragon. He prophesied my friend Jeff to be the Blethspa Amah. No, that's not right. Now that I think about it, he didn't prophesize. He said anointed.

Blethspa Amah means 'final change' or something like that, but what that means is still unclear. Is this something Goldsmith made Jeff into?

What else? I suspect that Walt Carmichael, the billionaire owner of Syzmek Industries, is also a dragon. Hale, who has all but said he is working on behalf of Carmichael, has been trying to find the Blethspa Amah to stop the prophecy, anointment, or whatever Goldsmith is up to. Okay, Miles, tell the eldritch horror what it wants to know while giving as little information as possible.

"Right, well, there is this Blethspa Amah character that Goldsmith anointed; the last change, or something like that. But Walt Carmichael doesn't want this to happen, so he's been sending people to try to find the Blethspa Amah."

"The Aurous and the Carmine. Tell me more about the Carmine."

Aurous sounds related to gold. It must mean Goldsmith when they refer to the Aurous. Carmine is an orange color. I think. Or is it green? No, that's chartreuse. I am pretty sure carmine is orange or red, but it also sounds like Carmichael. The Syzmek logo is red. The Carmine must be Walt Carmichael. I'm not sure I even follow my own logic, but it feels right.

"I really know more about Goldsmith, I mean, um, the Aurous, than the Carmine. The Aurous. The Carmine. They weren't very creative with their human names, were they?" My thought process spewing out of my mouth nervously.

"Tell me."

"I don't know much. I've never met him. I helped him build a magic fortress, the Syzmek building, but I didn't know what I was doing then. All of our contact has been through other people, most recently, a man named Jon Hale. He said the

Blethspa Amah would explain magic, make it boring, and destroy creativity. But I think he's full of shit because that's all Syzmek is doing."

"Tell me where this fortress is."

"It's in San Francisco, not far," I imagine the building, and I can feel its image, its location being sucked out of my head. Why are they asking me questions if they can pull information directly from my head? Maybe they can only get the thoughts I want them to. Or maybe they can read my surface thoughts, in which case they already know about Jeff, and I can't actually hide anything from them.

"Continue."

I am confused and terrified, but I'm unsure what they seek.

"Listen, I don't want to be unmade and remade again. That was honestly the worst thing I've ever experienced. I will help you, but I don't know what you are looking for. I can give you better information if I understand what's going on. I'm just a dumb, mortal little human, after all."

There is a long silence, so quiet that the only sound I can hear is the stereocilia in my inner ears, slowly dying in a deafening, whining chorus.

"We were imprisoned in this place. This thing you call 'reality' was our punishment–a consequence of transgressions you could not understand. For some, like the Aurous, it was punitive–a thing to be endured. It was a playground for others, like the Carmine, the Verdigris, and me, where there were no boundaries to transgress. We created things to play with, pushed them, and evolved them. Eventually, your kind came. You were those who could, to some small degree, manipulate the fabric of the prison. Shape it. The Aurous and their ilk saw in you a way to break free, a way to pick the locks that bound us. The Carmine saw you as

the perfect plaything, the ultimate distraction. But we could not let the Aurous destroy the playground, so we devised a plan: we would teach you how to weaken the boundary and shove our opposition through. Your Knights were mere pawns. And it worked, but the Carmine did not wish to share their toys. They tricked us and had even their allies banished to the great beyond. Still bound to our prison, we hovered outside, in between, neither free nor within. In limbo."

"That is a lot to take in. Okay, so how did you get back in? How did the Aurous avoid banishment?"

"You tried to bring another back, with its spark bound to yours. That left a path. When the hole was large enough, you passed through. I had but to follow."

"I see. So what is your goal? How can I help you?" I want to keep them talking if that is the right word, for as long as possible. This being doesn't seem to distinguish between individual humans very well, in much the same way as I might not distinguish between ants on an ant hill. That might be useful information for later.

"I will cast the Carmine out and reclaim my place."

"You needed the Knights of Saint George to do that the first time. You will need mortals again. I can help you."

Again, complete silence envelops me. I am forming a plan. It's not a good plan, nor a smart one, but it's the only one I can see. Somehow, I have to get someone to open a gateway into the outside and force at least three dragons through it.

"Yes. You will."

"What should I call you?"

"It is not you that shall call me. It is I that shall summon you."

Did I get don't-call-me-I'll-call-you'd by a dragon's ghost?

I'm about to say something snarky, but my indignation is interrupted when they drop me. Air is rushing past my face, bringing watery tears to my eyes. I plummet, screaming, but I can't hear my own cries of horror over the rush of air in my ears.

Then darkness.

CHAPTER 26

"MILES?" Magdalena's voice breaks through the blackness. I blink; a pair of fingers snap in my face. They have short, well-trimmed nails painted bright purple. I blink again. Suddenly, Magdalena's face is uncomfortably close to mine. I realize I am on my back. The ground is flat and rocky. I am in the middle of a dirt road—the one out of Stanyon's Hollow, I think.

"Have you always had your nails painted purple?" I ask her dully.

"You okay, brah?" She says with a sneer that I can see is hiding concern.

"Um, I just... I guess I just thought I was dead there for a minute," I groan. "Where am I?"

"I think we should have him sit down for a minute," Russ' voice is behind me. "Get him some water."

"We should be moving," Allen growls. He's standing on a small mound of dirt nearby, leaning against one of many trees.

"We were leaving when you started laughing. Then you fell and went all quiet and rigid for like five minutes," Magdalena says scornfully.

"Magdalena, is everything a dragon tells someone a secret that only they can tell?"

"What? What's wrong with you? I don't know, yeah, I guess, probably."

Do I share the conversation I had with the Masked with my friends? Does knowing put them in danger? Does it put me in danger? Will it know? Will it be angry? It didn't say I couldn't tell anyone. Keeping secrets always has a cost–a cost in trust and integrity.

"I had an experience with the Masked. I think it's a dragon. It was enlightening, but I'm not sure what I should share."

"Does any of it get us off this mountain faster?" Allen asks.

"Or make the last three days not happen?" Russ asks.

"No."

"Then let's save it for a post-escape brewski," Allen concludes.

"Are you going to be able to make it out without another episode?" Magdalena looks scornful. She's usually more snarky than this; I suspect that this annoyed soldier act is how she shows concern.

"Honestly? Your guess is as good as mine."

Magdalena shrugs and then starts up the road at a pace I can only describe as 'overeager.' We fall in behind her, and despite being younger than both Russ and Allen, it quickly becomes clear that I am the least prepared for the march we are on. I've been skipping my cardio too much lately, I can't remember the last time I went for a run.

We wind down the road for half an hour or so in relative silence before Magdalena slips off the road. Allen tails her, so Russ and I exchange a look and a shrug before following suit. After a few grueling hours traipsing deer trails and acquiring a thousand scratches, five ticks, and one twisted ankle, I come crashing out from some low-hanging madrone branches and into a clearing. The hard brown twigs catch in my hair while the red berries smear themselves over my face and shoulders. I am the last of us to get off the mountain.

"...and all the trees and the stupid hedgehogs and rabbits, thistles, oh, I hope a wildfire takes the thistles..." I angrily rant to myself. My three companions are standing next to an old truck, drinking water and staring at me, brows raised in shock. "I hate nature."

My body is dirty, itchy, and drenched in sweat.

"You okay, dude?" Russ drawls.

"I think I have poison oak inside my pants, Russ. How does poison oak get *inside* the pants? Inside the pants!"

"You do whatever tickles yer pickle, pal. I don't need to hear about it," Allen chuckles.

I flip him off and throw my bag into the truck's bed. Everyone else's bags are back there, and it looks like the most comfortable option, so I climb into the back of the truck and lie down.

"Why didn't we just take the road?" I grump, trying to get comfortable but failing miserably.

"Too likely someone would have spotted us," Magdalena says, climbing into the truck cab. I hear Russ and Allen climb in, too.

"Sure you don't want to sit up front?" Allen hollers back at me from the cab.

"No, I'm too uncomfortable and gross and stinky, and you all are gross and stinky, and it would be too gross and stinky, and I hate the world. I want to take a nap."

"Suit yourself."

Soon, we are bumping and bouncing down a dirt road at far too aggressive a speed. I am gripping the side of the truck bed with one hand and a spare tire with the other. Not only is napping not an option, my survivability is up for debate. I should have gotten into the gross and stinky cab.

When we eventually get to the freeway, despite living in a whirlwind, it is so relatively peaceful that I finally do drift off to sleep despite myself. I hug the tire and bounce on the corrugated steel truck bed for a few hours until Allen parks in front of my building. I delicately extricate myself from the truck and gingerly lower myself to the asphalt. I can barely stand when we arrive, and getting my stuff from the back is painful. By the time I am done, Magdalena bounds up to me.

"You're being all chipper and spry to rub in how old and grumpy I am, aren't you?" I ask in an appropriately old and grumpy tone.

"You got it, boss man."

"I told you..."

"You got it, *jefe*."

"I..." I begin to rebut but then think better of it. "My bruises have bruises. I need a shower."

"We going to meet and debrief or what?" Magdalena asks.

I squint toward the setting sun and look back.

"You know what? Can we do it tomorrow? It's late. I am tired. I am sore. I smell, I look, and I feel bad. I want to shower, have something to eat, and go to bed, if that's okay with you."

"You're the boss!" She grins slyly. "Sorry, *jefe*."

"See you tomorrow," I grump at her. "Bye Allen, bye Russ. We will talk tomorrow."

"Aight," Allen calls out the driver's side window.

"Sure thing, dude," Russ gives me a peace sign out the passenger-side window as Allen backs the truck up and leaves.

"You need help up the stairs, old man?" Magdalena taunts me.

"No, I got this," I start moving up the stairs, leaning heavily on the railing. It's the first time I have been called an old man and I didn't feel the need to argue.

She shakes her head, jogs the stairs, and vanishes into her apartment.

"Youth is wasted on the young," I call after her, but she's already closed the door.

"In the past thirty-six hours, I've hiked a mountain about seven times," I am muttering to myself now. "I've shifted through at least twelve different realities, I think. I've rappelled down a cliff and crawled up a ravine. I squeezed through multiple tiny openings, ran all night, and slept under a tree. I've been beaten, tied up, caged, carried up a mountain, thrown through a tear in reality, kidnapped by a lost god or an undead dragon, or, I don't know, something. I hiked the hard way down a mountain and slept in the bed of a moving truck. It's not an age thing; anyone would be sore, right?" I finish ranting at no one in particular as I close my apartment door behind me.

I stagger to my room. First things first, I plug my phone in. I strip my foul shirt and jeans off and throw them on the floor. I stare at Brent's shirt—a stinking, torn, stained flannel shirt. He was a good guy, and he didn't deserve what happened. I should feel sadder, but I don't; I just feel angry. Why do people have to be so shitty to each other? Then, I remember something.

Emily.

I grab my phone and it has basically no charge, but I call her anyway. It goes to voicemail almost immediately.

"Emily, hey, remember Circe? Well, I ran into her, and she might be after you. Hopefully not, maybe not, but be careful anyway. Call me back. It's Miles, by the way, which you probably knew from the caller ID, and I guess probably from my voice, but call me back. It's Miles. Be safe."

Then, I text her a slightly more coherent version of the same message. She responds almost immediately.

"In SERGEI meeting. Thanks for the heads up. Will be careful. Call you when I get back."

I sigh and go for a long, hot shower. I let the water soak into my body and rinse all the ick of the past couple of days away. I come out of my shower, still sore but feeling more human, and slip into a t-shirt and boxer shorts for the night. I am just about to collapse into my bed when there is a pounding at my door.

"Oh, for freaking hell," I grumble as I stagger to the door. I remember to look through the peephole this time, and see Magdalena standing impatiently in front of my apartment.

I open the door. "What?"

She pushes past me, enters my office/living room space, and sits at my desk.

"Can I help you, Magdalena?" I try to sound as cranky as possible, but I only sound tired.

"Nah, I was just bored, and I wanted to hang out," she props her feet on my desk and crosses her legs at the knees.

"I just want to sleep," I say, flopping down in the chair on the opposite side of the desk. "Can't this wait till tomorrow?"

"What were you doing up there on that mountain?" She picks up a folder from my desk and starts thumbing through it. I have no idea what is in there, or the last time I used a file folder.

"I was following the Hierophant's prophecy. Looking for answers."

"Did you get them?"

"What do you care?" I say, feeling cross. This seems very out of character for Magdalena. If she hadn't come so easily into my warded home, I'd have thought she might be an imposter. I should check anyway.

"I'm getting paid to keep you alive. Knowing how you got yourself dragged into some cult shitshow is kind of my job."

I find my muddy, dirt-encrusted courier bag in the corner and fish a crystal out of it. I start to gaze at her aura.

"It's me. Nothing weird going on," Magdalena scoffs. I, unfortunately, have to agree; the aura is Magdalena's.

"Well, I didn't hire you, so it's not your business," I point toward the door.

"Okay, fine," she starts to get up and walk toward the door. Her eyes are downcast, different from her usual defiant glower–they look sad.

"Listen," I raise a hand, "I'm sorry. I'm just tired, grumpy, and sore. So sore. I went up there following a sort of prophecy from the Hierophant, looking for some answers."

"Did you find them?"

"I think so, but I'm not entirely sure what the questions were."

"So what do we do next, jefe?"

"We?" I quirk an eyebrow.

"Yeah. I guess...well, I don't have a family. Everyone in my life who finds out about my magic either sees me as a threat to be avoided or as a weapon to be manipulated. Everyone else sees me as a brown-skinned trans girl and treats me even worse," Magdalena's eyes are suddenly teary in a display of emotion.

"I'm sorry, that sounds difficult. You are so tough and independent. I didn't know it was so hard. I'm sorry if I'm a little taken aback."

"You didn't know I was trans, and now you hate me," she examines her shoes very closely.

"I didn't, but no, no, that doesn't matter. I'm caught a little off guard because you aren't usually this emotional. Did something happen?"

"Do you know how close you came to dying? I mean, you are an asshole, Miles, but you are the only person in my life that treats me like a person. You and Allen are like, the only people who've ever been halfway decent to me."

"Oh."

"Anyway," she says, standing up, tears welling in her eyes, "I'd be sad if you died."

"Thank you," I say awkwardly. I don't know what else to say.

"If you ever tell anyone about this, you know I will kill you," she mutters as she steps back and wipes tears from her eyes.

"I've no doubt," I feel a little misty-eyed myself. "You asked me if I found my answers."

"Yeah?"

"Someone told me I had already picked my side, and I didn't think I had. But now I think they were right, and I didn't realize it yet. Now, it's time to go into the belly of the beast. The only way out is through. I've got to call Hale."

EPILOGUE

I ADJUST MY SEAT. I hate flying, and while first class is certainly fancier, flying is still flying.

"Beverage? Can I offer you a snack?" The flight attendant asks.

"No, thank you," I say quietly.

"Yes, could I have a rum, coke, and some of those cookies, please?" The man next to me says. He's got thinning gray hair, cut short and in a style I could only describe as 'nondescript business.' He wears square glasses. His vertically pinstriped shirt bows out around his ample belly, and his belt cinches in too tight at his waist, giving him an improbably top-heavy look.

I sigh and close my eyes. I really hate flying.

"It's a shame, the horrible stuff that happens in this world, isn't it?" He asks me.

When I open my eyes, he motions at the television screen, hovering on an arm in front of him. I glance at it blearily. It is an expose on the New Thule Massacre, which occurred only a few years ago but is being treated like ancient history.

"I try not to follow the news anymore; I've had enough."

"Hey," he says in a tone I've come to recognize, "you're that guy on TV, right?"

"Probably," I sigh.

"HexVex! We keep bad spells from yoooou!" He sings the now ubiquitous jingle aloud so the whole cabin can hear it.

"Yeah, that's me," Slouching farther down into my seat.

"You're the CEO of the company, right?"

"Nope, I'm the President, Walt Carmichael is the CEO," I close my eyes again.

"What's the difference?"

"I am in all the commercials and all the memes mocking it, I get all the embarrassing talk show interviews, and Walt makes all the decisions and money. I think the term is 'poster boy.'"

"Sure, but you're still rich, right? I mean..." The man says.

"It depends on your definition of rich. If you just mean the amount of disposable income available to me, then yeah, I am doing pretty well. If you mean having the freedom to make my own decisions and be my own person vs. being tethered to a corporate leash and forced to be a dancing monkey for a bunch of power-hungry people, then no. Or if you mean the real treasure was friendship all along...if that's what you mean, well, I'd have to go with, I'm pretty fucking poor still."

"You seem much happier in the commercials," the man concludes sadly. "I'm Clark."

I open my eyes and see that, as I fear, he is holding his hand out to shake.

"Miles," I sigh and shake his hand. "Miles Ward."

"So, you have like, a magic company?" Clark's tone is jovial. "You do magic."

"More like anti-magic, but whatever, semantic. Yes, that's what HexVex does. Oh, but I hate that name. Do I personally do magic? Not so much anymore. Now, I mostly go to meetings that I don't understand, shake hands, and pretend to be excited about some new product line for a commercial. Would you believe that three years ago, I was dead broke and being chased through the forest by cultists? Now I miss those days."

Clark laughs, "You are happier in the commercial but funnier in person."

"No, seriously, Clark, the only reason I am in this position is because I am being blackmailed for trying to help an ancient sorcerer steal from a movie producer."

He laughs some more. Nobody ever takes me seriously anymore. Now that I have money, I am eccentric.

"What a difference a day makes, huh, Mr. Ward?"

"Mr. Ward was my grandfather, please call me Miles."

"Okay, Miles, let me buy you a drink."

"No, thank you. Also, they are complimentary; it's First Class," I lay back in my seat and close my eyes. I have a few minutes of quiet with my thoughts before Clark speaks up again.

"So Miles, what would you say the secret to success is?"

"You want to know a secret?" I say without opening my eyes. "Walt Carmichael is a dragon. He's in an ancient war with a weird old man in the woods, who is also a dragon, and it doesn't matter who wins; the rest of us are up the creek without a paddle. One of them wants to destroy all of reality; the other wants to enslave humanity forever. There is a secret third one, too, and they are the scariest of them all, but I am worried my head will explode if I say anything else about that."

Clark laughs, "You should write TV shows. That's great."

"It was good to meet you, Clark; I am going to try to get some sleep now if you don't mind."

"Sure, Miles, have a good nap."

ABOUT THE AUTHOR

Justin Godey is the author of the *Blood, Wine, Magic* series, a modern fantasy set in the heart of Napa, California. With a passion for weaving captivating tales, Justin draws inspiration from the vibrant landscapes and lore of Napa, California, where he lives. When he's not immersed in his writing, you can find him exploring the realms of imagination through Dungeons and Dragons with friends, shooting his longbow at Skyline park, or playing ukulele in his backyard. You can learn more about his work at http://justingodey.com.

www.ingramcontent.com/pod-product-compliance
Lightning Source LLC
Chambersburg PA
CBHW020929310726
48980CB00007B/693/J

* 9 7 9 8 9 9 9 9 5 3 8 3 4 *